MARGARITA NIGHTS

MARGARITA NIGHTS

PHYLLIS SMALLMAN

McArthur & Company
Toronto

This paperback edition published in 2009 by
McArthur & Company
322 King St. West, Suite 402
Toronto, ON
M5V 1J2
www.mcarthur-co.com

Library and Archives Canada Cataloguing in Publication

Smallman, Phyllis
     Margarita nights : a Sherri Travis mystery / Phyllis Smallman.

ISBN 978-1-55278-763-2

     I. Title.

PS8637.M36M37 2009   **C813'.6**   **C2009-900033-4**

Cover design by Tania Craan
Printed by Webcom

The publisher would like to acknowledge the financial support of the Government of
Canada through the Book Publishing Industry Development Program (BPIDP) and the
Canada Council for our publishing activities. The publisher further wishes to
acknowledge the financial support of the Ontario Arts Council for our publishing
program.

10 9 8 7 6 5 4 3 2 1

To my husband, Lee Smallman,
I succeeded because you believed.

And to my children
Shawn Smallman and Ellen Wild.

Acknowledgments

Special thanks to my husband, Lee Smallman, and my friend Jim Ordowich for reading the manuscript multiple times and making it better.

Thanks to everyone who read *Margarita Nights* in the manuscript stages and offered emotional support through a long learning process. Myrna Hardcastle, Mary Lou Leitch, Margaret Morison, Gwen Morrison, Sharron Orovan Johnston, Elizabeth Turpin-Pulley, Jenny Smallman, and Judy Wood.

I would also like to thank the Crime Writers of Canada and Louise Penny for instigating the Unhanged Arthur Award which led directly to the publishing of this book. And thank you to Kim, Ann, Taryn and all at McArthur & Company for not only sponoring the Unhanged Arthur Award but for launching Sherri Travis with such brio.

CHAPTER 1

The *Suncoaster* blew up at four-thirty on a Tuesday afternoon in late January while I was setting up for the rush hour at the Sunset Bar and Grill.

I love bars. Like people, each one has its own personality; some are boring, some are stimulating and some are downright dangerous. When you enter a new one it's always best to stop just inside the door, taking your time until you decide just what kind you've got.

The Sunset is the *crème de la crème* of watering holes. On the second floor of a pink stucco building decorated with white Bermuda shutters and tall graceful palms, etched glass doors lead from the lobby of the restaurant into the bar. Black-and-white photographs of Key West in the thirties line the Cypress-paneled walls. Overhead, two giant fans on pulleys stir air smelling of old leather chairs, long ago Cuban cigars and expensive perfume.

Early evening is my favorite time of day at the

Sunset. Quiet, but with a sense of waiting in the air—waiting for something that hasn't quite arrived but you know it's coming. That day, Sinatra was singing in the background about Nancy with the laughing eyes while the ceiling fans slowly turned.

Across the bar from me sat the same two guys who were there every day about that time. The three of us, Brian Spears, Clay Adams and me, Sherri Travis, had the bar to ourselves. It was early yet. Things would heat up fast enough, but in the meantime we were doing what we always did, sharing life.

"Time to feed the kitty, children," Brian Spears announced and began collecting everyone's donation for the weekly Florida lottery. A lawyer in his late sixties, Brian would be retired except for an ex-wife, twenty years younger, with a better lawyer. He tells anyone who will listen that he'll be practicing law until the grim reaper closes his case. The buttons of his dress shirt strained under the load of his paunch as Brian, at least fifty pounds overweight, shoved my contribution to improving Florida into his shirt pocket.

"Heard from that godawful husband of yours, Sherri?" he asked.

"Not since he climbed up my balcony Sunday night." I went back to slicing lemon wedges. "And if I never hear from him again it will be too soon." I'd married Jimmy when I was nineteen and stuck it out for damn near nine years, but last spring I'd finally left him. It was over but Jimmy didn't get it, didn't think I really meant it. For Jimmy, his lying, drinking and sleeping around just didn't seem to be real good reasons for me to go off him and he was sure I'd be back. My ways of saying no were becoming more and more dramatic.

"That man has made you bitter," Brian complained, pushing his glasses back up his nose. "He's spoiled you for the rest of mankind. What good is a woman who doesn't believe in love?"

"I believe in love," I protested. "I love lots of people. Even you guys. It's romance that took the fall. For me, Cinderella is dead and the prince is gay."

They made rude sounds so I tried again. "Moonlight and roses hide muggers and thorns." Again with the raspberry chorus.

"Well, I tried to enlighten you," I told them. "It's hard to see grown men who still believe in Santa Claus and fairy tales."

Brian began to tell a story about some other woman's godawful. Seems she fed him to the gators in little pieces. Stories of revenge are the only joy Brian takes in life these days. He collects them, weighs them and considers them for the qualities of revenge and suffering they inflict on the errant partner. I was beginning to worry about the mental health of this friend of mine but I paid close attention to this story for future reference. Such drastic action was not only beginning to seem necessary but also downright attractive if I wanted the man I'd married to stay gone.

When Brian finished his story of extreme spousal abuse, Clay Adams said, "Have you thought anymore about selling real estate for me?" His handsome dark face was real serious, but then it always is when he talks about money. Accumulating wealth is his reason for breathing, the altar he worships at. "You'd make real money. You know everyone in town and have more friends than God."

"Ah, but when would I play golf?"

Clay looked as if his beer had gone off.

I pointed a paring knife at him. "If I was in an office, working regular hours, I'd only be able to golf six months of the year. Winter it's too dark to play after work. Where's the fun in that? This way I get to golf every day and work at night."

He pointed at his empty beer glass, frowning at my non-success ethic.

I grinned. "A man of your position should drink Scotch, Balvenie at least. Beer doesn't have the same image as a twelve-year-old single malt Scotch."

"I like beer," he replied.

"What you like is the price."

"We're talking about you. Don't change the subject."

I sat a sweating mug down on a cardboard coaster

in front of him. "Of course you could ask me to marry you. Take me away from the Cypress Island Municipal Course to the Royal Palms."

His broad forehead wrinkled in a frown. "You're just crazy enough to marry someone for a golf membership."

"I'm going to consider that a maybe," I told him and went off to serve some newcomers.

It was nearly nine when Cordelia Grant slipped in. She was dressed in a crisp white blouse and navy skirt, probably on her way home from choir practice. She stood just inside the door, holding her pocketbook in front of her with both hands. She looked around, about as wary as a virgin at a Hells Angels reunion. For a Fundamentalist Baptist like Cordelia, stepping over the threshold of a bar was like crossing the town line into Sodom or Gomorrah.

Everything about her was pale—pale gray-blue eyes, pale eyebrows, pale face and hair so blond it was almost white—and this lack of accent lent her face a strangely naked look. Her eyes locked on me. She walked stiff-legged to the bar, ignoring Jeff when he tried to serve her. She hadn't come in for a drink.

CHAPTER 2

"I have to talk to you," she said in her breathless, childlike voice. I led the way down the hall, past the washrooms, to the emergency exit where I held the door open for her. Nudging a wooden block into place with my toe so the door wouldn't lock me out, I stepped out onto the metal grill into a balmy Florida night smelling of asphalt, fried food and garbage. I leaned back on the metal railing and waited.

Cordelia took a deep breath and said, "Please let him go, Sherri. The children and I need him."

This was not what I expected.

"He's all I've got," she whispered and lowered her face onto her hands. She started to cry.

"You think I'm having an affair with Noble?" I asked just to be sure I hadn't misunderstood.

Her shoulders spasmed and there was a soft meowing sound.

"Cordelia?"

She raised her face and her tears shone in the dim light from the Exit sign.

"You came here because you think Noble and I are having an affair?"

She nodded.

"Why? Why do you think it's me?"

She didn't have to think about it. "Because when we go out with you and Evan he's different. More animated. And you and Evan are the only people he really wants to spend time with anymore."

"Cordelia, the only person I'm sleeping with is Mr. McGoo."

"Who?"

"Mr. McGoo, my teddy bear. Noble . . ." How could I tell her that Noble Grant was the last person I'd ever go for, even if he wasn't gay? "Noble and I have never done more than peck each other on the cheek with you standing there. There's less than nothing between us." It was true but still I felt like a liar.

"Then who is it?" she wailed.

"You should be asking Noble. Not me."

"I can't," she whispered.

"Why?"

"If we talk about it and it's out in the open there's no going back. He might leave me."

"Is that the worst thing that could happen?"

"Yes," she said and started to cry again.

I reached out tentatively and patted her shoulder

before I slid my arm across her sharp-boned back. She was a grown woman of thirty-two, three years older than me, with two kids of her own, but her fragility awoke protective feelings in me. Her body felt small and delicate beside mine; her head barely reached my shoulder but there was a correctness about Cordelia that would soon turn matronly, taking her from girlish straight into middle age.

Her stiff body relaxed and sank into my side for only a few seconds before she pulled back and began tucking in the starched blouse and smoothing down her skirt, putting her temporary weakness behind her. "You must think I'm being silly." She brushed the tears off her cheeks with long white fingers, then searching through her bag for a tissue before dabbing at her nose and sniffing delicately.

From down the alley came the raucous laughter of a boisterous group leaving the Sunset. I glanced out to the mouth of the alley before shaking my head in denial and saying, "Being cheated on isn't silly. I know. I've got the T-shirt. It must have been hard for you to come here tonight."

She opened her bag and put away the tissue. "I don't like scenes."

I laughed. "Trust me, Cordelia, this is no scene. I've been at the center of too many of them to be fooled."

"Don't tell Evan," she pleaded. "I don't want him to know."

That was something I wasn't going to promise. I had rather a lot to say to Evan. You see, I was the skirt that Evan hid behind, the woman he dragged along on those social occasions where he couldn't go stag, the female he used to keep other women away I was the way he socialized with his lover so his lover's wife didn't suspect. It hadn't bothered me before but now I felt dirty, conspiring in Noble's betrayal of Cordelia.

Two hours after Cordelia left, the cop arrived to tell me that Jimmy, my godawful husband, was dead— blown up with his boat, the *Suncoaster*.

CHAPTER 3

I looked at Detective Styles as if he'd told me it was raining outside. Actually, rain in southwest Florida in January is rarer than violent death, but the thing is, I'd always waited for this news, knew it was coming sooner or later. Jimmy was never meant to die easy . . . or old. He was probably dead drunk when his boat went up and thought it was fireworks. "Hee haw," as Jimmy always said.

Detective Styles asked, "Would you like me to drive you home, Mrs. Travis?"

Did I need to go home? Was I going to fall apart? I didn't know. There was just a great big void of nothing: no pain; no feelings; no nothing; just Peggy Lee singing in the background about the final disappointment.

Jeff said, "Go on home, Sherri. Leave me the keys. I'll get someone to follow me with your car." Middle-aged and chronically tired, Jeff was always the first one out the door and the last one in, so this was a sacrifice for him.

I nodded, relieved to have someone else make the decision.

In the car Styles said, "Fasten your seat belt, please."

I asked, "Do Jimmy's parents know?" This worry was running round and round in my head.

"We only notified you as the next of kin."

Next of kin was a strange way to hear myself described.

"Would you take me out to Indian Mound Beach to tell them? I can't do it alone." I clicked the belt into place. "And even my shaky knowledge of deportment says this isn't the kind of thing you announce over the phone."

We stared at each other for a few seconds. His features were even, not remarkable or memorable, unlined and pale as if he spent too much time indoors, but it was a face I was never going to forget. Mercy, meek and mild, Grandma Jenkins would say. If I'd met him on the street, I'd bet he sold insurance.

He sighed, a dry exhausted sound. I guess he was hoping to ditch me quick and get home to bed. Or maybe he just hated the thought of delivering one more piece of bad news to more next of kin.

He put the car in drive. "Where are they?"

I gave him the number on Spyglass Court and asked, "How did it happen?"

"Best guess at the moment is he didn't turn on the

exhaust fan to clear out the fumes in the bilge. The boat exploded when he hit the ignition." He glanced over at me before going on in that same dry, level voice. "We didn't find much. The tide was going out. We'll search the mangroves along the shore in the morning."

"But that doesn't make sense. Jimmy was always warning me to hit the exhaust fan before I turned the key. Even dead drunk it's hard to believe he'd forget something as basic as that."

Unmoved he asked, "When did you last see your husband, Mrs. Travis?"

Jimmy's mom, the Wicked Witch of the South, was Mrs. Travis, I wasn't—but it didn't seem like a good time to complain.

"Sunday night," I said.

"When officers Mackle and Reese were called to remove him from your apartment?"

"Yes."

"And did you threaten to kill him, Mrs. Travis?"

"Jimmy just didn't get it. Our marriage was over. I came home and found the idiot asleep on the old steel lounge on my balcony. He must have stood on the railing of the balcony underneath mine and pulled himself up," proving that he was still fit and still out of control. That he was still stupid was proven by the fact he fell asleep on the bare metal lounge. I never left the cushion out because the guy living below me fed the scrub jays. They perched on my railing and shit all over the concrete of my balcony while they waited for their turn to dive down for dinner. It was just one damn big birdcage with dying plants, the hot afternoon sun and bird shit. Come to think of it, it was the perfect place for Jimmy.

"Tell me about your husband," Styles said.

"I'm the wrong person to ask about Jimmy—too much history and I only remember the bad stuff." If I started talking, it might all pour out. How could I explain to this neat bland man that Jimmy could make you want to do all kinds of crazy things, including kill him?

But he wouldn't leave it alone. "How did you meet?"

I searched for pitfalls before I answered. "I first saw Jimmy the summer I turned twelve. He did a pike off the high board at the public swimming pool and flowed out of the water right at my feet. He was blond and beautiful and shining like a god. I fell in love with him instantly. It was an illness that took a long time to run its course." It felt good to be talking. Good and dangerous. "I've no idea what Jimmy was doing at the public pool that day, probably the one and only time he was ever there. Jimmy spent his summers playing golf and tennis at the Royal Palms Golf and Country Club, where he was club champion at eighteen, the same year he was the star of the high school track team and captain of the basketball team when Jacaranda

High School won the state championship. High school sports are a real big deal around here, which made Jimmy a really big deal. After high school Jimmy went to Florida State on a golf scholarship, although his parents wanted him to go to Harvard or Yale . . . anything Ivy League with a good Northern address. His parents also didn't want Jimmy to marry me. I mean, really, really, didn't want him to marry me, which is probably why he did." I told myself to shut up.

Styles drove in silence for a while and then asked, "What was he like?"

"He's charming. My god, is he charming." He could charm the birds out of the trees or his playing partner's wife out of her underwear.

"Is that why you were having trouble?" His voice sounded almost bored.

I wasn't fooled. I kept silent.

After a bit he asked, "What can you tell me about your husband's death, Mrs. Travis?"

I searched the pocket of my black leather jacket for cigarettes. I already knew there weren't any but I needed a cigarette bad and addiction, like hope, dies hard. "Are you sure he's dead?"

He let out a big frustrated breath. "Your husband's truck was in the parking lot. The *Suncoaster* went up in a huge ball of orange flames. It could be seen for miles. Plus we found clothing."

"Jimmy was living on his boat. Of course, you'd find clothing."

"Come daylight, we'll search for his remains."

Remains, what a horrible word, like something leftover and unwanted. Like what was left between Jimmy and me. I rubbed my forehead to clear away the ugly thoughts. "It just doesn't seem possible. Jimmy is the most alive person on earth."

"What can you tell me about the explosion?"

"Nothing."

"Did you have anything to do with your husband's death?"

"No." I shifted my body away from him and stared out the window into the blackness over the water. On this stretch of Beach Road only sand dunes and the odd clump of palm trees separate the road from the Gulf of Mexico. Come May, sea turtles lumber ashore and lay their eggs on the beach. The town removed all the street lights where Beach Road is exposed to the gulf, ensuring newly hatched turtles will head for the moon over the gulf instead of coming inland to the street lights and dying under the wheels of cars. But there was no moon now, only dark. Were there pieces of Jimmy floating out there in the blackness, being eaten by fishes and crabs and other unnamed creatures? I shivered and huddled deeper in the seat.

Styles exhaled heavily, a sound of bone-weary frustration.

CHAPTER 4

The lights were still on in the Travis mansion. No worry about nature there. Maybe they left them on all night because it looked so pretty all lit up. The mansion was a fairy-tale castle, with a steeply pitched roof and a round turret like the castle I saw Sunday nights on Walt Disney when I was a kid. Covered in pink stucco, it didn't belong on a beach in Florida.

Just pulling into the pink concrete drive made my stomach contract into a hard knot. I didn't even have to go in or see Jimmy's parents to feel the panic.

The drive led to a curved flagstone path edged in tightly clipped geometric shrubs. Ground-hugging lanterns set among bushes to cast small puddles of brightness in front of us.

I rang the doorbell and we waited in silence while my courage melted like the ice cubes in some forgotten drink. "Maybe it would be better if you break the news," I suggested. "I'll wait in the car."

Before Styles could answer, more lights flicked on and a disembodied voice demanded, "Who is it?"

Detective Styles and I looked at each other, waiting for the other to respond.

"Who's there?" the impatient voice demanded.

I leaned towards the grill set in the wall and said, "It's Sherri. May I come in, please?" I hoped he'd say no, so I could run away and let him read about Jimmy in the morning paper. Instead the door swung open on an older version of Jimmy. Dr. Travis was dressed in crisp chinos and a blue dress shirt, open at the neck with cuffs neatly turned back at the wrist. The gray hardly showed in Dr. Travis's fair hair and his good looks surely made checking into his clinic for plastic surgery a whole lot easier.

He held the door open for us without speaking and extended an arm in the direction of his study off to our left, but before we could reach the safety of Dr. Travis's lair, the wicked witch of the South flew out from the back of the house. Rings sparkled on each finger wrapped around the highball glass.

"What's she doing here?" Jimmy's mom hissed. Her given name was Bernice but I'd never been invited to call her that.

I hadn't seen Mrs. Travis in a couple of years, but she was still blond and beautiful. Of course she would never have accepted anything less. The only imperfect thing in her life was me, and she didn't like to be reminded of this temporary failure of the system. Tall, at least as tall as my five seven and a half, she was so skinny she looked like a prison-camp survivor. The close-fitting knit top and pants, in bands of hot pink and raspberry, clung to her and accentuated her thinness.

Bernice marched forward, intent on getting to me and doing some damage, but Dr. Travis shot an arm across her shoulders and held her back saying, "Bernice, please," in a tone of voice that said he already knew his request was useless.

"This is Detective Styles," I said quickly. "He has something to tell you." Well, I'd done my part. Take it away Detectives Styles.

Styles frowned. "I'm afraid it's bad news."

They exhaled in unison, reaching out for each other, clinging together, their faces saying they'd known as well as I did how Jimmy would end.

"There's been an accident."

The veneer that made them special—special and above mere mortals—melted, and they sank down into middle age, becoming just ordinary people in the midst of a tragedy.

"I'm sorry," Styles said.

Bernice gave a whimper and sagged at the knees. She would have collapsed on the floor but her husband grabbed her under the arms and lowered her gently onto a high-backed antique chair. Then he turned horrified eyes to us.

I raised my eyes to the gilded mirror over their

heads as Styles began, "Your son's boat exploded. His truck was in the parking lot so it's believed he was on board at the time." The crystal high ball shattered on the parti-colored marble floor.

"How . . . ," Dr. Travis started, but Mrs. Travis came alive. "It's your fault," she hissed at me. "Trash, nothing but trash . . . if he hadn't married you . . ."

My feet were moving with her first words and the door closed behind me before she finished the last.

The unmarked police car was locked so I leaned back against it, taking deep breaths and fighting for control.

The smell of the Gulf of Mexico, a hundred yards behind the house, mingled with the smell of fresh-cut grass. The sprinkler system came on, adding a soft mist to the air. The rains didn't come last summer and now, deep in winter, we were under a drought watch, with water strictly rationed. Drought doesn't matter in South Beach, where the thick Bermuda grass, up to the ankles, must be maintained at all costs.

I watched the beads of water form on the black leather boots I'd just blown a week's pay on and tried not to think or feel. Instead, I concentrated on cataloging my litany of injustices at the hands of the Travis family. Anger, always my refuge in times of trouble, was easier to handle than other emotions. And the rage at being blamed for one more of Jimmy's screw-ups was easier to deal with than the creeping sense of loss and pain that was trying to beat down my defenses.

Styles emerged from the house and the door closed quietly behind him. He came to the passenger side of the car and unlocked the door. I lounged back against the car, hands stuffed deep into the pockets of my coat, as he swung the door open.

"Well," I said brightly, "I think that went rather well."

His eyes opened wide and his mouth followed before he closed it, in a hard thin line. He went around to his side of the car. Looking at me over the roof of the car, he said, "Your in-laws . . . ," he paused, searching for words.

"Feel I leave a little to be desired in a daughter-in-law?"

He opened his door. "I think they feel you led their son astray."

I thought about that for a moment. "I'm not sure if I led Jimmy astray or he led me. I only know we both enjoyed the ride."

He slid in behind the wheel and softly closed his door.

I followed, slamming my door hard and imagining the witch's pained wince.

"What changed?" Styles asked. "Why did you separate?"

"I decided to grow up."

Styles backed carefully out the drive. He pulled slowly away. Everything about this man was cool and deliberate, not flashy or quick, just relentless. I wrapped my arms around my chest and hugged myself tightly against an inner chill.

"Mr. Travis said that your husband carried a rather large insurance policy and you were the beneficiary."

I laughed. "Not likely. I remember Grandma Travis making Jimmy take it out when we were first married. She even paid the premiums for a while. Grandma Travis was the only one in the Travis family that liked me. 'You'll be the making of my boy,' she said. Well, I guess she got that wrong."

"So there isn't a life insurance policy on your husband?"

"Jimmy never wasted a dime on insurance. He lived for now, not the future."

"And you no longer had a future together?"

"Not anymore." I rubbed at the goose bumps on my arms.

"Tell me about it."

My family motto is "The police are not your friends." That and a well-honed survival instinct, learned from a thorny childhood, screamed at me to shut up, while a need to explain, if only to myself, pushed me on. "There were some really great things about Jimmy." I leaned back against the headrest. The voice of caution whispered in my ear. I ignored it. "Life with Jimmy was exciting and almost enough fun to make the agony that always came after the fun worthwhile."

We rolled slowly to a stop at a red light. The streets were deserted but still we sat there waiting for the light to change.

"Was your husband into drugs?"

I turned to study Styles in the dim light. "Why?"

"Just a question."

"He was a chipper. A tweaker."

"Occasional user?"

I nodded. "He tried everything. First in high school and then in college."

"It was a flirtation with him, not a commitment. For a few months, when he was first in college, all the money his father sent Jimmy went up his nose. It scared the hell out of me. But it ended."

"People don't just quit doing drugs."

"He did. It just stopped, unlike the job in a bar I got to keep us alive while he was experimenting. I wasn't even legally old enough to drink."

"Why did he quit?"

I lifted my shoulders and let them fall. "Booze, drugs, sex and gambling . . . the only thing that Jimmy liked better was golf. Drugs interfered with his game and at the level he was playing he needed everything he had to win. He'd have quit anything that interfered with getting his pro ticket. Golf was the only thing he took seriously. He dreamed of leading the pro tour, but ended up a club pro instead."

"Doesn't sound like a bad place to end up, playing golf for a living." he said in a wry voice. I suppose playing golf for a living sounded like a whole lot more fun than talking to next of kin or hunting for body parts in the mangroves.

"A club pro spends most of his working hours teaching or doing office work. Jimmy was a super teacher but he still talked about trying to get on the tour again, talked about practicing and getting his game in shape and going on the pro tour."

"Lost dreams," Styles said. "We all have them."

When I let myself into the apartment the little red light on the answering machine was doing the chicken dance, but I didn't want to think about the daily dose of reality waiting for me on the machine. All I wanted was oblivion.

Later, I wished I'd listened to my messages.

CHAPTER 5

The slamming of a door down the hall brought me instantly awake and I watched the dust motes dance in the sunlight coming through the Venetian blinds while I searched for the thing I should remember. The ache was there but not the why. Slowly memory crept in and slammed me in the gut.

Jimmy was dead. I drew my knees up to my chest and wrapped my arms around them with the pain of it.

How could he be dead? How could all that joyous energy that was Jimmy just cease to be? I turned it over and over. It didn't feel right, didn't feel true; even dead drunk, Jimmy would never make the mistake of turning on the engine before clearing the bilge of fumes. And the accident happened at four-thirty in the afternoon, early even for Jimmy to be blitzed, although I'd heard around town that Jimmy was drinking heavily.

So where had the mistake been made? I could

believe the *Suncoaster* was gone. After all, as Styles had pointed out, people had seen it burn from a mile away, but I couldn't believe Jimmy was dead. Couldn't believe he had screwed up like that. Slowly a new conviction grew in me. My lying, cheating, scam artist husband was up to his old tricks. Jimmy wasn't dead! That son-of-a-Bernice! If he'd been there in the room with me I would've killed him. Enraged, I kicked off the covers and jolted out of bed cursing and raging until the first wave of fury passed, leaving me shaken with the violence of it.

Too many times I'd believed Jimmy had changed, that he'd never do what awful thing he'd just done ever again, and too many times I'd been disappointed. I just wanted to be free of his craziness. I didn't want to be sucked into another of Jimmy's disasters. No matter what was going on, it didn't involve me. I had my own life now.

Evan Beckworth, my friend and next-door neighbor, let himself into my apartment with the key I kept under the mat. "Lucy, I'm home," he called as I came out of the bedroom, dressed in my newest golf outfit in black and red. I'd pulled my long black hair into a pony-tail and now I unsnapped the back of a baseball cap and fitted it around the elastic holding my hair.

Evan's hands were full of fresh donuts and coffee. "How are you doing?" he asked. His face said he thought I might crumble into a hundred pieces if he wasn't careful.

"I'm perfectly fine."

Evan is drop-dead gorgeous. All the women I know want him . . . and quite a few of the men. Blond hair, soft hazel eyes and, I swear to god, a cleft chin like some bloody cartoon superhero. Tall and bronzed, he has a body that could advertise the gym he spends most of his free time at.

"I don't have to go into the paper today if you need me." I'm sure Evan could've worked for a better paper than the *Jacaranda Sun*, but he'd followed Noble here after college and stayed to be near Noble.

I opened the refrigerator door and took out a carton of orange juice. "It isn't as though I'm going to cry my eyes out over a guy who cheated on me the night before our wedding and as quick as he could after." I yanked open a cupboard door, ". . . someone I'd have divorced if either of us could have afforded it. A guy I have more restraining orders against than I have tax returns. It isn't as if I still loved him," I explained and poured the juice right over the rim of the glass and onto the floor.

"Shit." I slammed the cardboard container down on the counter and more juice slopped over the top. I grabbed the paper towels, pulling off great lengths until toweling spilled over the counter and followed the juice onto the floor.

Evan came and took the roll of paper towels out of

my hand, pushing me towards the living room. "Go and sit down."

I slumped on a stool at the bar separating the living area from the kitchen. The *Jacaranda Sun* was beside the takeout coffee. Jimmy smiled up at me from the front page. "This was taken when Jimmy became the pro out at Windimere Golf Course." You couldn't see the blue of his eyes in the picture but the square jaw and broad forehead came through just fine. Even the small scar, high on his left cheek, where I'd caught him with a fishhook, showed up. The smile on his face said, "Isn't life grand?" Even from a picture, he could melt your heart.

I turned the paper over so I couldn't see his face and watched Evan finish wiping up the juice. He sprayed cleaner and wiped it down again, scrubbing away like a demented housewife.

"The floor hasn't been this clean in years," I told him.

Evan asked, "Where were you last night?"

"Here." I pulled one of the coffees out of the cardboard container and took off the top.

Evan stopped mopping and looked up at me. "But your car wasn't in the lot when I got home."

I told him about Jeff and blew waves across the black liquid.

"I know how hard this is on you," he said. "I would have come over if I'd known you were here."

I slipped off the stool and headed into the living

room. "I'm so over Jimmy. Besides . . ." I didn't go further. My survival instincts were working just fine now. There was no reason to explain to Evan that my lying, cheating husband likely wasn't dead. Evan was the press. He might be my friend, but he still worked for a newspaper and the story of the *Suncoaster* blowing up must be the biggest headline Evan ever covered in Jacaranda. What a coup to report that Jacaranda's favorite son might not be dead. What a temptation! And I knew all about temptation. I've given into it way too many times to expect others to resist. I rooted around under the couch for my runners.

The lid slammed on the trash container. "If you are so over Jimmy, how come you've been sleeping alone this past year? You're beautiful and single, yet there's no man in your life," he said, coming into the living room.

"Men are like going to the dentist. I want to know how much pain and trouble it's going to be before I get involved." I threw myself down on a wicker chair and pushed my feet into the runners. "Besides, a tattoo on your butt that says 'Jimmy's' puts you a bit off your stride."

"Oh, I'm sure you could get past that." He sat down on the couch across from me. "And anyone can afford a divorce. Is it so hard to admit you still cared for the guy?"

I made a face. "Jimmy and I had our moments." I

planted a foot on the coffee table and yanked hard at my shoelaces. "It wasn't all bad. Just mostly bad." The laces were probably going to cut off my circulation. I'd go lame and be crippled for life. "Jimmy did teach me to play golf. I'm grateful for that. Well . . . ," I gave him a broad wink, ". . . that and the other fun thing he taught me on the *Suncoaster* the summer I turned fifteen." I slumped back against the cushions. "She was thirty-two feet of ivory fiberglass and mahogany trim. Her name was on the prow in elegant black script." I sketched the name in the air.

"And as Katherine Hepburn said about another boat, 'She was yar.' What the hell do you suppose yar means anyway? But that's what she was. Yar. And watching the *Suncoaster* fly before the wind out on the gulf was pure joy." I sat up straight. "Now the boat is gone and so is Jimmy. I'm really going to miss that boat. But hey, look on the bright side, I still play scratch golf."

Evan had his disapproving-grandma look on and couldn't stop himself from saying, "You don't mean that."

"You didn't know Jimmy."

There was a flicker of something in his eyes before he looked away. "I did actually," he said lightly. He picked at the rim of his cardboard coffee cup.

I sat perfectly still. "Where did you meet him?"

With a soft lift of his shoulders, he said, "He was

popular guy and was invited to every party in town. I met him several times. I didn't like to tell you."

"Why?"

Again the soft lift of his shoulders. "I didn't want to hurt you."

"What happened, Evan?"

He started to deny it, and then he rubbed his hand across his mouth and gave a huge sigh. "About a month ago Noble and I were out sailing. We anchored in the lea of Little Jose Island and were swimming in the nude when Jimmy sailed in. Jimmy knew Noble, of course, and understood the situation immediately." Evan looked up at me. His jaw was set like granite. "He just got this big grin on his face like it was the best joke he'd ever heard. Noble has been terrified ever since, waiting for Jimmy to out us."

"Sooner or later it has to come out."

"Yes, but not yet. Noble needs time. I don't want him pushed into it."

We had this discussion about a million times a day. I popped to my feet. "I've got a tee time." I went to get my sunglasses off the counter.

"You're going to play golf?" His voice went up an octave and his eyes grew round at this latest example of my poor social graces. Evan was my arbitrator of good taste and he'd been working hard to take off my rough edges, but even with all his hard work the Junior League wasn't coming to call anytime soon.

"Today?"

"Why not?"

"It's not a good idea."

He looked so serious, I laughed. "You mean people will talk 'cause in polite society you don't play golf the day after your husband is blown to Kingdom Come."

"Not usually, at least not anywhere I've ever been." He followed me to the door, still fussing over me. "You can be your own worst enemy sometimes. Stay home and we'll hang out."

I opened the front door and leaned forward to kiss his cheek. "I wish I had a mamma just like you."

I ran down the stairs, opened the car door, and slung my bag onto the passenger's seat.

I looked back up at Evan leaning over the railing. "Oh, by the way, Cordelia came into the Sunset last night." Spread the joy, I always say. "She thinks I'm having an affair with Noble." Well, that should take his mind off my troubles.

CHAPTER 6

I swung out on Airport Road and drove the two blocks to Main. Jeff had changed the radio from my normal Tampa Bay rock station to a golden oldies one, but I was too preoccupied to care. At Main the light changed just as I got there and I was making the left when some stupid song about a guy named Jimmy Mac coming back started playing on the radio. Then it hit me. Jimmy wasn't coming back. The angry conviction that this was all a scam fled and I bumped up onto the center median and stopped with the ass end of my puke green Dodge hanging out in traffic. I couldn't breathe.

A rush of traffic caught up to me. Cars with out-of-state license plates dodged around me, blasting their horns while I bawled and cursed them, not knowing who I hated more at that moment, the tourists or Jimmy. Hell, I wasn't even sure if I was crying for Jimmy or myself, I only knew my life was never going to be the same again. Lost dreams, Styles had said. I sure as hell had a few.

When the light changed again, I eased carefully back out into traffic without killing anyone. By the time I hit Jacaranda Boulevard I was back to believing that the fraud artist I married was at it again. Call me Ms. Inconsistency if you like—you just had to know Jimmy to understand.

When I hit Raintree Avenue, I turned south without thinking, instead of north towards the golf course and pulled into Harry's Diner. I saw Clay's white Lexus parked out front before I realized why I was there. I left my sunglasses on and headed for the door.

Harry's is a tiny place, one long counter with a dozen stools and about five tables pushed up against the outside wall. Left over from the fifties, the diner's chrome shines from all its edges and a large glass pie shelf sits in the place of honor on the center of the counter.

I stepped inside and waited a moment while my eyes adjusted to the light. The buzz of conversation dropped and finally ceased. Clay Adams, always tuned to the world around him, glanced over his right shoulder to see what had caused the sudden silence. His eyes lit up when he saw me and a grin pulled at his lips. I crossed the black-and-white-tiled floor to the counter where he was having breakfast with Brian Spears.

"Bacon and eggs are bad for you," I told Clay as I slipped onto the red leatherette stool next to him.

He looked hard at me. Those sharp obsidian eyes always see more than you want them to. "Not doing so good, are you?"

"Says who?"

"Tough girl. If you were all right, you'd be on the golf course instead of here."

"Damn. Can I use your cell phone? I need to cancel my tee time." He reached into his suit jacket for his phone and handed it to me.

Clay went back to his breakfast while Brian studied me anxiously over Clay's back as I made the call. Brian's gray eyes are set deep in a fair-skinned face covered in sunspots from years of sailing. He shows up regularly with tape over the latest blemish he's had removed. Even this early in the day Brian's suit was rumpled and his tie was undone.

Clay is the exact opposite of Brian; with dark hair and skin, he is always meticulous about his person and perfectly presented no matter what hour of the day or night. Lean to the point of gaunt, there's a hungry look about Clay that no food could ever satisfy, and his restless eyes always seem to be searching for something they can't quite find.

Clay has never married, likely because he gets a bigger thrill seeing someone sign on the dotted line for one of his overpriced properties than he ever gets from seeing a woman in his bed. He lives to make deals. Seven days a week he's buying and selling properties up and down the west coast of Florida, making his real estate company the biggest in the county.

Val arrived with a cup of coffee for me. "Sorry for your loss, honey," she said, her plump brown face full of concern. She reached out and rubbed the back of my hand. "Sorry."

"Thanks." I had a hard time meeting her eye, uncomfortable and wanting to tell her that there was really nothing for her to be sorry about—it was just Jimmy being an ass again.

The silence around us was palpable now. Jacaranda is mostly a small town where everyone knows everyone else, except for the tourists, and they don't count. Like one big family: acrimonious, battling and often nasty, but still family, so everyone had heard about the explosion on the *Suncoaster* and was feeling real sorry for me.

Only Clay seemed comfortable. He just went on neatly eating his artery-clogging breakfast without worrying if I was falling to pieces beside him.

"Can we go outside, guys?" I whispered. I wanted to get out of there before everyone in the diner started coming up to me one by one to express their condolences. "I need to talk."

Clay pushed his plate away and threw some money on the counter. "See you tomorrow, Valentine," he said and led the way to the door. Brian took my hand as we followed him out. Hand-holding wasn't normally the kind of relationship Brian and I had. Our bond was more like insult and injury, so a big lump came up in my throat.

"What can I do?" Brian asked as the door closed behind us.

"Let's sit in my car," Clay suggested, leading the way.

I started by telling them about Styles. "The thing is . . . well, you know Jimmy." I ran my index finger under my nose.

Clay pulled some tissues from a box in the glove compartment and held them out to me.

"You know all the things he's done in the past. Get-rich projects with other peoples' money. Selling things he didn't own. This is just one more scheme, but I don't know why."

"Sherri," Clay said, "denial is a normal part of grieving. I know it's hard to believe he's dead, but you have to know the police wouldn't tell you this lightly."

Clay turned in his seat to look at Brian. "They must know Travis is dead, right Brian? They wouldn't just say someone was dead if they didn't have a body."

Brian adjusted his glasses, thinking it over. "I wouldn't think so, but from what I read in the paper there was an explosion and then a fire. How much would be left of him? Sorry, Sherri." He patted my shoulder with his sausage-sized fingers.

"Do you think you can find out how certain they are Travis was on board?" Clay asked.

"I know a few people. I'll make some calls."

Clay turned back to me. "You just have to sit tight, Sherri, and wait 'til we know more."

"If there was someone on the boat and it wasn't Jimmy, who was it?" Saying my fears out loud made them real.

"We have to know that there was a body, before you start worrying about that," Clay told me.

But I couldn't wait. "Someone had to start the engine. I'm worried it might be Andy Crown. He's Jimmy's best friend. Jimmy takes him out on the Suncoaster a lot."

"Is he that paranoid guy?" Brian asked.

"Yeah." Of all the other ways of describing Andy, like funny and clever, it had come down to this.

"I know the Crowns," Brian said. "Nice people. Shame they got a kid like that."

I swung violently around to face him. "Well, schizophrenia was no great present for Andy, either." The look on his face stopped me. I slid down into the white leather. "Sorry, Brian."

"It's okay, kid." He patted my shoulder again. "Only natural to be upset."

All of this went right by Clay. He handed me his phone and said, "Call him."

Clay switched on the ignition to roll down the windows while we waited. Andy didn't answer. I slapped the phone shut. "No answer."

"That doesn't mean anything," said Clay.

"True. He thinks the CIA can control his thoughts through the telephone. Plus he thinks his telephone is bugged." I tried to laugh. "All things considered, if I were him, I wouldn't answer it either."

Depression reached out and grabbed me. All our bright promise had fallen into madness, death and failure. I opened the door. "I have to go."

Clay leaned over and called, "But keep in touch," as the door slammed shut.

Cypress Island is a barrier island situated halfway between Tampa and Naples. There's a metal lift-bridge over the inland waters at the north end of Cypress Island and another lift-bridge at the south end connecting the island to the mainland. In-between the two bridges there are about eight miles of paradise and Florida's best-kept secret. Most visitors to the west coast of Florida stop at Sarasota or hurry on down the interstate to Fort Myers without ever knowing our island exists—a bonus for those of us who don't want it to become another Dade County.

I drove through the town of Jacaranda, past houses sheltering under live oaks dripping with Spanish

44

moss, past old Florida-style houses with wide verandas running across the front and metal roofs shining in the sun. There's a whole parcel of white clapboard churches, and everywhere you look scarlet bougainvillea and orange trumpet vine climb on fences and sheds. The tourists love it.

When I was a kid it was still mostly a fishing village, but in the last ten years it has become gentrified, sending prices skyrocketing and pushing all the fishermen off the island.

At Banyan, I turned left onto Beach Road and headed for Indian Mound Beach, which is two miles past the south bridge and the most exclusive part of Cypress Island. The road twisted and turned around trees and bends in the shoreline. Overhead, the trees met, forming a living canopy. At middle beach, where the land narrows and the inland waters and the Gulf of Mexico nearly meet, the beach was full of colorful umbrellas, pink and blue and yellow, their borders dancing in the breeze while their owners walked along the edge of the water, heads down concentrating on finding shark teeth. This beach is famous for its teeth, ancient reminders of sharks long dead, and it draws people from all over the country.

Most of the owners on this part of the island are either from up north or they're the most successful doctors, lawyers and Indian Chiefs in the whole county. The houses, set in lush tropical jungles overlooking the Gulf of Mexico on the west side or bordering the inland waterway down the east side, are all worth millions of dollars. It has always been my belief that nothing bad or chaotic could possibly happen out here. It just wouldn't be allowed.

I pulled into the drive of number three Spyglass Court. Fill had been brought in to raise the house up on its own little knoll, where it rose above the palms like a fortress. Built of concrete and glass with a flat roof, the house's circular stainless-steel balconies jutted out on either side of the second floor and glinted in the bright morning sun.

I looked around carefully before getting out of my Green Puke. Even though the lots were large and thick plantings separated this house from the Travis house next door, I still felt uneasy. Everyone knows that being an evil witch gives you superpowers. Bernice Travis just might have some sixth sense when it came to me, might fly over the dense lady palms to cast a spell on me and turn me into a toad. I power-walked to the front door and rang the bell, still scanning the greenery for the evil one.

A voice with a Spanish lilt answered my ring and asked me to wait one minute and she would see if Mrs. Crown was at home. From the silver Jaguar sitting in the drive it seemed pretty likely. The question was would she be at home to me.

CHAPTER 7

The front of the house was all glass, even the door, opening the house to the most casual of visitors. Inside everything you could see was all chrome and glass with hard edges with no place to curl up. It was a house that had always made me uncomfortable. Past the great room another glass wall at the back of the house showed the borderless pool. With water spilling over the far edge, it looked like an extension of the gulf beyond the house. Standing there, it seemed as if you could swim from the great room to the pale blue line where the water met the sky.

I watched Betsy Crown float down the curved steel stairs towards me wearing a short white tennis skirt and a white polo shirt, looking totally elegant and composed. Like her house, she was sleek and cool with nothing to hide. She glided across the pale granite floor with a tight little smile, a woman determined to be pleasant no matter what, and opened the door with a flourish. "Sherri, how nice."

She was old enough to be my mother but I had to look real hard for the proof. Only two little vertical worry lines showed between her eyebrows and judging, from the taut skin stretched across her face, she'd paid a visit or two to Dr. Travis.

"I came to see you about Andy," I told her.

"Let's go out by the pool." She led the way without speaking.

The caged pool was set in a two-storey, sixty-foot-long screened room facing the beach. At the deep end of the pool, a pair of stone dolphins arched into a dive through a spray of water.

Betsy Crown sank down into a black wrought-iron chair, crossing her slender brown legs at the ankle and gestured to a matching chair across the glass table from her. The satin air coming across the gulf from Texas was warm for that time of year and scented by the pungent smell of the gardenias spilling out of a crystal vase on the table.

I perched tentatively on the edge of the cushioned chair and said, "I'm trying to find Andy. I'm not sure he knows about Jimmy and I don't want him to see it on the news or hear it from someone else."

"He isn't here." She looked out to the gulf, where a sailboat skimmed across the water. It was worth watching. You'd swear the boat could sail right up to the edge of the tiled pool and join us. Betsy Crown seemed mesmerized by it.

"Have you told Andy about the *Suncoaster*?" I prompted, wanting her to relieve my fears.

"No." She watched the sailboat. "I haven't seen him."

"Has he called?"

She gave a little shake of her head, keeping her eyes fixed on the horizon. "No."

"Then he probably doesn't know."

There was no response from Mrs. Crown for several moments. We just sat there like two idiots watching that stupid boat while I tried to think of a nice way to get what I needed out of her. At last she turned to me and said, "Jimmy was here looking for Andrew."

That was jolt. "When?"

"Sunday afternoon."

"Did he say why he was looking for Andy?"

"No." She looked at me now, a hesitant smile teasing the corners of her lips. "Jimmy was in a very good mood. He danced me around the foyer. He was always so much fun." She smiled a real smile now. "You know Jimmy."

I did indeed know Jimmy. "Is Andy still on Hess Street?" Was there a polite way to ask if he was under lock and key in some hospital? I blamed Evan for this new concern with propriety.

She began to neatly press the pleats into her tennis skirt with the flat of her hand. "I don't know where he is exactly. He cashed the check I sent last month. I sent it to him at that address." She looked up at me, eyes bright and eager, wanting to help. "I could call the bank and see if he cashed the one for this month."

"I don't know if it would help in finding him. Does he have a car?"

"I'm not sure. I understand you and Jimmy hid his car the last time he went off his medication."

Now that had been a real fun time . . . Andy flying around the island, accusing people of all sorts of things: out of control and scary. "He really wasn't safe to be driving. The paranoia was too strong," I don't know why I was trying to justify our actions to Mrs. Crown. She knew the situation better than I did.

"I appreciate what you did. Did you give the car back to him?"

"I don't know what Jimmy did." We'd basically stolen the car and Jimmy had taken it out to the golf course where he worked and parked it. We'd barely spoken when I'd driven him back over to the island to pick up his truck. "Jimmy and I haven't been on chatting terms lately."

"Jimmy always looked out for Andy." She went back to ironing her pleats. "They met in the eighth grade when we moved here." Her eyes flicked up to mine. "Did you know that?"

I nodded. "That's why I'm worried about how Andy hears. Perhaps it would be better if you called and told him."

"No!" Emphatic and final. She straightened in her chair, feet and knees together, hands cupped on her lap. "You can't know how hard it is to watch your only son live with this disease, never mind the embarrassment and humiliation we've suffered, having him rant and talk crazy in front of our friends, seeing him carted off by the police, seeing him on the street like . . . like some vagrant." She spat out the last word and clapped her palm over her mouth to staunch the flow. She took a deep breath and straightened her shoulders. Her hand settled back on her lap. "It isn't nice."

"I'm sorry."

"None of this needs to happen if he'd just stay on the Clozapine."

"Andy hates feeling sedated all the time." Plus, knowing Andy, he just flat out forgot to take them. I loved the guy but even on his best day he wasn't organized enough to have any kind of routine. Even brushing his teeth was probably hit and miss.

"Nevertheless, Vernon and I have decided that we will have no further contact with Andrew until he gets himself straightened out and stays on the drugs. We can't help him and it just distresses us to see him that way."

She brushed a non-existent stray strand of hair back from her face. "Of course we will continue to support him financially." Her voice was refined silk, her composure flawless as she made this pronouncement. On the ladder of social climbing, she was right near the top, all that one of Jacaranda's leading matrons and the wife of a successful stockbroker should be, but at that moment she made my mother, Ruth Ann, look like a queen. Whatever she might be, Ruth Ann would never abandon me.

I picked up my bag. "If Andy calls, please have him get in touch with me."

"He won't." The words and the voice left no room to argue. She rose gracefully from the chair and led the way back through the modern art gallery house.

Betsy had known Jimmy most of his life but hadn't expressed any feelings about his death. I guess she didn't feel anything and from the way she was dressed, her day would go pretty much as usual. Hadn't I reacted the same way? But then, I didn't think Jimmy was dead, whereas she had no reason to doubt it. Also, Betsy Crown's eyes were a dead give-away. With that much stuff in her it would be hard to feel anything but numb.

CHAPTER 8

I live in the mile and a half of Cypress Island that is north of the upper bridge, the least desirable part of the island. It's mostly small businesses, boat storage, marinas and the like. The Jacaranda Airfield, water purification plant and sewage plant are all up at the north end too. Makes you think, doesn't it, when the sewage plant and water storage facilities are within a John Daly drive of each other?

To compensate for this, the north end also has the world's greatest fishing pier, and fishermen line both sides of it at all times of the day and night. Sticking out into the gulf like a great big concrete finger, the pier is lit at night to keep boats from piling into it. It makes a great place to take a walk when I'm too hyper to sleep after work. There's always someone there to pass the time with.

The municipal golf club is also up there, conveniently close to the sewage plant, and the outflow from the sewage plant is used to water the golf course.

They call it gray water, as though changing the color alters what it is, and the golf course is covered with signs warning golfers not to kiss their balls. After you're done laughing at that mental image, the fear of what bacteria might be out there, just lying around and waiting to infect you, can scare the hell out of you. I just keep repeating to myself, "I trust my elected officials. Of course it's safe. I trust my elected officials." Whoever heard of elected officials who didn't have the people's best interests in mind?

I live at the Tropicana Apartments, in an orange-colored, two-storey walk-up with miserly little single-glazed aluminum windows that don't keep out the heat or the cold. I swear they don't even keep out the palmetto bugs. There's no pool, but there is a nice drainage ditch out back for a water feature, provided you don't mind green slime and the odd gator. And in lieu of landscaping there are scrub palmettos and cabbage palms.

It's my guess the place will never make any edition of *Southern Living* but for me it's better than living on the mainland and spending half my life waiting for a bridge to go down. Every morning there's a line-up on the mainland of support staff, gardeners and maids waiting to cross over to the island to keep it functioning.

I turned into the building's parking lot, which was made from crushed shells like most unpaved parking lots around here. There was Detective Styles, leaning against his beige sedan with arms and legs crossed and looking like he was settled in to wait forever.

"Shit!" For a brief second I thought of throwing my car into reverse and peeling out of there, but that's what the old Sherri would have done. The new grown-up Sherri pulled into the parking space beside him.

He uncrossed his arms and pushed away from his car as the Green Puke shuddered and died.

Most of the middle-aged men I'm real familiar with are overweight and reeking of things. They belch and fart and let things roll, so when a man of this age is scrubbed up and looking serious, he always means big trouble for somebody. My guess was Styles meant trouble for me.

He leaned a hand on my car door and looked in through the open window at me. Bland and non-threatening, he said, "Hello, Mrs. Travis."

I nearly wet myself. Mercy, meek and mild was gonna get me. I tugged on the door handle and he backed away as it screeched open.

"I'd like to ask you a few questions," he said, all polite and calm. I could deal with drunks, wannabe rapists and drug addicts, but this man just flat out frightened the piss out of me.

"Come upstairs." I started for the stairs without waiting for him to say aye or nay, walking fast as if I could outdistance him and get away. I tilted my head to my right. "My unit is at the end."

A gecko sunning in the heat scurried off the edge of the concrete steps and disappeared into the dying Pampas grass. I thought about joining him.

Instead I said, "Being at the end, I can light my barbie without worrying too much if the rest of the tenants get out before the building burns down." My nervous jokes are seldom funny but that never stops me. My mouth goes into overdrive when I'm panicking.

I stopped outside my door and asked, "Where you from?'

"Here."

I bit back a caustic remark. "I mean before."

"Sarasota." We waited a heartbeat and then he said, "New Jersey." He sure didn't look happy to be admitting this and I could understand his reluctance.

"How long have you been here?"

"Four months. I was in Sarasota five years." As if that counted. A newcomer.

I unlocked my door and waved him in. Normally I liked my apartment, liked my two white wicker chairs rescued from someone's garbage on my way home from work one night. I spray-painted them white and the paint flaked off like dandruff every time someone sat down but I liked the way they creaked and groaned and sagged around my body. Ruth Ann made seat cushions for them in a black material with green palm fronds and pink bird of paradise, amazing both of us.

But it's the floor that was my masterpiece. I'd complained so loud and so long to the landlord about the velvet carpet in a rotting-mushroom color with pathways worn into it, that one day while I was at work he came in and ripped it all out, leaving only powdery gray concrete behind. After another war of words, which I also lost, I painted the floor dove gray, with splashes of green and pink and black, to match the chairs. It's delightfully cool on bare feet and easy to clean, so when the landlord finally offered to replace the cheap carpet with something even cheaper I said no thanks.

But none of these decorating achievements caught Styles' eye. He was looking at the books. The walls were covered with bookcases and books overflow onto stacks on the floor. There are books piled up in pillars to hold boards that make shelves for more books under the long narrow window looking out onto the communal walkway. A surprising number of these volumes have yellow stickie notes of stuff I want to remember and come back to. These yellow flags do nothing for the room's appearance.

"I love to read," I explained, picking up the leftover Styro cups from the morning. The hot room smelled of stale coffee. "I love books and everything about them." I went to the sliding doors and opened them.

"And Jimmy brought me books from all over Florida and any other state he played golf in. He used to walk into libraries in every town he passed through and help himself. It was never any use telling him not to do it. Jimmy never listened."

The words "receiving stolen property" floated into my head. Is there a statue of limitations on book theft? Holy shit, of all the things I could be done for, how come I never worried about this one? "I really did try to stop him," I pleaded, getting my defense lined up. "He'd come home with the trunk of his car filled with books, golf clubs and dirty laundry." I filled the coffeepot with water and put a fresh filter in the basket as I watched this white bread cop turn full circle, taking the room in.

"Those years on the tour meant a lot of towns and a lot of libraries." I'm a cracker born and bred, although from the size of my butt there was more bread than cracker involved and though I try to hide the drawl and drop the Piney woods talk, in times of stress it comes back in spades. It was back now, thick as year-old honey.

Styles' eyes took in all the signs of not so gracious living before they settled on my vibrator. Lying on a pillow on the floor, Evan's anatomically correct present for my last birthday caught his attention. At the end of a shift it's exquisite to roll it back and forth under my feet but why spoil the fun for Detective Styles?

He blandly raised his eyes to me, giving nothing away, and asked, "Was Mr. Travis living on his boat full-time?"

"Yup." Was this a crime? "People like me move into their cars when they hit bottom. People like the Travises move onto their boats."

"You lived on the *Suncoaster* with you husband for a few months, didn't you?"

"Yeah." I got two mugs out of the cupboard.

"So you know the boat well?" His hand described a hazy circle, "Know all about bilge pumps and things like that?"

The cups thunked onto the counter as I stared at him, knowing the important bit was coming.

"You know about boats, don't you, Mrs. Travis?"

"My grandpa was a shrimper. I know about boats." My drawl passed Scarlett O'Hara's.

He waited a heartbeat before he said, "Your husband's death wasn't an accident." He said just that and no more, waiting for me to jump in.

The coffee maker gurgled into the silence.

Finally he said, "The exhaust fan had been tampered with. It's a murder investigation now."

I sucked in my breath, my hands curling into fists.

"We found enough wreckage to tell that the blades weren't attached to the fan. It would sound like it was working when it was turned on but it wouldn't exhaust the fumes."

"Maybe they fell off." A silly suggestion even to my ears—he shook his head in denial.

"Are you sure someone was on board?"

"Yes."

How did they know? Human remains obviously, but how could they tell that from bits of raw meat left in the fridge and blown to bits? Bad thought, bad thought.

We stared silently at each other before he added, "We've asked Mr. and Mrs. Travis for DNA samples. It will take a while for the tests to confirm that it was your husband onboard."

My stomach rolled over, but he wasn't done with the good news. "There's one other thing. One of the residents along there was motoring by in his boat about three o'clock yesterday afternoon."

Jimmy didn't have his boat in a marina. He anchored it in Hidden Pass just down beyond a public boat-launching ramp at the foot of the south bridge. The ramp was at the end of a white-shell parking lot with a long boardwalk out along the mangroves where Jimmy left a small runabout, against all regulations, under the boardwalk so he could get out to his boat. If the runabout was stolen, well, no worries. Hell, he probably stole it in the first place.

Squatting on water this way was cheaper than paying for dockage and, besides, Jimmy was at the mouth of the Intracoastal Waterway, his idea of heaven. Jimmy had been cruising up and down those waters his whole life and most of the people who went by in their boats had known him since he was a kid and didn't make a fuss.

"This witness saw someone aboard the *Suncoaster*," Styles told me. "The person on the *Suncoaster* ducked back down the companionway when the witness waved."

"That is strange. Everyone waves at you on Cypress. If they didn't wave back, they were definitely from away."

"The witness thought it was a woman on the *Suncoaster*." Why do my chickens always come home to roost so much faster than anyone else's?

"Down here, women wave too. It was a tourist for sure."

"Where were you yesterday at three, Mrs. Travis?"

"Here, getting ready for work." And inspiration struck me. "But it didn't need to be yesterday. Everyone knows that Jimmy moves his boat once a month—not far, just enough to give his neighbors a change of scene. If the fan was messed with, it could have been anytime since he last moved the *Suncoaster*." This was good stuff, really saving my ass here.

"The witness also said the only car in the parking lot was green."

I swung away and poured myself a cup of coffee. The drops falling on the heating element made loud pinging sounds.

I turned back to Styles and held up the second mug to him. He shook his head. "Tell me about . . . ," he paused and took a small notebook out of his inside pocket. We both knew he didn't need to refresh his memory. ". . . Ray-John Leenders." He drew the name out slowly, pronouncing it carefully.

I went to the fridge and got the milk, trying to give my stomach time to stop doing back flips. Then I started pulling out the kitchen drawers, searching for cigarettes. I knew that I wouldn't find any, but I looked anyway. I'd picked a very bad time to try yet again to quit smoking.

"Tell me about Mr. Leenders." His voice was soft and polite, encouraging me to hang myself. Oh sorry, in Florida I think it's the electric chair; either way you're just as dead.

I gave up the hunt. "Ray-John Leenders is just someone the world would be better off without."

"I understand that you threatened him with a shotgun."

"The son of a bitch was beating up on my mamma." I hadn't used that word since I was six. I was regressing real fast here.

"First you take a shotgun to your mother's lover and then you threaten to kill your husband in front of witnesses. I'd say you have a little problem with anger management, Mrs. Travis."

I made a rude sound.

He stood quiet, hands folded in front of him, waiting. Well he could wait 'til hell froze over as far as I was concerned.

I turned away. Maybe there were still cigarettes in the utility drawer between the fridge and stove. I'd hidden them everywhere for emergencies, telling myself if I only had one cigarette it wasn't really smoking.

"How old were you?" he asked.

"Fifteen." No cigarettes in that drawer either. I turned back to face him and planted a fist on my hipbone. I stared at him hard, waiting.

"It must have been upsetting for you to see your mother beaten."

Routine would have been the way I'd have described it.

We did some more of the waiting and then he said, "So first you threaten Mr. Leenders and then your husband. You don't learn, do you?"

"Yeah, I learned. I learned I should have shot the bastard the day before when he tried to rape me instead of waiting and telling Mamma. I would have saved her a tooth and a fractured skull. He's probably still out there somewhere beating up women and abusing their kids."

He changed tactics. "I've been told your half-sisters were taken away from your mother."

"Their grandma didn't take to my daddy when he came along. The twins went to North Carolina to live but I'm sure you know more about that than I do."

"You don't have the same father? And then your mother took up with Mr. Leenders."

"So I come from a family that's Jerry Springer's wet dream, what's that got to do with the *Suncoaster*?"

"You know, Mrs. Travis, your attitude doesn't help you."

It was my first good laugh of the day. People had been telling me the same thing my whole life, but without my attitude I would have been curled up somewhere in a corner sucking my thumb.

"Tell me again where you were yesterday about three, Mrs. Travis."

"Here, getting ready for work." Little did he know how much time it took to perfect my white trash look, long straight hair, too tight clothing and too high heels, with more makeup than was wise or necessary.

"Alone?"

"Yes, unfortunately." I had a question of my own. "Was anyone with Jimmy?"

"What do you mean?"

"Jimmy has a friend, Andy Crown. I'm worried that Andy might have been on the *Suncoaster*."

"His death would bother you, would it, Mrs. Travis?"

"Yes."

"More than your husband's?" Outside on the communal walkway someone slammed a door.

"I haven't been able to reach Andy. His parents haven't heard from him either."

"There was no indication of more than one person on board."

I heard the sound of feet running down the stairs. "Are you sure anyone was on board?"

"Someone hit the switch."

"But did . . . did you find any real evidence that someone was on board?"

"What do you mean?"

"Jimmy was mechanical." I worried my bottom lip. I really didn't know where I was going with this. I only knew with Jimmy there was always a twist. "Maybe he just wants us to think he's dead."

"Why?"

"Dozens of reasons. Take your pick: drugs, debt or an angry husband. Maybe even an angry woman. Who knows what kind of trouble Jimmy was in this time. I just figure he wants to get away without anyone looking for him."

"Would he let his family believe he was dead?" Styles asked.

"Hell, yeah! That boy just never thinks things through."

"His truck was at the boat ramp."

"But it would be if he wanted you to think he was dead. Besides, if the past is anything to go by, a finance company will be along real soon to reclaim it."

"Would your husband send this Andy Crown out to move the boat if he knew it was rigged?"

"Good god, no! Never! He wouldn't hurt Andy. Or anyone else for that matter! He's a lot of things, but he doesn't kill people."

"Andy Crown's name did come up . . . unstable, maybe even dangerous. Do you think he could be responsible for your husband's death?"

"No! No way! He has schizophrenia but he wouldn't hurt a fly." Anger made me confident for a rash minute. "What the hell do you think we are anyway, murderers and maniacs?"

"I'm just asking questions." He was all reason and control. "Someone tampered with that fan. If Mr. Crown didn't do it, then that brings us back to you."

"And about half the population of Jacaranda! If you look hard enough you'll find more than a few people who would like Jimmy to disappear from their lives."

"Let's concentrate on you. When were you last on that boat?"

I shrugged and turned away to pick up the coffee cup. "Ages ago."

"Could you be more specific?"

"Before I left him."

His cold unblinking eyes stared at me as if they could read my soul. I forced myself to meet his eyes: tried not to let him see my guilt.

The doorbell rang and I jumped, jarring hot coffee over my hand. Styles still didn't blink.

CHAPTER 9

The door opened. Evan, carrying a container of flamboyant flowers in each hand, side-stepped into the room to protect the arrangements. "Three of these whoppers arrived before I got my ass out the door this morning."

I went to help him.

"They're from the three amigos." He leaned forward and kissed me. "Lovely cards."

"This is Detective Styles." My voice was louder than it needed to be.

Evan looked towards where I was pointing.

Detective Styles was taking it all in. I knew what he was thinking, "So this is the new guy in her life." Evan would look like one more reason for me to want Jimmy dead.

Evan put down the flowers on the coffee table and became the most respectable of men.

"Hello, I'm Evan Beckworth," he said, holding out his hand and walking towards Styles. "I work for the *Jacaranda Sun*." I so didn't want Evan to tell Styles his name. In twenty-four hours Styles would know everything about Evan except that he was gay and we weren't lovers.

"Detective Styles, Jacaranda Police Department."

Men sure like to get those credentials right out there, don't they? Give these two another minute and they'd start telling each other where they went to college and what clubs they belonged to.

Detective Styles started for the door. His hand was already on the knob when he turned back and said, "I'll be in touch, Mrs. Travis."

"Give me a cigarette," I demanded and threw myself onto the ratty couch that Grandma Jenkins had donated to the décor. For once Evan handed the package over without telling me he couldn't afford to have both of us smoking and went to help himself to coffee.

"What are the police telling you?" I asked.

"Just the fact that a boat, owned by Jimmy, blew up."

"Nothing about foul play?"

His back straightened. "Foul play?" If he'd had antennae they would have gone up too and if I'd had the energy to stand up, I would have kicked myself.

"They just have to check in case."

"In case what?"

"Well, boats don't normally blow up. They're just

checking to make sure it's an accident. What else is happening?"

"Oh, I almost forgot to tell you," Evan said, "your mother just called. She's been trying to reach you. She's on the way over."

I shot off the couch, grabbed my bag, and headed for the door.

"Wait," Evan said behind me.

"No, you wait. I'm out of here." The last thing I wanted was to get trapped by Ruth Ann.

Marley Hemming was on the stairs coming up as I went through the door. I felt the smile spreading across my face. I met Marley at Kittridge Elementary School and we'd been cheese and crackers ever since. She hasn't changed much, just gotten taller. With curly red hair and freckles, she's half an inch taller than me but ten pounds lighter. I never can understand why she's so skinny when all she ever does is eat, or talk about eating or plan to eat. I hate her.

"Hi, Juice," I said, the old nickname slipping back.

"Hi, yourself. Going someplace?"

"Dodging Ruth Ann."

"I'll come with you," she said and started back down the stairs.

"Call your mother," Evan yelled out the door after me.

For once that bile green piece of shit didn't argue about starting.

"Where we going?" Marley asked.

I shrugged and put the car into reverse. My brain was working overtime, poking in corners, turning over rocks, and sorting things out. There was nothing left for conversation.

"Let's get something to eat," Marley suggested.

"All right, but off the island. I don't want any more sympathy today."

"Hey, who's sympathizing with you? Isn't this what you've been yelling you wanted to do?" She lowered her voice in a bad imitation of mine. "I am gonna kill the bastard, I swear."

"Don't give up your day job."

"Seriously, are you all right?"

"Barely." It was the first time I'd admitted this even to myself.

"Pull over," she ordered.

"Why?"

"Just do it."

I did as I was told and Marley got out and came around to my side. "I'm driving," she told me. I slid across to the passenger seat without arguing.

The bridge was up so we waited for a Seafarer sloop to make its way out the channel. A pair of osprey had made a nest on the arm of the stoplight hanging over the road and one of the pair hopped around the nest while the young osprey stretched out their necks for lunch. It seemed strange that life around me was going on as normal when my life had been turned upside down.

I stared out the windshield at the faded board fence screening the neighbors from the parking lot of the burger takeout. "I go from believing he's dead to thinking it's all some goddamn gigantic mistake." I took the hamburger Marley offered me. "More than that," I could hardly bring myself to continue, "I keep thinking it's some stupid hoax."

"I know," Marley agreed. "That was my first reaction . . . like he'll just pop back up at any minute, yelling surprise. Remember the time he was missing for three days and you thought he'd drowned? He walked in like nothing had happened. He knew he was safe so what was the big deal? Hadn't even thought to call and tell you he was safe."

"I swear to god if that son of a bitch strolls back into the Sunset and orders a beer, I swear, I'll take the bar knife to him. I'll kill him for sure."

"And I'll help you," she promised. "But let's face it—even for Jimmy this is a bit extreme. He's never blown anything up before. Did the police find anything that says Jimmy was actually there?"

"I think it's mostly his truck being there that has them convinced he was on board."

"The cops must have something, Sherri. Maybe you should ask for more details."

I set the hamburger on the dash. "Have you got a cigarette?"

She opened the canvas shopping bag that she trucks around and threw a pack of Camels into my lap and then dipped her fingers into my fries and said, "Dr. John always asks a lot of questions about Jimmy and he was awfully cheerful this morning."

"Because Jimmy's supposed to be dead?" Dr. John was John Zampa, the dentist Marley worked for.

"Yeah," she said, helping herself to more fries.

"Why would he be interested in Jimmy?"

She chewed carefully while she thought about this. "My guess is Mrs. John, cute, tiny, flirty eyes, bored and on the make. She's got a nanny for the baby and little John is in school now. The Junior League and the Garden Club probably don't do it for her." She stopped talking and tore into her burger. Tucking lettuce into the corner of her mouth with a finger, she continued, "Lara Zampa was taking golf lessons at Windimere from Jimmy and we both know what Jimmy's like."

"Did Jimmy ever hit on you?" I asked.

She turned to face me and gave me a look that made me regret my rash question. I changed the subject. "Still it's a long walk from being a jealous husband to blowing up a boat."

73

"Dr. John owns a piece of Windimere. I heard him on the phone saying, 'I want that bastard Travis out of there.' This was just before Christmas. He definitely had it in for Jimmy."

"Do you think Dr. Zampa is capable of blowing up the *Suncoaster*?"

She gave it some thought. "A boat yes, a person no." She finished her burger and said, "Dr. John came up the hard way. It took hard work and grit to get where he is. He was the first one in his family to finish high school. Went to college on a scholarship." She took a sip of her soda. "Then he married his dream girl. He's told me more than once how lucky he was to snag her and I know her papa set him up in business. I don't think he'd let all of that go too easily."

"Well, there you are. Dr. Zampa blew up the *Suncoaster* and Jimmy just walked away . . . used it as an excuse to take a powder. Thank god there are other possibilities besides me. Styles has me half convinced I did it."

"Well, my money is still on you." She plunged the straw in and out of her cup as she thought it through. "What if it was someone else on the boat? Someone had to hit the switch to start the engine." She turned her head to look at me, the green eyes, big and round, stared at me over her soda. "If not Jimmy, who was it?" She hesitated, put down the soda and whispered, "Andy?"

CHAPTER 10

"Andy," I agreed. "Thinking about the *Suncoaster* and Andy, it seems not exhausting fumes from the bilge is exactly the kind of mistake Andy would make. Even on a good day he's forgetful and accident-prone and it's been quite a while since he's had a good day."

"Shit," she said.

I stubbed out the cigarette.

She drew herself up in indignation. "There's no way Jimmy would hurt Andy."

"I know that. But what if it just happened? Maybe someone rigged it or Andy got careless." There was one other possibility I hardly dared think of, one I had to take a deep breath before I could say aloud. "Or Andy used the boat to commit suicide. I've been doing a lot of reading. A huge percentage of schizophrenics commit suicide. Styles said the blades were off the exhaust fan."

"But where's Jimmy?"

"If the boat blew up with Andy on board, Jimmy might use it as a way to get out, to disappear and start over."

"Would he let you and his folks think he was dead?"

"Depends on how much shit he was into. I know he owes a ton of money. He tried to borrow some from me before Christmas and there were a couple of guys who came into the bar looking for him last week that I wouldn't take home to mother and you know how welcoming she is."

"Wouldn't he just ask his dad? Daddy always got him out of trouble before."

"I got the impression from Jimmy that Dr. Travis has set new rules."

I pulled the elastic out of my hair and ran my hands through it. "There's something else."

"What?" Her voice was wary as if she was unsure she really wanted to hear this.

"The cops think I fixed the *Suncoaster* to blow up."

"What?" They must have heard her inside the restaurant. "Why?"

"They have a witness that saw someone on the *Suncoaster* that afternoon. A woman."

She waited a heartbeat and then asked, "And they think it was you?"

"Yeah."

She tossed the last of my fries back into the bag,

put both hands on the wheel and stared straight ahead as she asked, "And was it?"

"Yes."

"Oh shit." Her fists pounded the steering wheel. "Why?" she growled. "I thought you couldn't get far enough away from that asshole." She turned to face me. "Why? For god's sake, why?"

"There were some pictures."

"Of what, as if I couldn't guess?"

"Me. Polaroid nudes Jimmy took years ago. He's been calling me up and describing them in detail, telling me how much he's enjoying them now that the real thing isn't there."

"No wonder you never answer your phone! Did you find them?"

"Yeah. I burned them in the kitchen sink . . . well, all except one." I could feel the broad smile splitting my face. "Something to remember when I collect my pension."

"If you live that long."

I sat up straight. "That's what's scaring the hell out of me. Styles likes me for the fit of an electric chair. Last night, the Travises told Styles Jimmy still had an insurance policy and when Evan came in . . . well, that pretty much clinched it. I bet Styles thinks we're having an affair."

"So does everybody else in town. Will Evan come out of the closet and tell Styles you're not his type?"

"I hope it doesn't come to that, but I just don't

think Styles will look beyond me. He's a tidy man. This is tidy. Maybe that witness can't identify me but this shitty puke green car is unforgettable."

She didn't argue or try to make me feel better, just worried the skin along the edge of her thumb as she thought about it.

"If Jimmy is alive and I think he is, where would he be?" I asked.

"Easy," Marley said. "Up in the redneck Riviera, hunting and fishing and screwing the native women."

I shook my head in disagreement. "That was my first thought but I've had more time to think about it. The Panhandle wouldn't be a very good place to hide. Somebody who knows somebody would tell somebody and sooner or later we'd all hear it down here. No. If Jimmy is gone he'll want to stay gone. He won't want anyone to find him."

"Well where then?"

"I've been thinking about this. He used to tell me how easy it is to hitch rides on boats. Down in the Caribbean, there are always boats cruising from one island to another that need crew. He figured you could work your way from Florida down to South America and never need a passport, just hopping from one port to the next. You know how he loves boats and the Caribbean. That's where he'd head."

She stared at me, emerald eyes wide and a little surprised, working it out. At last she gave a small nod of agreement. "Honey, you are so screwed."

"I have to find him."

"Do you think he got someone to drive him across to Miami?"

"Why bother? There's a guy that Jimmy knows down in Boca Grande who captains a boat for a bunch of doctors up in New York. When they aren't using it, they charter it out. Jimmy crewed on it one May during tarpon season, one big booze-out."

"And you think . . . ?" she asked, making little circles with her forefinger.

"And I think Jimmy may have paid him or sweet-talked him into taking him across to Texas, Louisiana or even the Bahamas or Mexico."

"How do we figure out which?"

"It's a good day for a drive down to Boca."

She started the car and was backing up before I'd finished sweeping the debris from her snack off the dash.

CHAPTER 11

We went south down Tamiami Trail, now designated a scenic highway, which is fine if you happen to think strip malls and motels are scenic. Outside a Citgo station a rusting magnetic sign left over from Christmas said "Happy B-day Jesus."

At State road 776, we turned west, going past white-walled and gated communities, citrus groves, cattle ranches and a million billboards selling everything from real estate to sex and religion.

"Do you suppose anyone has ever done a book on the billboards of Florida?" I asked Marley. "You know, one of those big, glossy, coffee-table books. Look at that one," I pointed to a weathered billboard up ahead. "'Have you talked it over with Jesus?'" I read out loud. "There's the answer to all our problems, girl. Let's give him a call."

"The long-distances charges would be a killer," said Marley.

"There's one." A huge sign stood above a field of grazing cattle, with small white birds riding their backs and picking bugs. Overhead, buzzards soared.

"Gator Bill's Pawn and Gun Shop," I read. Gator Bill also offered the added service of bail bonds.

"One-stop shopping," Marley put in. "Do the crime and we get you out before you have to do the time. You might want to write down his number just in case."

At the Mercury motor test station we crossed out onto the causeway to Gasparilla Island. This is the place the Bushes, governor and past president, come for their Christmas holiday. Sometimes they even bring the current president.

About now I'd normally be in heaven, but the huge blue dome of the sky and sparkling azure gulf, with a little bitty strip of causeway in between, didn't give me the customary kick. I stared at osprey nesting on tall poles, at diving pelicans and even at a lone dolphin surfacing twenty feet offshore and felt dead to it all.

We drove through the quaint town of Boca Grande, past the hotel that looks like an old planta-tion house with twenty-foot white pillars holding up the second storey and wooden rockers sitting in a line along the porch. The theme from *Gone with the Wind* always plays in my head when I see this old hotel. We turned east, past the dense green hedge blooming with scarlet flowers and enclosing a jewel-green croquet lawn along the back of the hotel.

Beyond the golf course, the road twists and turns leading out to the Sandbar Marina, a weathered gray building with three docks stuck out into a sheltered bay embraced by mangroves.

"The *Hollidaze* is berthed out at the end of the center dock," I told Marley. We walked along the gray planking between the rows of boats, out to the spot where the forty-two-foot Bertram with twin 435-horsepower engines normally would be tied. The giant cruiser with the stupid name wasn't there. There was a new boat, a power launch called the *Jersey Queen*, in her place.

"Do you suppose it's owned by a transvestite from New Jersey?" I asked Marley.

Marley replied, "What now, oh fearless leader?"

"Beats the hell out of me." Not finding the *Hollidaze* made it seem all the more likely I wouldn't find Jimmy either.

"Let's ask around. Maybe someone knows where she is or when she left," Marley said.

I slumped along behind Marley, letting her do the asking while I worried about clothing options for my trial.

Most people we talked to seemed to be transients, only there for a few days. They'd never heard of the *Hollidaze* and couldn't care less.

But Marley won the prize when she talked to a guy filleting fish at the gutting table that jutted out over the water. A troupe of brown pelicans were perched on the floodlights above the table waiting for him to toss out the remains of the fish for their dinner.

"The *Hollidaze* isn't here anymore," he said in answer to Marley's question. "It's berthed on the north side of the island, up past the hotel, in a private slip." He told us all this without once stopping the filleting or taking his eyes off the flashing silver blade. I guess the thought of losing a finger and having to throw it out to the pelicans with the rest of the refuse kept him focused.

Under a rusting metal roof we found the boat slip backing onto a narrow canal out through the mangroves. There was room for six boats, three on either side of a long wooden boardwalk. Five of the slips were full. One yacht had a for sale sign and the number of the Silverton Yacht Brokerage Company on it.

But there was no *Hollidaze*. Just a nameplate over the empty berth.

And there didn't seem to be anyone about to ask either. We yelled hello at each of the other five cruisers but no one came out to see what the racket was about. Madness. Each one of these suckers was worth well over a quarter of a million bucks and there wasn't anyone about. The floating fortunes just bobbed gently in the wake of any passing boat, waiting for rich guys to come out to play. How hard would it be to hotwire one and be out of here?

"Hello," I called again at each boat as we made our way back to the parking lot, sure now that Jimmy was somewhere faraway.

A Ford Explorer pulled in and parked as we stepped off the dock. A tall black man got out, dragging a box of supplies behind him.

"We're looking for Captain Whiting and the *Hollidaze*," I said. "Do you know when he'll be back?"

"Nope," he said, basically ignoring me and starting to move along the dock.

I followed him. "Do you know where he's gone?" Maybe it was the sound of desperation in my voice that stopped him.

He looked over his left shoulder at me. "I think they ran over to the Bahamas."

"When?"

"This morning." He didn't wait for any more questions, just boarded the second yacht, the *Merriweather*, and disappeared below deck.

"You've got as much chance of finding Jimmy as you have of catching a fart in a hurricane," Marley said.

"I didn't want to be this right." It was a Prozac moment.

"C'mon," Marley said, poking me in the ribs.

I followed behind her, depressed and beaten. "No one is ever going to believe me that Jimmy's out there somewhere, are they?"

"Nope."

"Well don't sugarcoat it, will you?"

"You need honesty, not 'There, there, dear, it will be all right.'"

"That son of a bitch," I said in reply.

"You're coming to my place," Marley stated as the car coughed to life. "I'm going to make you a good dinner."

"Marley's answer to every problem, more food."

"You didn't eat your lunch." Her voice accused.

"That's because you did."

When we hit Tamiami I said to Marley, "Maybe I should just do what Jimmy did. Why don't I drive down to Miami and catch a boat leaving for the Bahamas and just keep on going. Better yet, why don't I head to Key West and strike out for Cuba. They can't bring me back from Cuba, can they?"

"And here I thought I'd heard every dumb idea you had in your head."

"Why shouldn't I do it?"

"Let me count the ways. Never mind that you'd have to run the rest of your life, what are you going to do in Cuba?"

"Stay alive."

"How will you get there?"

"I don't know. Steal a boat and motor over."

"Have you lost your friggin' mind?"

Apparently, but running was an option I wasn't giving up on. I'd just keep my idea to myself until I needed it. "Let's go look where the *Suncoaster* blew up."

"Another bad idea. You're just full of them today, aren't you?"

I think she was afraid of what we might see there and how I might react. "Okay, okay. Take me to Andy's instead. I can't get in any trouble there, can I?"

CHAPTER 12

Andy lived in a bad neighborhood . . . a really bad neighborhood. Houses grew wrecked cars in the front yards instead of trees or grass, and every building looked like it was ready for demolition. Some looked like the deconstruction had already started. With night coming on, it felt like Beirut.

The Palmetto Motel wasn't used by tourists anymore. A new road had left this place stranded between urban sprawl and industrial wasteland and now it was home to a different type of person looking for temporary lodgings. Women fleeing abusive mates, hookers, people supporting a habit, or folks just plain down on their luck, they all fell into the Palmetto with its broken screen doors, missing numbers and air conditioners leaking rust down cracked stucco, telling the resident they've hit the end of the line and had no future.

Marley parked in front of Andy's unit and we stared out the windows, taking it in. Marley muttered, "What a dump."

"I'm about one paycheck away from here." I got out of the car and crunched across a small strip of sun-fried grass bordering the parking area.

Andy lived at number nine. The screen was missing from the outer door so I reached through the aluminum frame and knocked on the warped wooden door.

If he was in, he wasn't answering. I pounded again, just to make sure. I moved sideways to the window, half of which was boarded up to accommodate the air conditioner, and tried to see through the bamboo blind. I couldn't see anything.

Marley stuck her head out the car window and yelled, "He's not here. Let's go."

"Wait." I rummaged in my bag and found an old receipt for gas. I wrote, "Please call," and signed it. I stuck it in the crack between the warped frame of the aluminum screen door and the door jamb.

A black woman, looking exhausted and hot, dragged herself towards me down the sidewalk. I gave her my biggest smile but something in my stance, or maybe I just moved too suddenly, set off alarm bells in her.

Warily, she stopped six feet from me, trying to decide what new kind of trouble I might be.

"Hello," I sang out cheerfully. "Do you know Andy Crown?"

She shook her head in denial. She was wearing a

violent purple tank top paired with faded denim shorts; both were way too tight and didn't meet at the middle of her body. Her plump arms hung straight down by her sides, a plastic bag of groceries in each hand. I wondered just how small a movement it would take on my part to make her drop them and pelt back out to the street.

"He lives here." I jerked my thumb at the door. "His name's Andy. He has a little problem."

A light went on in her eyes and she blew air out between her lips. "He got a big problem!"

"Have you seen him lately? I want to help him."

"I ain't seen him for days. Good riddance, I say." She stepped around me onto the grass and walked away as Marley laid on the horn.

Somewhere about midnight, after a bucketful of margaritas, I was telling Marley yet again the story of my life, never mind that she'd been there for it, telling her what a screw-up I was. She'd been there for that too. "Why did I think I'd be any smarter than Ruth Ann? It's as clear as our D cups, we're never going to find decent men. Losers and disasters, that's all that's in store for me."

"Maybe you have to look in different places than where Ruth Ann finds her men."

I shook my head in wild arcs. My head seemed to be working on a system all its own. "Nope. Just got to look at her to see what the future holds for me. Why don't I just shoot myself right now and save myself the misery?"

"Okay, now you're being dumb. Dumb and self-pitying."

"Oh thank you. Thank you very much for your understanding."

"I do understand. That's not the problem. The problem is I've heard it all before and it's gotten old."

"If I could stand, I'd leave."

That's when I decided I needed a new audience.

The phone rang. I would've let it ring but I couldn't bear the pain.

"Yeah." I groaned into the receiver.

"So, how's the margarita girl this morning?" asked Clay.

"Shithead."

"I think I liked you better last night when you called."

"What do you want, Clay?"

"Oh, nothing. Just to talk."

"I can't right now. Have to throw up."

I pressed down on the phone rest to cut him off and dropped the receiver on the floor beside the couch. The last thing I needed was for it to ring again.

I swore off margaritas forever while kneeling before

the porcelain shrine. After rinsing my mouth and taking more aspirin than was recommended, I dragged myself out to the kitchen and made some coffee.

Marley's apartment is like her, full of color and movement, not a good place to wake with a mouth like a trash bin and a head the size of Alaska, but I gave it a shot. I sat on a chair with my elbows on the table and my head propped up in my hands while I waited for the coffee maker to work its magic and counted how many times I'd promised myself never to do this again.

On the wall over the kitchen table was a clock that looked like a black-and-white cat. Its eyes and tail moved back and forth, back and forth, in a manic motion. It was making me sick. I turned the wooden chair, painted lime green and pink with black-and-white dots, towards the sink. Lime green walls didn't help either my head or my stomach.

The coffee maker gurgled loudly and I could smell the first faint whiffs of the beans. This wasn't working out. I turned it off and crawled back onto the couch, pulling the blanket over my head to keep out the vicious sun and telling myself I was too old for margarita nights.

Sometime in the afternoon I resurfaced. This time I thought I might live but I still wasn't able to handle lime green and pink so I didn't even try for coffee.

I drove home carefully, afraid any sudden movements might disturb the precarious perch my head had on my shoulders. A huge sigh of relief escaped me when I turned into the Tropicana, but it immediately turned to a groan when I saw Detective Styles once again waiting for me. "I've been trying to call you," he said.

"Why?" I managed to croak out. Even behind dark glasses I was squinting against the light, too ill to be rude or smart-mouthed. Why is it that the memory of how awful I feel never stops me from doing this to myself, living proof that aversion therapy doesn't work.

"I need an official statement from you," said Styles. "It's just routine." He started to walk towards me and I took a careful step backwards.

He stopped. "I'll drive you to the station." The soothing tone of his voice said his intent was to reassure me. "And have you brought back."

"Can I have a shower first?" He couldn't help but notice I was in the same black golf outfit I'd been wearing the day before.

He frowned. "Now, if you don't mind."

I did mind, but my head hurt too much to argue. I just followed him to his car like a whipped puppy, sagging down in the seat and closing my eyes, praying I wouldn't hoop all over his pristine upholstery.

CHAPTER 13

When we arrived at the police building, just following him inside had me feeling like a criminal. By the time he led me through the reception area, down a corridor to a small closet-sized room with no windows, I was ready to confess to anything.

Styles turned on the fluorescent lights and pulled a wooden chair out from a small oak table. "I'll be back in a minute. Make yourself comfortable."

There wasn't much chance of that happening. I lowered myself carefully down, concentrating on keeping my two areas of pain, my head and my stomach, from colliding. I waited. And then I waited some more. If this was the new form of police brutality it was very effective.

A troop of cops going by the open door looked into the cubbyhole to see what kind of criminal it contained, studying me as if they were memorizing my face for the next time they saw it, which would probably be on a police bulletin in the post office.

They went away and left me to sink back into my misery. I sat there for another half-hour. I needed water, lots and lots of water. I was contemplating how much extra trouble I'd be in if I just walked out when a voice said, "Hi, Sherri."

Jadene Scarlotti smiled at me from the door. It was easy to see that her teeth were brushed and she'd had a shower that morning. And I'd have bet any money that she hadn't spent the night before drinking margaritas and smoking way too many cigarettes. Jadene was always a responsible adult—even at sixteen when we'd sat next to each other in Chemistry class and she'd ratted me out on a silly practical joke that filled the lab with the sulfur smell of rotten eggs. She'd always been middle-aged, respectable and well over on the side of authority. Now she worked for the Jacaranda Police Department as a dispatcher . . . polyester police from the get go.

Maybe that's why I'd never liked her. Far too perfect for me. Today she was dressed in a severe beige suit, a little too tight around the ass, but hey I understood how that could happen, and a high-collared lace blouse, about as sexy as a bowl of prunes.

"Hi yourself," I replied. Now call me a cynic, but wasn't it strange that she showed up at this door out of all the rooms in the building? And she wasn't the least bit surprised to find me there, didn't even ask why I was there.

"Are you all right? Can I get you anything?" she asked.

I shook my head, a big mistake.

"I was sorry to hear about Jimmy."

I stretched my mouth at her and looked away.

Never one to take a hint, she came into the room and sat on a chair across from me. She reached out to touch me but I jerked back and buried my hands in my lap beneath the table.

She looked a bit startled but this girl was a stayer. "What do you think happened?" Her blue eyes were all sincere behind her blue oblong glasses.

"I think there has been a gigantic mistake. I think Jimmy is still alive and the sooner you people start looking for him, the happier I'll be."

"Well," she said and gave me a weak little smile while she hunted for the perfect question to make me confess. The pale pink lipstick barely defined her mouth. "I'm sorry for your loss anyway."

She sat there for an uneasy moment. "I understand you and Jimmy weren't together anymore."

I had the silence thing down to an art form. I dug around in my bag and found a hair clip at the bottom. I pulled the hair back from my face, rolling it into a knot and set the clip in place.

Jadene wasn't done yet. "When did you see Jimmy last?"

I didn't owe her anything, even politeness. I dug out my nail file and set to work.

The girl could take a hint. She pushed up from the table and left the room.

Within two minutes, Styles came through the door. And he started in on all the questions he had asked the day before, but this time there was a tape recorder. Finally he ran out of questions or grew bored with the same answers I'd already given. "Is there anything you'd like to add?" he asked.

"Jimmy wasn't on the *Suncoaster* when it blew up. I think he left for the Bahamas yesterday morning on a boat called the *Hollidaze*. It's out of Boca Grande and captained by a Captain Jessie Whiting."

He wasn't impressed. "Tell me about Mr. Beckworth? Are you having an affair with Mr. Beckworth?"

CHAPTER 14

"None of your business."

"This is a murder investigation." Close to losing his cool, Styles' voice now held an edge of anger. A small victory. "A murder investigation makes it my business," he said.

I reached up and resettled my hair clip.

"You don't seem to realize a crime has been committed here."

I crossed my arms and gave him my eat-shit stare, the one I used on guidance counselors back in high school.

Styles looked like he had indigestion. "Your husband's truck is still in the parking lot at the boat launch. You can move it now. We're done with it."

"What about the *Hollidaze*?"

"I'll check it out." He stood up and reached into his suit jacket. He laid a small brown envelope on the table in front of me. "The truck wasn't locked. We found these under the floor mats."

I smiled. "Jimmy never locks anything."

"He's dead, Mrs. Travis. And right now you're the only one with a reason to kill him. You can drop the 'my husband's still alive' act."

The black-and-yellow cruiser dropped me off at the public boat ramp where Jimmy's cherry red four-door Ford pickup sat in the empty parking lot. The sun glinted off the ton of chrome lining its sides, running board and dual exhausts. It yelled, "Hey, look at me"—bold and exciting just like Jimmy.

Seeing the truck, a huge emptiness opened up inside of me. I turned away from the last tangible piece of Jimmy. Crossing my arms tightly over my chest, holding myself together, looking everywhere but at the stupid truck Jimmy loved, I walked over to the concrete ramp where people backed their boat trailers into the Intracoastal Waterway.

It was a day designed by the board of trade to lure tourists and their money from the snow up North, a clear fine day, a good day to be out on the water with temperatures in the seventies, warm for January. The incoming tide gently lapped at the shoreline at my feet. I stood there between clumps of seagrapes and searched the water, looking for some sign that would tell me what had happened, why a ball of flame had shot into the sky. A light breeze smelling of saltwater and fish was blowing, but I was sure I could smell gas and burning wreckage. Only the remains of a horseshoe crab at my feet spoke of death. There was no debris. No charred remains of boat or man. No sign left on the water of the *Suncoaster*, or of Jimmy—just sunlight dancing off water nearly as blue as the sky. A brown pelican flew north up the Inland Waterway towards Jacaranda, its wings going up and down in the same unhurried peaceful rhythm all pelicans seem to use, like they're going to fall out of the sky at any second if they didn't flap harder.

The truck cab was hot as hell. Careful to avoid any scalding hard surfaces, I slid onto the old towel Jimmy had thrown over the vinyl upholstery. Jimmy sure hadn't gotten any tidier living alone—there was more flotsam and jetsam in the cab than along the waterline. The passenger's seat and floor where covered with fast-food containers, dirty clothes and empty cigarette packs, the miscellany of his life.

Who did the truck belong to now? Likely the bank or a lease company; for sure Jimmy hadn't paid for it. I started the truck as the police cruiser pulled slowly out of the parking lot.

The radio was playing a song about a guy that was a long time gone. The witch must have been shaken by Jimmy's music choices. Jimmy had even less class than I did and, whether his parents liked to acknowledge it or not, Jimmy was even more of a redneck than I was.

Outside my door a basket of white lilies waited. The card said "Thinking of you," and was signed Cordelia and Noble.

I let myself in, leaned back against the door with the pungent lilies cradled in my arms and listened to the emptiness. Evan, sweetie and good housekeeper that he was, had closed all the windows before leaving my apartment. A cloying smell of floral scents assaulted me. I opened the sliding door and waved a tea towel madly about to move the air.

I showered and dressed in what the witch would call my white trash clothes—a cropped stretch top in pale pink, with a heart cutout edged in red glitter to show maximum cleavage, and ragged-ass cutoffs, low enough to show off my navel ring. I looked like nobody's idea of a grieving widow, except maybe the grieving ho widow from hell. I should stop by and see Bernice . . . see how she was coping.

I headed for Big Red with a garbage bag. Styles said the police had checked the truck and hadn't found anything, but they didn't know Jimmy like I did. Somewhere there had to be a clue to what he was up to.

I checked all the crumbled bills and receipts I found in the glove compartment before I dropped them in the bag. In a plastic sleeve behind the visor on the driver's side I found an old picture of me in my red cheerleading costume. I threw it quickly in the trash and then just as quickly retrieved it and shoved it in my back pocket. It was a picture that had been in Jimmy's wallet for years.

The Ford had a crew cab and the seat was piled with a dozen boxes of new golf shoes, stock probably belonging to Windimere. I opened every box and took a good look inside. All I found was a bill with the supplier's name on it. A name and telephone number was written at the bottom in Jimmy's handwriting. It went into the pocket of my shorts with the picture.

After I finished emptying out the truck, even looking under the seats and running an old T-shirt of Jimmy's over the interior to take off the dust, I wasn't any the wiser. The hinged cap that covered the bed of the Ford was locked but its key was on the ring with the ignition key. The box contained mismatched golf clubs, fishing equipment, the spare tire, a plastic garbage bag containing what looked and smelled like dirty washing, and a cooler with crushed Coors cans, melted cold packs, as well as some food thing gone green and slimy that I didn't even want to think about. I didn't find any travel brochures for South America.

Upstairs, I ignored the blinking message light and called the number Jimmy had written on the bottom of the bill. The wall clock read a quarter to five. If it was an office number they might not answer but if it was a cell phone I might get lucky. A man answered and identified himself as Bill Jackson.

"Mr. Jackson, my name is Sherri Travis. My husband Jimmy has some shoes that you supplied."

"Look, Mrs. Travis, I am sorry to hear about your husband but this has nothing to do with you. I supply Windimere with product and if someone on your husband's staff is padding the cost it isn't my problem. I told him that two days ago when he called. There was no need for him to fly off the handle like he did. He had a real mouth on him."

"Which staff member is doing the fiddle?"

Silence thundered down the line. At last he said, "I think that's all I have to say, Mrs. Travis. Goodbye."

If someone was skimming off the owners out at Windimere and Jimmy was about to blow the whistle, was that a good enough reason to make the *Suncoaster* disappear?

And did I have anything better to do with my time then take a trip out to Windimere? The shoes were a perfect excuse.

It was getting dark. Everyone would either be gone or about to leave. I'd have to hustle. Nothing happens on a golf course after dark—well, nothing good.

CHAPTER 15

I climbed into the pickup. Until someone came to claim Big Red he was all mine and I planned on enjoying him.

I turned to a Tampa rock station and drove back over the bridge and out Killman Road to Windimere, out where slash pines grew above undergrowth so thick not even the longhorn cattle raised out there can make their way through it. Starting in early February, the male pinecones produce yellow pollen to blow down and cover cars and boats and mobile homes. You can forget about trying to keep anything outside clean around here in the dry season. The pollen seeps into houses and into cars, turning every surface and every piece of upholstery yellow. The pines are always the first things to go when the developers move in.

But development hadn't spread to this little wilderness between I-75 and Tamiami Trail. Here feral pigs, longhorn cattle, snakes and birds of every description ruled. Only the golf course infringed on this backcountry. Windimere was owned by a group of businessmen and professionals, lawyers and doctors, who sank every spare cent of change they could beg, steal or borrow into this bet on the future. So far they only had a great golf course, but one day soon gated communities will surround it. Already, red stakes with yellow plastic ribbons fluttering on them had been driven into the ground along the western boundary. Things were about to happen out here.

The manicured entrance, with stone pillars and tropical flowers, divided deep jungle on either side of the drive. A bevy of quail scurried across the road in front of me and disappeared into the thick brush. The winding drive opened to a parking lot, empty except for three cars and the huge clubhouse with the golf course behind it.

The Windimere owners hadn't stinted on the landscaping. A full-grown Jacaranda tree, with beautiful silver bark, had been planted in the center of the parking lot. In early April it would turn periwinkle blue with flowers. The flat-roofed pro shop sat under bottle bush trees, heavy with their distinctive red flowers. I'd stayed away from Windimere because of Jimmy's connection to it, so this was all new for me. In the soft light of early evening, it looked magical. But without people coming and going it had a lonely feeling and wild untamed nature crouched around the perimeter of its carefully tended area waiting for the owners to fail so the jungle could reclaim its own.

In the pro shop, a foursome was at the cash register. A handsome man behind the counter, who was handing over a bag to one of the golfers, looked my way at the sound of the door. His smile faded.

The other men turned around to follow his stare. Their faces were a whole lot friendlier than the guy's behind the counter. But this late in the day, after an afternoon of golf and a few beers, these guys would be friendly to just about any female. I wasn't exactly dressed for golf, more dressed for a night of mud wrestling out at Big Daddy's. My wooden platform sandals, with the Chinese red toenails sticking out, struck loudly on the ceramic tiles as I moved to a display rack. A soft whistle came from behind me. I held up a 250-dollar rainsuit as a shield. I was still studying it when the four guys left.

"Hi, Sherri."

Surprised, I shoved the hanger back on the rack and clacked up to the counter. The guy was smiling now. The smile worked well. Tall, dark and athletic-looking, he was wearing a soft pink shirt with black trim on the collar and sleeves. He and Jimmy must have been quite a pair with the ladies' membership.

"Have we met?"

"No, but I know you're Jimmy's wife."

I smiled and told him, "I haven't been Jimmy's wife for a long time."

"I . . ." His response was cut off by the door opening behind him. An older man, dressed in work clothes, came through the half-opened door and said, "We're done. See you tomorrow."

"Okay. Lock the back door on your way out."

"Sure," the man said and closed the door.

We were all alone.

"I'm Tony Rollins, by the way," handsome said and went to lock the front door to the pro shop. "I'm the assistant pro." He came back towards me, moving in too close, stopping inside my comfort zone. I eased away. "I had a call," he said and gave me a strange little smile. "Let's go somewhere more private."

Private? We were surrounded by hundreds of empty acres, just us and the wildlife. It didn't get more private than this.

Alarm bells started jangling but I clattered along behind him. That's the amazing thing about dumb people like me—we go on making the same mistakes over and over, trusting to luck or divine intervention. Since everyone had left for the night and nobody would be coming out here after dark, if things went wrong divine intervention was the only thing I could count on.

I followed him through the merchandise, down a hall running past washrooms to a door at the end, trying to remember what Jimmy had said about him. There was something evil bouncing around in my head but I couldn't identify it.

CHAPTER 16

"This is Jimmy's office." He stood aside for me to enter. A faint memory of expensive cologne hung in the air, bringing Jimmy back.

A big desk sat in the center of the back wall. Beside a dead computer screen, a large silver-framed picture of Jimmy and me sat on the desk, which explained how Tony Rollins recognized me. Jimmy's normal chaos was at work here as well. Bills and invoices floated to the very edge of the desk.

"This room looks like Jimmy." Half stockroom, half office, the room was crowded with boxes of shoes and clothing. Golf clubs and bags, new and used, were stacked on top of each other or leaning up against the walls.

Tony Rollins laughed. "No one could ever find anything in here but Jimmy."

"Not the tidiest person in the world was Jimmy." Watching Rollins carefully, I asked, "Have the police been here?"

A small nod, "Yesterday. They came out and looked through everything and asked a lot of questions." He didn't look worried so they hadn't asked the right questions. "They said it was just routine."

Either they hadn't known it was murder when they came or they weren't spreading it about yet. I walked around the room taking it all in. "Did they ask about Jimmy's extracurricular activities?"

Tony Rollins didn't answer. I glanced back at him. He looked uncomfortable.

"Don't worry." I gave him a bright smile, pushing my shoulders back and jutting out my chest. "I have no illusions about Jimmy."

"They didn't seem to have anything in mind, just nosing around." He hoisted a hip unto the desk. "I hear you made a call."

"I want to get rid of those damn shoes."

"Bill Jackson called me to say he'd heard from you."

"They're taking up space."

"That's all?" He polished the edge of the scarred desk with a forefinger. "Jimmy hasn't been sounding off about things around here, has he?"

I gave a snort of disgust. "Jimmy and I weren't talking." I flashed him my biggest tip-generating smile. "At least not about shoes. I have them in the truck."

He was happy now. "Good."

"But Jimmy wasn't too pleased about your scam, was he?"

His head jerked around to the closed door. We were the only people in the building but still he didn't like me talking about it.

"It's all right," I assured him. I flexed my shoulders and his eyes went back to the cutout heart of my top. When in doubt pull out the big guns. "It's nothing to do with me but it sounds like a pretty good gig." I put my hands on my hips and pushed my shoulders back to hold his attention.

"Everyone does it," he said, his eyes never leaving my heart.

"The accounts show one invoice but you pay a lesser one and keep the difference, right? Jimmy found out about the double invoicing and he didn't like it."

He frowned. "He just went crazy. Said a whole bunch of stuff there was no need to say. He was acting weird lately."

"Maybe he wanted in on the action."

He shook his head. "I offered him that."

"Did the police ask about it?"

He was on his feet. "No."

"Hey, don't worry." I was backing up as I said it. My hands were out, palms up trying to calm him down and take the scary look off his face.

"Keep it to yourself, okay?" The tone of his voice made it somewhere between an order and a threat.

"I'm cool. They aren't going to hear about it from me."

He sat back against the desk, arms crossed and legs stretched out. "I don't know what was wrong with Jimmy. It wasn't as though he didn't have some things of his own going on."

"Yeah? Like what?"

"Poker games. He used to hold poker games here after hours. He picked up some nice change at those games."

"Who was the big loser?"

"Not Jimmy."

"Did he leave some unhappy players?"

He shrugged, not interested in poker. "He shouldn't have ragged on me like that."

The memory trying to dig its way out of my mind finally made it to the party. "What about drugs?"

"Jimmy didn't have anything to do with drugs."

"But Jimmy told me you sold great stuff," I said softly.

"You should be careful what you say." He was on his feet and I was backing away again.

"No worries." I was suddenly conscious of how quiet it was in the building and how black it was outside the window.

He loomed over me. "Who else have you been spouting off to?"

I edged further away. "Nobody." I gave him my big

warm "come to Mama" smile. "Do I look like I care?" Sexual heat and preconceived notions about a girl in cutoffs and a tight top are a great boon to a girl on a quest. "Don't worry about me," I said, jutting out a hip. "A girl like me knows how to keep quiet."

His eyes dropped to the cutout for reassurance.

"I was just wondering if Jimmy was using again." I told him. "He's been known to in the past."

"Naw." He waved away my suggestions and gave me a warm smile. "But if you need anything I can get it for you. I know how to take care of my friends." He moved in closer, not touching me but his body covering mine just the same.

I tried a little laugh. "I'd have thought Jimmy would be your best customer."

Rollins shook his head. "He was going around like my mother, having a hissy fit over a little pot." He looked flabbergasted and confused at this failure in Jimmy. "Purer than the pure! Very uncool."

"Jimmy didn't like you dealing? That doesn't sound like the Jimmy I knew."

He swung away from me. "Well it was the Jimmy I knew." Agitated and angry, he picked up one of Jimmy's golf trophies from the desk and wrung it between his hands. "These last few months he's been a real pain in the butt, riding me about everything." His eyes were on me but his hands didn't stop working on the trophy, twisting it between his hands like a rag and he was getting every last drop of water out. "Jimmy changed over this last year. Actually, he was doing a good job." Jimmy's reformation came as quite a surprise to Tony Rollins. It came as a revelation to me as well. After a lifetime of being irresponsible and out of control, this was a hundred-and-eighty-degree turn for Jimmy.

"He just didn't want the stuff around anymore. I never had anything to do with hard stuff, but that didn't matter to Jimmy." The nameplate came off the marble base of the trophy and fell to the carpet. Tony Rollins didn't notice. "He told me he would break my fucking neck if he caught me dealing drugs here again." Indignation fought with stunned disbelief on his face.

"He even stopped the card games though he was the big winner. It was like he'd found Jesus or something."

"Not being able to sell out here would be a problem. All of your customers must be here."

He frowned.

"Come on. I work in a bar remember? I know the score."

"It's only small time. Just to keep the members happy." He smirked, sure of himself, sure he was irresistible. "I like making people happy. I'm good at making people happy."

He moved towards me, his eyes telling me he'd like to make me happy and he knew just how to do it.

I reached out and took the trophy from him. He didn't resist. I eased away from him saying, "I bet you're real good at making people happy." The back of my legs butted up against a pile of boxes. "Right now, I'm still dealing with Jimmy." I had a real good grip on the trophy, ready to use it on his head if he got too close.

His eyes rose from my chest and he gave me a weak smile. "Yeah, sure, I understand. But soon. We'll get together, won't we?"

"Sure. Did Jimmy have any special friends?"

He smirked and I said, "I didn't mean women necessarily, there were always women. I was wondering if there was anybody he was really close to, played golf with, holidayed with, like that. For the funeral. People I should notify." Lots of the people playing out here would have more than one home. An empty house up in Ohio or Michigan would make a good place to hide out for a few months. Or maybe the person on the Suncoaster when it blew up was a member who was using Jimmy's boat for a little on the side. "Tell me about Jimmy's friends."

He shrugged my question off. "I don't know of anyone special. He pretty much got along with everyone."

"Except Dr. Zampa."

"You know about that? He was trying to get Jimmy fired."

"Because of Mrs. Zampa?"

"Yeah, but Zampa hadn't a prayer. Jimmy was really popular. He was going to be the pro for as long as he wanted."

His thoughts took a u-turn. "Look there's lots of Jimmy's things around. The cops went through the drawers here but there's a locker of Jimmy's and his golf bag. I didn't think about those 'til after they left."

His memory had likely been hindered by a need to clear out anything incriminating. "Why don't I help you load them up?" he offered.

"Great idea." I wanted to see anything connected with Jimmy. There had to be something to tell me what he was up to and where to find him.

Tony started peeling the photos of Jimmy from the walls. "It'll be good to get these down and start fresh. No use clinging to what's over."

He looked over his shoulder at me. "I've put in for Jimmy's job."

"Of course." One more reason to play mechanic. "You'll be able to run things the way you like." I dropped the trophy I held onto the desk and picked the nameplate up off the floor.

"I've got some ideas." He dumped a box of golf shirts still in their plastic sleeves on the desk chair and piled everything of Jimmy's into the box. Then he carried Jimmy's stuff out to the truck.

Beyond the small pools of light dotting the parking light it was midnight black and with the sun gone it had turned cold. I shivered.

"I'll stop by the Sunset and see you," Tony promised as he closed the cap on Jimmy's truck. He moved in close, near enough to me so I could feel his warm breath on my cheek. I got a strong impression that Tony Rollins might be one of those guys who didn't really get the word no.

"And anytime you want to play here, just call me." His voice promised more than eighteen holes of golf. He brushed up against me, touched me, not even subtle. "Jimmy said you were real good."

"Sure," I said, sliding backwards, opening the door to the crew cab. "Don't forget the shoes." I held the crew door open, keeping it between us and asked, "Do you know Andy Crown?"

"Yeah." He reached in and started taking out the boxes, piling them on the ground at his feet. "He came out with Jimmy sometimes to hit balls. Not much of a golfer."

"Has he been around the last few days?" As he took out the last armload of boxes, I hopped in the cab, my hand on the door, ready to slam it shut.

"Nope." He closed the crew door.

"Has there been anyone else here looking for Jimmy?"

"Just that guy from the newspaper."

"What guy?"

"Evan Beckworth."

CHAPTER 17

At the Tropicana the air held the smell of a distant barbecue, reminding me I hadn't eaten, but I wanted to go through Jimmy's things first, so I humped everything up the stairs. I spread the contents over my living-room floor. It wasn't a lot.

I opened every zippered pocket on the golf bag, dumped out the clubs and then chased the balls that ran away across the concrete floor. Nothing. There wasn't anything unusual in the cardboard box either, just memories. I stacked the pictures and trophies back in the box.

Now I had to decide what to do with his nice set of graphite Pings. I ran my hands lightly over the leather head covers. Jimmy was a freak about equipment, always buying the newest and best, always looking for that one special club that would take his game to a new level. Should I drop them off at Indian Mound? I'd rather eat shit and die than give anything up to that bitch. They were going back into the truck.

But first I called Evan. Why had Evan gone out to see Jimmy? Evan's recorded voice urged me to leave a message. "Hi. It's me. Call." How do you leave a message like, "Did you blow my godawful husband to Kingdom Come?"

I stood by the truck, keys in my hand, trying to decide what to do next. Staying home alone wasn't an option—I was too juiced for that. I headed for Hess Street to see if I could find Andy.

Andy wasn't home, but then if this were my place I wouldn't be either.

At the takeout window at Hog Heaven Barbecue I ordered pulled pork on a bun with a side of slaw. As I handed over my money, Eddy Ortiz's cab pulled into line right behind me. We'd gone to high school together. Actually, Eddy was the only reason I'd passed Spanish, correcting my homework, or more often, doing it on the bus going to school in the morning.

Jacaranda High had fewer than five hundred students, so you pretty much knew everyone. Those few who stayed in Jacaranda after school had a special bond. That feeling of belonging was one of the things that I missed when I went away and I'd slipped back into the comfort of it like a pair of worn jeans when I came home. Seeing Eddy now gave me the warm feeling I needed.

I got out of the truck and went back to talk to Eddy while I waited for my order.

"*Que pasa, calabaza?*" he asked with a big smile. And then he remembered Jimmy and his face fell. "Sorry, Sherri."

This was generous of him. Eddy's father was a migrant worker from Mexico, so Eddy spent the first ten years of his life drifting from farm to farm following the harvest with different schools and new kids every month or so. While Eddy was in high school, his father had found permanent work with one of the landscapers in Jacaranda, and nine of the Ortiz family moved into a two-bedroom, metal-clad mobile home at the edge of a field where nursery stock grew. There was no protection from the sun and the yard was trampled down to sand. The whole structure could have easily fit into the Crowns' caged pool, but it was the Ortizes' first real home.

Living out in the back of beyond, east of I-75, even if they had a permanent residence, did little to make Eddy's life better. The off-island kids, driven in over the north bridge every day in a big yellow school bus with the roof painted white to try to keep it cool in the broiling sun, were dirt to the townies, no matter what their family circumstances. In a way, I was a rare exception. While not exactly accepted, I crossed the invisible line, carried first by my looks and nasty attitude and then by Jimmy's popularity. I was the token white trash that all the girls wanted to emulate and the boys wanted to shag. A little danger in their white bread lives. Eddy and I still shared this bond of outsiders. But Eddy had had it worse than the rest of us. Older then the others in his junior year, he sat like a Mayan warrior in a sea of creamy complexions. Eduardo Ortiz lived in a have-not world surrounded by have-everythings. Graduating grade twelve had been an act of rugged determination on his part.

"It was a terrible accident," Eddy said. "A terrible thing." Eddy genuinely felt sorry for the golden boy who'd thrown it all away. Everything had come easy to Jimmy. Nature had blessed him with good looks, charm, brains and a physical ability to do all the things so highly prized in our world. And his daddy was rich. Life, and all its bounty, was handed to Jimmy on a golden platter for him to take, and he'd screwed it all up. Less of a man than Eddy would feel a little joy at someone like Jimmy losing big.

"Thanks Eddy, but Jimmy and I were no longer together."

"I know, Sherri, but all those years . . . since you were kids really, all that just doesn't go away."

I swallowed hard and nodded.

"It's gonna take you a little time, *calabaza*."

"Your order's up—" a voice called me back to the window. A server in her forties, looking dog-tired and wearing a nametag that said Helen, offered me a paper bag and a weary smile.

I pulled into a parking spot and went back to talk to Eddy while he waited for his order.

He leaned out the window as I came towards his cab. "You're still the prettiest cheerleader Jacaranda ever had."

"Are you flirting with me, Eduardo?" I asked, leaning on the door of his cab.

He shook his head and flashed his white teeth at me. "Know better. I'm just stating a fact."

"You should know better. Melly would kill you."

The smile got even bigger. His beautiful dark-skinned wife was a spitfire.

"Eddy, I want to find Andy Crown. I don't think he knows about Jimmy. It's going to be hell for him."

He scratched his head. "I saw him . . . probably a week, ten days ago, walking over North Bridge, talking to himself and waving his arms around. He isn't in good shape."

"You haven't seen him since?"

"Nope."

"Keep an eye out, will you? I really need to find him." I wrote out my number for Eddy while he paid for his food.

He took it and said, "I'll tell the other guys. If I hear anything I'll swing by the Sunset to let you know. And I'll give Clint Longo a call. He's in the sheriff's department and patrols the area along Tamiami. We'll find him for you."

When I got to Marley's apartment she was already in her pj's.

"Bad day?" I asked.

"Bad night. I can't keep up with you and the margarita nights anymore. I'm going to crash. Are you staying?"

"Nope. Just came by to bum a cigarette."

"They still sell these things, you know," she told me, picking up the pack from the table and handing it to me, along with a blue plastic lighter.

"If I buy them, I smoke them." I lit the cigarette and tossed the pack back onto the table, setting the lighter down beside it.

"And if you don't buy them, you still smoke them."

"Not as much."

She shook her head at my logic. "Listen, Styles came by the office today."

"To see you?"

"No. Why would he want to see me? To see Dr. John. I came back after lunch and heard them in the office. The door wasn't quite closed."

"And you listened?"

She gave me a look. "Styles seemed to be trying Dr. John out for size as the guy who made the *Suncoaster* go bang."

"Why?"

"I told you . . . Mrs. John. Maybe he thought he

was going to lose his sweetie along with her daddy's money."

"At least they're looking at someone besides me."

"Well, my money's still on you," she said and handed me the rest of the pack of cigarettes. "Here, enjoy, knock yourself out. I'm going to bed."

"Sweet. Your kindness is only exceeded by your thoughtfulness." I headed for the door. "And I just want you to know I've been kicked out of better joints."

The smell of lilies was strong. The reminders of death weren't doing anything but depressing me and I promised myself that I'd take them to a local nursing home first thing in the morning. But perhaps the aged were the last people who wanted to see flowers of condolences. Another of life's little conundrums, but the flowers had to go.

Mr. McGoo was sitting on the bar. His left ear and one eye were missing, sacrificed in a war with my cousin Emily. I picked him up and hugged him to me. The light on the answering machine was still dancing.

"It's nice to be popular, but hell to be the rage," I told Mr. McGoo as I hit the rewind button. I went to the fridge while the messages began replaying. I poked through the limited possibilities for food and a cold drink. "What will it be, McGoo, water, orange juice or water?"

The first message was from Ruth Ann. "Oh god." I hadn't thought to call her back. I really am the world's worst daughter.

Ruth Ann's wandering message was from before the world crashed. She told me she'd been given lots of oranges so she was making marmalade; she told me the news from Sarah and Julie, my sisters in North Carolina . . . the normal sort of thing, while country music played in the background.

Ruth Ann's life was the epitome of the country and western songs that twanged from her radio from the moment she woke until long after she was asleep. In that occasional brief space when there was no man in her life to be disturbed by the noise, her radio played all night, probably to cover the fact there wasn't anyone snoring on the pillow beside her.

Country music was the background to every conversation we'd ever had, every meal and every argument. I only had to hear certain songs to have those times and emotions come rushing back. Mostly these memories didn't make me happy. They just made me remember the men in my mom's life, men with names like Buck or Junior or some double-barreled name like Ray-John.

Next came a message from a lovely-sounding lady at MasterCard, asking me to call. Last November, ten of us had gone off to the Bahamas on a four-day junket. I had no idea how much I'd enjoyed myself until the bills came in. On top of that was the shopping I'd done getting ready for the trip; then there was my cold, which made me miss about four shifts in December; and then Christmas and a new battery . . . yes, I am sure MasterCard would like to speak to me. I needed speaking to.

The next call was from Jimmy.

CHAPTER 18

His voice could always seduce me. Even as my brain was cursing, "You son of a bitch! You can't even die straight," my body was reacting in the same old way to that smooth drawl.

"Hi, Babe. Go out and look under the dead fern on the deck. There's a videotape out there. Bring it in before you water the fern. I know you'll water it, dead or not. Put the tape somewhere safe for me and forget about it. Why don't you just give me a key so I won't have to climb the balcony next time? Better yet, why don't I just move in? Love ya!"

I stood there staring at the answering machine on my kitchen counter, diamond shards of broken glass around my bare feet. The next message played. Ruth Ann again, telling me she'd heard about Jimmy. "Are you all right, honey?"

"Yes, Mom, I'm friggin' wonderful."

The messages droned on, several from friends and one from an insurance man, but still I stood there, hugging McGoo and rubbing his remaining ear back and forth between my fingers.

When the tape ran out, I reached over and pushed the rewind, hunting for Jimmy's message and played it through again. Then I took a giant step over the broken glass and went to retrieve the video.

The black plastic tape had a label on it saying "Holy Grail" in Jimmy's bold handwriting. I remembered watching *Monty Python and the Holy Grail* with Jimmy and Andy. The three of us had watched hundreds of old movies. Long nights spent drinking beer with Jimmy and me making out in the flickering light as Andy went on and on about what made the movie we were watching so wonderful. Sometimes we would watch two or three in a night. Later on it was just Andy and me watching them as Jimmy chased his dream.

Andy had been a film major in New York when the schizophrenia finally swamped him. That September he'd left Florida looking forward to living in New York but by Christmas his parents had flown up to drive him back. Hallucinations had taken over his life.

Looking back, we all knew something was wrong long before his disease was full-blown. We made excuses, like he had things on his mind or he was artistic. We even worried about substance abuse, but we never once thought it was all in his head. At one point I was totally convinced that he had fallen into some giant conspiracy and no one was listening to Andy. Jimmy had been the most clear-eyed and the first to realize that Andy needed more help than we could give him.

I switched on the television and slipped the tape into the VCR. There wasn't much on it. I watched about twenty minutes of guys hitting golf balls at what looked to be the driving range out at Windimere. Jimmy taped the swings of people he gave lessons to so he could replay them and show them what they were doing wrong. He was a natural teacher; never losing his temper or thinking someone was stupid if they couldn't do what was so easy for him. He just went over and over and over it as if it was the first time he'd ever talked to someone about swing plane or weight shift. That's why I'd become such a good golfer. It wouldn't have worked if he'd been too critical; I don't take too well to criticism.

All of a sudden the tape went wacky and then there was a shot of parked cars before it went crazy again. After a few minutes of up and down stuff— what looked like a metal ceiling and parts of golf carts—there was a clear shot of cars, of a guy putting a package into another guy's golf bag and then a close-up of the two guys. One was sideways to the camera so you couldn't see him very well but the other, a white, middle-aged guy, looked directly at the camera. I didn't know him. Then there was a close-up of an SUV and the license and then the camera went funny again. After this there was a good shot of the two guys shaking hands.

Then Jimmy came on mugging for the camera. I played the part with Jimmy about a dozen times before the night caught up to me.

Next morning I went for a jog, hoping it would clear my head. When I got back to the Tropicana, there was a white business card stuck in the door from an insurance guy by the name of Huff. Insurance being just one of the many things that I had no use for, I flicked it onto a pile of unopened bills before I dragged the cushion out to the lounge.

With a cup of coffee in my hand, and the hollow sound of the bamboo stand to the left of my balcony serenading me, I stared down at the red pickup. The parking lot had been full the night before so Big Red sat next to this old motorhome that had been there so long that the tires had gone flat and a chartreuse green mold had spread all over its roof and sides.

I was a little surprised to see Jimmy's truck still there, figuring either a finance company would reclaim it or Jimmy would come back for it before morning.

What was Jimmy up to? The tape was important, must have been for Jimmy to climb onto my balcony and stash it there, but why was it important? The mess that he was in, the trouble that had made him disappear must have something to do with Windimere and golf. And had the message been left on my machine before or after the *Suncoaster* blew?

I needed help. I called Evan at the paper and told him about the tape. "I want you to see it and tell me what's happening. You'll know what it means."

"I'm jammed up until late tonight. There's another special meeting about the King Ranch starting at three. It'll be after supper by the time all the yelling and screaming is done. Then I have to write it up."

Most of the news was pre-packaged from the mother ship so Evan only had to worry about the local section. With the land boom going on, most of the local news was about developers and the people who opposed them. In Florida, land speculation is as popular as the lottery and a lot more profitable.

"Why didn't you bring it over last night?" he asked.

My brain said, "Because I need to decide how deeply you're involved in this." My mouth said, "As if. Noble was there and there are some things I'm still too young to know about."

"Oh, yeah." His voice sounded funny.

"Are you and Noble having problems?"

"You mean new problems or just the same old problems?"

Why do I ask? That led to about twenty minutes

of him telling me what it would take to make him truly happy. After five years you'd think he would have figured it out, Noble was never going to come out of the closet. It just wasn't going to happen but every day we talked about it so now I just let him run on while I tried to decide what came next. As Jimmy's wife, even one that didn't live with him, I had this sneaky feeling there were things I should be doing. Even dead Jimmy was turning out to be a pain in the ass.

When I grew tired of wandering the same old path, I ended Evan's whine with, "I hear you went out to Windimere looking for Jimmy."

Silence roared down the line.

"Evan?"

"I didn't see him."

"But why did you go there?"

"To talk to him . . . make him see sense. He needed to leave you alone. Needed to leave all of us alone."

"Us? What us?"

"Well, you. I wanted him to leave you alone."

Clang! His huge whopper hit the floor. Evan wasn't a person to confront anyone, especially not Jimmy. Not for me anyway.

"Detective Styles came to see me," Evan told me.

"Lucky you."

"He wanted to know if we are having an affair."

"And you said . . ."

"Yes."

I thought about this as I showered, weighing and judging our conversation. There was something Evan wasn't telling me. Or maybe it was just the effect Styles had on him.

I called Ruth Ann, tucking the phone between my shoulder and chin, while I did my eyes and let her talk at me.

"Come over. I'll make something nice." Like Marley, Ruth Ann is convinced food solves problems.

"I have to go to work."

"So soon? Is it wise?"

Ruth Ann didn't know the state of my finances. "Yes." Not going into work would be truly unwise.

"There'll be a funeral," she told me.

"Why?" She was confirming this worm of anxiety eating into me. There must be something I should be doing but a funeral sounded ridiculous given the circumstances. "There's no body."

"Well, a memorial then. There has to be something, some formal thing, for what they call closure. Don't worry, I'll go with you."

Now there was something to really worry about. I remember the first time my folks met Jimmy's parents. Back from hauling citrus to New York, Dad had moved in with Ruth Ann again after a dozen final break-ups. Mr. and Mrs. Travis had invited us over for dinner. Not supper . . . dinner.

Ruth Ann, all friendly like, started telling Mrs. Travis about all the folks they knew in common. But the thing was, Mrs. Travis played golf with them and Ruth Ann cleaned for them. I thought Mrs. Travis would stroke out right then and Dr. Travis wasn't looking too healthy either. Jimmy and my dad just went on talking about what fish were running and where they might have the best luck. I think it was grouper season . . . or maybe pompano, or snook; they were always out there in the gulf killing something and it always seemed that Jimmy had more in common with my dad than he did with his own. Anyway, the tension in the air went right over their heads and when I tried to talk to Jimmy about it later he couldn't understand what I was going on about. The social status thing never mattered to Jimmy. He liked who he liked and disliked the rest. But really there were few people Jimmy didn't like.

Now I told Ruth Ann, "When someone tells me there's a memorial service for Jimmy, I'll worry about it."

"You seem very calm about Jimmy's death. I'm worried about you, Sherri. I hope you're not in denial."

"You've been watching Dr. Phil again, haven't you?"

I put on my black skin-tight leather pants, the black glitzy sweater that showed a tad too much cleavage for polite occasions, found the big pretend diamond hoops and added a little more makeup. The outfit said, "I'm doing just fine thank you." I sprayed the air around me with the expensive duty-free perfume I'd treated myself to in the Bahamas.

Before I headed for the Sunset I was going to make a stop.

CHAPTER 19

The phonebook showed the house was in a three-block section of Jacaranda built in the twenties with Spanish-style homes on large lots.

"Shit!" I said, as I pulled up in front of Dr. Zampa's residence.

It was my dream house, the one Jimmy and I chose out of all the others as we'd driven around Jacaranda playing "What will we buy when Jimmy wins the Masters?" Built of cream stucco, it had a red-tiled roof and arched windows. A cream stucco wall, with a crimson vine growing on it, enclosed a front lawn shaded by a broad old orchid tree. The black wrought-iron gate, set in an arch of the stucco wall, opened onto a rough brick path that led to the front door. Jealousy took a huge bite.

The woman who opened the door didn't look as if she were enjoying the house I coveted. "Mrs. Zampa? Lara Zampa?"

"Yes." Her highlighted brown hair hung limp and unwashed to her shoulders. Her green eyes were swollen and red-rimmed. But still she was pretty.

"I'm Sherri Travis."

She stepped back in surprise but I preferred to take it as an invitation and followed her in, closing the door firmly behind me. "I need to talk about Jimmy. I know you were his friend."

She took off to the back of the house. I tagged along.

She'd made a mess of decorating my dream home. Contemporary furniture in the living room gave way to a family room decorated in dark green with a primitive country feel to it. A room that cried out for dark wood floors and Spanish furniture, it ran the length of the house; a kitchen at one end faced out onto a backyard filled with brightly colored plastic toys and a pool. Another huge bite of jealousy.

The air in the room was stale, smelling of family living, forgotten meals and dog. Mrs. Zampa bent one leg up under her and fell into a forest green leather chair. She grabbed several tissues from a box on the end table that was already littered with crumbled tissues. My guess was she'd sat like this since she got the news. There was no need to ask if she thought Jimmy was dead.

She blew her nose and glared at me. "I don't know why you're here."

I let my breath out slowly and jumped into the deep end. "I know you and Jimmy were having an affair."

A jolt of shock went through her body and I hurried to add, "That doesn't matter. That isn't why I'm here."

But it seemed to matter to her. "How did you find out about Jimmy and me?" she asked.

"It doesn't matter." Now that I'd pushed my way in here I couldn't decide what I wanted from her. "You play golf out at Windimere?"

She nodded. "Jimmy was teaching me to play."

"He taught me to play too."

"I know. He said you were really good." She blew her nose again. "He said the two of you were going to own a golf course someday. Said he was going to teach and run the pro shop and you were going to run the clubhouse."

"Old dreams. Did Jimmy teach you to sail? He taught me."

She shook her head. "I already knew—spent my summers on boats. But that's where we got together, on the *Suncoaster*." She covered her mouth with her hand to stop the words. Then she said, "I'm so sorry." She leaned forward and buried her face in her hands. Her body shook with sobs.

"What are you sorry for?" I asked. "Jimmy and I were over."

She shook her head in denial. "I loved him. But it was still you," she croaked. "He told me that again the day he died."

Her words jolted me like a cattle prod.

"Were you on the boat the day it exploded?"

She nodded. "I wanted to be with him. Forever. But he said he was waiting for you to come to your senses, to get over whatever was bugging you. It wasn't important to Jimmy . . . ," her fingers shredded the tissues as she searched for a way to explain, ". . . what was between us. I was just a way to pass the time for Jimmy, 'til you came back."

She wiped the back of her hand under her nose. "He said . . . ," she swallowed and tried again. "He said that you two were starting over."

"That was never going to happen." My voice crackled with disgust and anger, bursting a new dam of grief in her.

Ashamed, I said, "You must have cared for him very much . . . loved him."

She bobbed her head and dropped the handful of sodden tissues on the table before grabbing a fresh batch. Her fingers started making confetti out of the tissues as she looked up from under a fall of lank hair. "I was going to leave John. Jimmy told me not to. He was angry with me, said it would mess everything up." Tears rolled down her face. "I was nothing to him."

"I'm sure that isn't true." Her pain was hard to look at. "Do you know what kind of trouble Jimmy was in?"

"Trouble?" Her delicate arched brows drew together, puzzled, as if it were a word she'd never heard before. "Trouble?"

"Do you know any reason he might want to go away? Why he'd pretend to be dead?"

"God, no!" And then a bright light of hope went on in her eyes and her body surged eagerly forward. "Jimmy's alive? It's okay?"

"No, no. I didn't mean that . . . don't know anything. I'm just finding it hard to believe Jimmy is dead."

The light went out in her eyes and her thoughts turned inward. "I've been wishing it hadn't happen, wishing I hadn't . . ." She grew silent and still.

I rubbed my forehead, searching for words to make her continue. "Did you do something to make Jimmy's boat blow up?"

No answer. She'd forgotten me and slid down into a hell of her own.

"When the *Suncoaster* blew up, I thought he might want to disappear . . . to use it as an excuse to walk away."

No response.

I tried again. "Was there anything different about Jimmy lately?"

She roused herself. "He said he'd come into some money. He bought me this." She pulled out a gold chain from beneath her crumpled cotton blouse. A small diamond slide hung from it. "He said there was more coming, his luck had changed."

"Was he talking about gambling?"

She shrugged. "He wanted me to find out if any of the investors out at Windimere wanted to sell their share."

"He wanted to buy in?"

She nodded.

"Then he was talking big money. A lottery ticket, an inheritance?" I turned my palms up, questioning. "What? I just don't understand."

She shook her head. "I don't know. He was as excited as a kid." Her lap was full of white fluff and she went back to watching her fingers work on it. "Jimmy was so alive, so impulsive and . . ." The sound of a child crying came from a red plastic intercom on the wall, interrupting her.

She looked towards it and said, "I have to go. My nanny is off this afternoon." She swept the mess of tissues out of her lap and dumped it on the side table where stray bits floated to the floor.

Reluctantly, I followed her to the front hall, sure that there was something I hadn't asked.

She stopped at the foot of the curving stairs to look up, and said again, "I have to go."

The banister was made of intricate black wrought iron that wrapped along the edge of tiled steps and jutted out in a small balcony in the hall above. It looked like delicate black lace—just the way I always knew it would.

"Do you know where Jimmy would be if he's still alive?" I asked.

"No."

The crying was getting louder and she mounted the first step.

"My number is in the book. If you think of anything . . . why Jimmy might go away, where he might hide, anything, please give me a call."

She nodded. "And if you find Jimmy, tell him I love him and want him to come back for me."

CHAPTER 20

At the Sunset, Billie Holiday was singing about the man that got away, and doing nothing to cheer me up. I signed on the till and was wiping down the gleaming mahogany bar when Styles came through the door. Some men work hard at making you think they're tough. Not Styles. He was way beyond caring. I watched as he looked around him, hands easy at his sides, taking it all in. Now this man knew how to enter a place. When he'd made up his mind what he had, he walked slowly towards the bar.

"Detective Styles," I nodded at him. "What can I pour you?"

"Nothing." He placed a hand flat on the bar and hoisted his behind up onto the edge of a stool. Turned sideways, one foot still on the floor, his body language said he wasn't staying. "I just came by to tell you that we've been in touch with the police in the Bahamas."

I got this sinking feeling in my gut. "You haven't come here to brighten my day, have you?"

"The boat is in Bridgetown all right but the only people on board are two crew, neither of which is James Travis, and two of the owners from New York," he ticked the names off on his fingers, "a Howard Cooperman and a Paul Zeller, and their wives."

I let my breath out. "Maybe he took off before you got there."

"Perhaps it's time you stopped playing games, Mrs. Travis."

"Tony Rollins . . . out at Windimere." I shook my hand holding the bar towel at him. "He had this thing going on with false invoices for merchandise. And he was selling drugs. Jimmy was giving him a hard time. Check him out."

"And your new theory is . . . ," he waved his hand in lazy circles as if trying to capture the thread of my thoughts ". . . what? Rollins killed your husband? Your husband was running away from Rollins?"

This man had a way of making me feel really stupid, something I don't need any help with. "I don't know. I just wanted you to know that there are things going on out at Windimere that could account for Jimmy's boat being blown up and for his disappearance."

"You mean you weren't the only person who didn't cry when your husband came up dead?" He slid off the stool and walked out of the room.

Why hadn't I told him about Lara Zampa? She was just as likely to have done it as Tony Rollins. Right, and Styles was just as likely to believe me about her as he'd believed me about Tony Rollins.

"Stick to pulling beer, girl," I told myself.

The crowd rolled in behind Styles and in a short while the three stools at the end of the bar were occupied by two of the usual crew and Brian was telling another story about marriage gone wrong as I set a dry vodka martini in front of him. Somehow these stories made Brian feel better, as if his marriage hadn't been the disaster he really knew it was.

"Do you think we should worry about this obsession of his or is it something he'll grow out of?" I asked Peter Bryant, the third guy who made up the three amigos.

"Don't worry until he stops coming up with new ways to get rid of a spouse. Then we'll know he's found the perfect one. That's when we'll worry."

Brian pushed his wire rims up the bridge of his nose with his forefinger. "It's the creativity I admire. So many ways to off your lover."

"He's still shopping. No worries." Peter said, tilting his glass at me. Looking sharp as always, Peter was wearing his normal floral shirt and crisp dress pants. The smell of Polo filled the air around him.

On the wrong side of fifty, he looks like early forties; at six two in his snakeskin cowboy boots and about 190 pounds he still scores with the women. Peter adores women. He always sits on the end stool by the waitress station so he can chat them up when they come out of the restaurant to pick up their drink orders. Plus, he faces lengthwise down the bar so he can check on any new game entering his territory.

Peter describes himself as an entrepreneur and he likes to pretend his business is more upscale than we all know it is. He owns the Pelican Motel out on Tamiami Trail where one of Ruth Ann's friends worked as a maid. She said Peter wasn't opposed to making the odd bed when someone didn't show up for a shift. The Pelican isn't the kind of place where anyone gets too particular about how the bed is made, so even an entrepreneur can do it.

The Pelican, where most of the rooms are rented for short stays, is right next door to the Kit Kat Klub, with its three Betty Boop dolls doing high kicks on a red neon sign that says "Girls, Girls, Girls." There was a whisper around that Peter owned a piece of the KKK . . . not a thing you'd admit to at the Sunset Bar and Grill, mind you. No, no, we're much too upscale for that.

Skating on the edge of the sordid, Peter would never get invited to join the Royal Palms Golf and Country Club. As Bernice would say, he's NOKD, the secret code of Indian Mound Beach for "not our kind, dear."

Peter smoothed back the curls of his mullet. One night I'd played the Beastie Boys' song "Mullet Head" in his honor. Brian, who up until then only knew he hated Peter's long hair and not that it had a name, started calling Peter "skullet head," as if Peter needed to be reminded his hair was growing mighty thin on top. But no matter how we insult him, Peter stubbornly clings to his hairstyle and the ringlets that gather at the nape of his neck. "Just how closely are the cops keeping in touch?" Peter inquired.

"Detective Styles kindly took me on a tour of the police station today. Showed me a nice little room and the latest in tape recorders and even gave me something to sign to say that I'd been there and how much I'd enjoyed my tour."

"Be careful what you say to the police," warned Brian. "In my experience, more people talk themselves into trouble than talk themselves out of it."

"Your advice may already be too late."

"Don't make any more statements unless you have a lawyer with you."

"Stop!" I sat a fresh Scotch in front of Peter. "You're scaring me, Brian."

"You should be worried. The police want to solve this. It doesn't mean they're going to find the right solution, just a solution."

"You misunderstood. It isn't the police that worry me." I shoved a fresh rack of wineglasses under the bar. "It's the thought of paying your legal fees that makes me weak at the knees."

Brian ignored this. "Lots of innocent people end up in jail," he said as Clay slipped onto a stool between them and ordered a margarita.

"What's wrong with you?" Brian asked at this strange departure in drink choice.

"I have it on good authority that everything goes better with margaritas." He gave me a big grin and added, "So what's happening, Sherri? Any news on Jimmy's accident?"

"The police have been in touch," I answered.

"Now there's something to worry about," Peter said.

"There's more to this mess than what was between Jimmy and me." I told them about Jimmy's new source of income. "How much would it cost to buy into Windimere?" I asked Clay.

He shrugged. "They've got money troubles. A million might get you in."

"Jimmy and a million dollars: an interesting concept." Then I told them about Jimmy's tape.

"You should have brought it along," Peter said. "Between the three of us, we know everybody between Sarasota and Naples."

Practical as always, Clay asked, "Just what do you plan on playing it with, Peter?"

"Oh yeah, right."

One of the delightfully odd things about the Sunset is there are no TVs and heaven help you if you don't turn off your cell phone when you come through the door.

Peter had one of his not-so-good ideas. "How be I come over to your place when you get off work and take a look at it?" he asked, all hopeful and eager.

"Yeah, as if that's going to happen. Even Huff the insurance man has more hope of getting past my door."

Things were busy so I didn't see Dr. Zampa come in. He was just suddenly there, looking mean and angry and scowling so hard his dark bushy eyebrows nearly joined over the bridge of his long nose.

"I want to talk to you," he growled.

I must have really upset wifey but I'm a bartender, used to handling drunks and crazies. He didn't scare me. Besides I would be charming, oh so charming. I smiled. Who could resist? "Of course."

But no one had told Dr. Zampa how charming I was. This guy was truly pissed off.

I came out from behind the bar. Dr. Zampa loomed over me. He was only two or three inches taller than me, but it was his intensity, rather than his size, that made me feel overpowered and threatened.

Still, I thought I could control the situation. He was a dentist for god's sake, how dangerous could he be? "Let's go down the hall. It will be private there."

He followed me closely as I went into the hall

leading to the restrooms. I turned to face him and he bumped into me, his chin jutting into my face as he demanded, "What the fuck do you mean comin' to my house?"

He didn't wait for an answer. "You got her started all over again." He was jabbing a finger into my shoulder with every word. "Now she's asking if I paid your shithead husband to stay away from her." I backed away, but he followed. "As if I would."

My back was up against the wall. "Easier just to blow up his boat, was it?"

"You sayin' I did it? What gave you that crazy idea?"

"Maybe your temper? And you hated Jimmy, didn't you?"

"You stay away from my wife, you hear me?"

I raised my hands between us. "I just talked to her."

"And now she's got it in her head the jerk's still alive."

"Are you so sure he isn't?"

"He's fuckin' dead!" It wasn't a poke now. It was the flat of his hand that rammed me backwards, slamming my head against the wall.

"Hey, what's going on here?" Clay came towards us.

Dr. Zampa stepped back but he wasn't through. "Stay away from my wife or you'll regret it." He shoved past Clay.

"Are you all right?" Clay asked

"Yes." My knees felt like sponge. "No." I was melting down the wall and then I was in Clay's arms. And his face was buried in my hair.

"Well, it's about time," I thought. For months we'd been swirling around in a heated dance of advance and retreat, a salsa of desire and denial, and I was more than ready for a new beat. My body relaxed into him, feeling the length of him against me as I turned my face up to his. He smelt of sandalwood. Warm words formed in my brain while laughter bubbled in my throat. There was so much I wanted to tell him. I wanted to ask why it had taken him so long to hold me.

Just as suddenly as he'd embraced me, Clay pulled away, leaving cool air where his warm body had been. His hands on my shoulders held me against the wall and away from him as he searched my face. And then he let me go, reached out a finger and pressed it to my lips. "Let Jimmy go."

"What are you talking about?" I was talking to his back.

The girl who was always quick on the uptake was left well behind, confused and trembling.

CHAPTER 21

When I pulled myself together and got back behind the bar, Clay was pretending we'd never met. Beside him a middle-aged guy in a gray suit lifted his hand to get my attention.

I kept my eyes fixed on Clay's drinking companion and went to take his order. Over six foot, the guy was built like a giant fireplug, with buzzed steel-gray hair and broad shoulders topping a powerful body. The total package gave the distinct impression he wasn't a man to mess with.

"Have we met before?" I asked when I brought him a gin and tonic.

"No," he said smiling. "I'd remember meeting you."

"It's just that you seem vaguely familiar but I can't place you."

"This is Hayward Lynch," Clay said, cool as if he'd never touched me. Maybe I'd just imagined the sparks between us. "Hayward is the biggest land developer between Naples and Sarasota," Clay added.

"My face is in the paper a lot," Lynch said, which would explain it if I ever read a paper, but for me the news is always the same old thing with new people doing it.

"I live up in St. Pete," Lynch added.

"I won't hold that against you," I told him. "I'm very broad-minded."

The cash registered pinged, telling me that the restaurant had a drink order. I started filling it, sure that I could feel Clay's eyes on me. Maybe I just wanted his eyes to be on me. How pathetic was that, acting like a sixteen year old with the hots for the quarterback?

It was a busy night and the bar was noisy but in one of those weird moments where everyone went silent at once I heard Clay's voice, telling Lynch that I was the widow of the guy who'd been blown up on his boat. I turned on the blender for margaritas and drowned out the rest.

When I returned with another martini for Lynch he said, "I met your husband last Christmas at a party at the Travises'. I'm sorry for your loss."

"Thank you."

"I took some lessons from him. He was a great teacher."

"Yes," I agreed. "Everyone says he was the best." I was working hard at not looking at Clay.

"Did he ever mention me?" Lynch asked.

He was staring intently at me. I've seen lots of vanity but this guy had cornered the market.

"Should he have?"

Lynch relaxed. "No, of course not."

It was a busy night. Fridays always are. Tips were good, so I wasn't feeling too down on life when I got home just after midnight. Not even the fact that all the spots under the trees were taken and I had to park near the building where the morning sun would bake the truck, making it about a hundred degrees when I opened the door—not even that could take away my good mood. That was tomorrow's annoyance.

I felt good all the way up the stairs and all the way to my front door. That's when the good feelings all went away.

The door was unlocked.

Okay, maybe I forgot to lock it . . . that could happen, but the fine hairs on the back of my arms stood out like antennae, telling me something else was going on here. I knew bad news was coming even before I turned on the light.

CHAPTER 22

Perhaps there's some primeval sense that tells us when our space has been invaded. In my case it was the smell of garbage. I listened, trying to decide if I was alone. Silence filled the space except for the sound of the dripping of the kitchen tap. I leaned in and flicked the wall switch that turned on the brass table lamp at the end of the couch.

"Holy shit."

Heaven knows, given my housekeeping, it might be hard to tell a normal break-in from my everyday untidiness, but not this time. The living room had been trashed with an angry frenzy, cushions torn from chairs and books pulled off the shelves, and the contents of the kitchen cupboards had been pulled out onto the counter. How desperate do you have to be to break into my hovel? And why the destruction? Not a drawer or shelf remained untouched.

I wavered at the threshold with the faint dim voice of reason, which resides deep in the back of my head, yelling "Call a cop." Another voice replied, "It's already too late."

I crept forward, exploring the disaster.

In the bedroom I pushed the mattress back onto the bed and picked up the bundle of sheets. Mr. McGoo lay on the floor under them.

"Did they hurt you?" I asked. I looked him over good before cuddling him to my chest. "Bastards."

I went in search of the phone and dialed the emergency number; while it rang I picked up the trashcan. You had to give the thief credit for hygiene. He'd used a pair of wooden kitchen tongs, the ones I use to get my toast out of the toaster when it got stuck, to pick through the garbage. Why would anyone look through the trash? Maybe now that everyone knew about hiding drugs in the freezer the trash was the hot new hiding place. But this wasn't an ordinary robbery, wasn't guys looking for anything they could sell. The television and stereo were right where I'd left them.

The dispatcher said she'd send a patrol car. All I had to do was wait. Easy for her to say!

Instinct told me to wash everything that the bastards had touched so I picked up the pots that had been dumped on the floor and put them in the sink. Under them were the salt and pepper shakers. Grandma Jenkins had given them to me for our first apartment, a green pepper for salt and a red one for the pepper. The red one lay broken on the floor. I started to sniffle. Over an ugly goddamn salt and pepper set that Grandma Jenkins had probably bought at a church jumble sale, I lost it.

My whole life felt cracked and broken and scattered all over the floor for other people to stomp on. Common sense said I'd got off lucky. What would have happened if I'd come in while they were here? Best not to think of those things.

How did they get in?

I wiped my nose on a piece of paper towel and went to the front door to check under the mat. The key was missing. Which meant the guy who used the key still had it.

The chain wouldn't keep a flea out, but I put it on anyway. Then I got a wooden bench off the balcony and wedged it under the door handle. A stick that I was using to stake up a dead tomato plant fit perfectly in the door track of the slider. I still didn't feel safe so I called a twenty-four-hour lock place and a sleepy voice answered and said he'd come right over. I didn't even ask how much it would cost.

Fear and rage pumped adrenaline into me and I flew around the room at double speed, putting books back on the shelves, cushions on chairs, and cans back in the cupboards. I saw the pair of gold hoops I'd left lying on the counter by the phone and thought of the watch.

In the bedroom, I sank to my knees in front of the old beat-up chest of drawers from my room back at the trailer park.

Someone had already been through the drawers but I searched for the dusty blue velvet box anyway, wildly pushing clothes aside until they flew out of the drawers and onto the floor. When Jimmy and I were together, I always hid the box so Jimmy couldn't pawn it. A few times I'd hidden it so well I'd forgotten down which register or on top of which curtain rod I'd put it, and it had taken days to find it. Now I no longer worried about Jimmy making off with it; I'd left it out for the burglars.

But it was still there at the bottom of the drawer. I opened the box, punching the air in triumph at the diamond face of the Omega smiling up at me. I caddied for Jimmy in the tournament where he won the watch and it stood out as one of the greatest days of my life. Playing like Tiger Woods, Jimmy was hitting long and true and making twenty-foot putts look easy. If he'd been able to play that way all the time he'd been on his way to Augusta.

There was one more thing to check on. I shimmied under the bed and looked for the package tapped to the frame with heavy gray tape. The little Beretta that had been my father's sixteenth birthday present was gone, leaving only the smell of oil and the drooping tape.

The cops were so not interested in my little event they could barely keep from yawning. When they checked out the door and heard where I kept the spare key, they gave each other a look. The investigation was over. They probably only came because it gave them a change from just cruising aimlessly up and down empty streets. I didn't tell them about the Beretta. That might have made them too interested.

"Would you like a coffee?"

"No thanks." The older cop spoke for both of them as he headed for the door.

"Something cold then?" I was nearly dancing with eagerness to keep them.

"No thanks. Lock the door behind us," the younger said on the way out the door. What kind of dumb-ass advice was that? The burglar had a key.

I barricaded the door behind them.

While I waited for the locksmith I answered the blinking light. The tape was half rewound. Why would burglars listen to my messages?

The first message was from Evan. "I'll be home on Sunday. I'll watch your tape then."

There was a message from the Huff guy about insurance. This guy was going to get to the top of the pyramid with his persistence but he wasn't winning a place in my heart.

And then, "It's Andy. Things aren't too good for me right now, but tell Jimmy the Holy Grail is safe." The tape whirred on.

"Where are you, Andy?" I yelled at the machine.

As if responding to my question, Andy said, "I'll try to get to you but don't worry if you don't hear from me. I've got stuff I have to do. It's cool. Bye."

Andy was alive. I'd cleared all the messages the night before. Andy hadn't been on the *Suncoaster*.

I bolted for the VCR and stuck my fingers in the tape holder. Empty.

The answering machine played the rest of my messages as I tried to call Andy. It rang and rang but no one answered.

There was a loud knock at the door. "Who is it?" I called, frozen in place by panic.

"Locksmith."

After a break-in the burglars would figure I'd send for a locksmith. If they wanted to ask me some questions, that would be an excellent way to get me to answer the door.

"What do you want?" My normal contralto turned falsetto.

"Look lady, you called me. I didn't call you."

True. I took a deep breath and pulled back the drapes to have a look at him. Pissed off and carrying a tool chest. Yep, a locksmith dragged out of bed. Sheepishly I opened the door and let him in. Like the cops, he was another bored person dealing with the routine of someone's misfortune. And also like the cops, I couldn't bribe him into staying one second longer than necessary to do the job, collect a check, which may or may not bounce and hustle himself out the door. I was on my own again and I didn't like it much.

Somewhere towards morning I woke up with my heart pounding and my hands scrambling around the bed.

Why was I awake and why was I so frightened? That's when I heard someone scratching lightly at the door and calling my name.

CHAPTER 23

I found the phone that I'd gone to sleep clutching and shot out of bed, already pushing the buttons. The red light was flashing. The batteries were out of juice again.

"Sherri," a voice whispered on the other side of the door.

"Go away. I've got a gun. I'll shoot," I screamed at the door as I ran for the kitchen.

"The police are on their way." I jerked open a drawer, frantic for a weapon.

I found a butcher's knife and swirled to face the door. I held the knife out in front of me with both hands like some damn martial arts superhero. "I'm armed," I yelled.

The sound of running footsteps was the only answer.

Knife still clutched in my right fist, I shot to the window to see my attacker. Through the light of the one remaining floodlight, Andy Crown sprinted across the parking lot. I dropped the knife and fumbled with the window latch. Sliding the window open, I called, "Andy, come back."

He didn't stop. Didn't even slow down. He just disappeared into the shadows of Raintree Avenue.

There was a parking space in front of the stunted shrub that grew at Andy's door. I listened to the pinging noises of the engine as it cooled. An eerie glow of a TV lit the thin curtains of a window a few down from Andy's but the rest of the Roach Motel slept.

The sound of the truck door opening, the sound of my runners on the gravel, echoed in the horseshoe enclosure so at first I rapped lightly at the door. "Andy?"

No answer. I pounded just to make sure Andy could hear me. "Andy, it's Sherri." The sound ran around the walkway and came back to me.

Louder now, "Andy."

Three doors down a door opened and a man's head appeared. "Shut the fuck up." Always a slow learner, I leaned my right ear against Andy's door to hear if there was any sound from inside. The mountain, posing as a man hitching the backside of his crumpled boxers, stepped out onto the walkway, unhappy that I was still there. I hustled to the truck, waiting for the man to go back inside and watching to see if Andy's curtains twitched.

The guy waiting for me to go grew tired and started for the truck.

I jumped in and locked the door, sweeping the darkness for any signs of Andy, any movement in the shadows. I searched the rear-view mirror, thinking he might be hiding in the parking lot until he thought it was safe to come out. Nothing.

Marley's call woke me in the morning sooner than I really wanted to rejoin the world. "Get over here," she ordered. "I'm cooking."

In the bright clear sunshine the green monster was looking even more depressing than usual. The cloth ceiling, which had been developing strange pouches of air, had finally let go and now the entire panel hung like a hammock from the visors up front to the edge of the back window. I just walked on by to the pretty red pickup.

Running east-west, Banyan Street is the main street of Jacaranda. Its traffic lanes are separated by a park full of banyan trees and their forest of roots, which hang down from branches to become more trunks, create a secret world. I remember chasing lizards among the smooth gray roots. Native to India, Florida purists think the banyans should be rooted out of the center of our city and replaced with palms. In the meantime, those banyans just keep on growing and three days a week the farmers from off the island bring in produce to sell in the banyans' shade. The market was going full tilt, so I bought fresh marmalade and a loaf of raisin bread on my way through.

The stucco building Marley lives in was built in the twenties, old by Jacaranda standards. Downstairs there's a drugstore that's been there since the beginning and is still run by the same family. All the original fittings, hardwood floors and tin ceilings are still in place. Upstairs there are two apartments with twelve-foot ceilings that overlook the park. A broad alley leads to the open stairs of a balcony along the back of the second floor. I tapped lightly on the lace-covered glass of the door, breathing in the smell of bacon. The door flew open under my knuckles. "What kept you?" Marley demanded.

The demented cat was still doing his thing on the wall. Underneath him the table was set with Fiesta ware in turquoise and orange. Even without a hangover it was a stretch.

"Shouldn't you be out tracking down bargains?" Friday's paper lists all the garage sales being held on the weekend, and Friday night Marley sits down and marks them on her map to plan the most efficient route. She starts out at six Saturday morning, when it's just Juice and the dealers, and hits them all. Everything in the apartment came from a garage sale or flea market someplace, but Marley had now slipped from need into obsession. Now she rents a storage unit to keep things the apartment can't hold.

"I'm taking a day off" she informed me. "I'll go tomorrow."

"Did you make this great sacrifice just so you could cook me breakfast?"

"Don't flatter yourself. Now tell me what's happening."

"Andy's alive. That's the good news. The bad news is my apartment got broken into, they took the videotape, and I chased Andy away."

She set the glass jug of orange juice down hard on the table. "Why didn't you call me?"

"I know how you are when you wake up in the middle of the night."

"What did they get?"

"Just the tape."

"And your only clue to what Jimmy was up to." She pulled out a chair and plopped down. "It really sucks to be you, doesn't it?"

"Hey!" I held my hands out, palms up. "Where's the food? I didn't just come for the chit-chat, you know."

She popped up and went to the oven for the plate of blueberry pancakes surrounded by bacon and sausage and set them down on little round hotpads that somebody's grandma crocheted back in the fifties.

"What was on that tape that made it worth breaking into your place?"

"I don't know," I said, helping myself to the food.

"It must be important. Why would Jimmy want you to take care of it if it didn't mean anything and why would someone steal it? That proves it's important."

"I have no idea and no answer to any of those questions."

"You must have some idea."

"The only part of the tape I really paid any attention to was the part with Jimmy making a fool of himself. I think it was just a test to see if the camera was working. No secret message. And the rest . . ." I lifted my shoulders. "The part of the tape that was important must have been the two guys. Jimmy zoomed in on the license plate but I haven't any idea why. I barely looked at it. I was waiting for Evan to see it. I was so sure that he'd know what it meant."

Over breakfast we went around and around the mulberry bush, but I didn't tell her about Dr. Zampa. Hey, she had to work with the guy. Neither did I tell her about Clay. I don't know why I kept that back.

By the time Marley reached out and rescued the last piece of bacon from my plate and I claimed her cigarettes none of her questions had been answered

I got up to get an extra ashtray from the cupboard. I knew exactly where to find it; unlike me, Marley is extremely neat, everything exactly where it was the last time, all the handles of her pots and pans lined up in the same direction. I guess it went with being a dental hygienist.

"The one thing I remember is the close-up of the license plate of the white SUV. It ended in OFF." I lit the cigarette and said, "The normal word didn't come first or that would have stuck with me for sure."

"Tell me again, who did you tell about this tape?"

This was a tougher interview than with Styles. I took a deep breath and began the list. "Evan. Then I told Clay, Peter and Brian. No one else knew. That's it. None of those four drives a white SUV." I ticked their vehicles off on my fingers. "Evan has a black Honda, Peter drives a red Porsche, Clay has a white Lexus and Brian an older white caddy. Not an SUV among them. The plate has nothing to do with them."

She sat on the chair with her knees pulled up to her chin and her arms wrapped tightly around them. "There's one person you're forgetting."

"Who?"

"Jimmy. I bet he broke in."

"I blame most bad things in my life on Jimmy, but this?"

"He left the tape there. He definitely knew about it." Marley had another question. "Did Jimmy know about the key?"

"No. He would have used it before if he did."

"Did you tell the cops about the tape, tell them it was missing?"

"I didn't know it was gone until after they left."

"Call Styles."

I shook my head. "He won't believe me. Without something to show him, he'll just think I'm trying to confuse things to keep him from arresting me."

"You're right." She jumped up and began clearing the table. One of the reasons she's so skinny is that she never sits still, a habit that got her into lots of trouble as a kid. "Styles is going to think it's just one more theory." She ran hot water in the sink before returning with the coffeepot to fill our cups.

"When I find Andy, I'll have a copy of the video to show Styles. That's the only thing I can do."

She settled back in her chair and picked up her coffee cup, looking at me over the rim, she said, "I think Jimmy blew up the *Suncoaster* and then came back for that tape."

I let my breath out in a huge sigh. My shoulders sagged.

"You're never going to see him again and no one will ever believe he isn't dead."

She had spoken my nightmare and she wasn't done yet. "Maybe Jimmy changed his mind about leaving the video behind. Maybe there was something on that tape that he didn't want anyone to see."

CHAPTER 24

"Leaving you once again in the lurch and on the hook for disposing of his miserable hide." She sat the coffee cup down in the saucer with an angry clank. Marley might just be the only person Jimmy ever met who was immune to his charms.

"Surely it would be too dangerous? Someone would be sure to see him."

"You can't find Andy and he isn't even hiding. Maybe Jimmy sent Andy over last night."

"Possible. Andy must have had a ride to the island but I've got Jimmy's truck."

"What about Andy's car? Jimmy still has that." Marley changed courses. "Who knew about the key?"

"Evan, you . . . but then the cops said the first place burglars look is under the mat. Next they check around any plants."

She was out the door in a flash. A long row of red geraniums sat in clay pots on the railing just outside the door to Marley's kitchen. She came back in and slapped down a key covered in soil on the table between us.

"*Et tu, Brutus?*"

Her mind was still on the problem of the missing tape. "You've got to tell the cops. They're talking murder, remember?"

"I'm hardly likely to forget that. What can I say? I had evidence but it's gone . . . trust me on this one?"

She heaved a great sigh. "So what now?"

"I have to find Andy. Talk to him. I know he's got a copy of the video. I'll take it to the cops and let them figure it out."

"The cops can find Andy faster than you. Tell them he's missing."

"I'm wondering if he's gone walkabout again." Off the drugs his life turned into one huge pit of terror. Voices yelling in his head every waking moment, voices telling him people were trying to kill him, buzzing in his head that his friends were really his enemies, whispering all kinds of horrible things until he was no longer able to judge what was real and what wasn't. God, I was beginning to know what that felt like. I was beginning to see friends as enemies. Maybe fear would soon overwhelm me and I'd just take off like Andy did. No one would see me for weeks. I'd start sleeping in parks and eating out of dumpsters. I gave myself a shake.

Marley pulled on one of her red curls as if she were stretching out a slinky and worried her lip. "What can I do to help?" she asked.

"Call around and see if anyone has seen Andy."

"Okay. I'll call everyone. If Andy is anywhere within ten miles someone will see him."

"Thanks, Juice."

"Do you want to stay here for a bit? At least until you're over the fear of who might be waiting for you when you go home." She nodded in the direction of the living room. "The sofa is still there if you want it. You have a key."

I shook my head. "Sooner or later I have to go back. And if Andy comes looking for me again, I want to be there."

"It's who else might come looking for you that gives me a panic attack."

"I really wish you hadn't mentioned that."

"Ah! Not as dumb as you look, are you?" She got up and started washing the dishes.

"Styles knows about Andy." I got to my feet and followed her to the sink. "I just hope the police don't start questioning him about Jimmy."

Marley gave a big humph sound. "They try talking to him and they'll commit him for sure." She ran the water, rinsing the plates.

"It isn't against the law to be crazy. He has to be a threat to himself or others."

"I know. And I know Andy wouldn't blow up

170

Jimmy's boat. But you can't judge a nut by its shell. The cops are only going to see he's psychotic and think dangerous. That might be a good thing, Sherri. At least he'd get treatment. Besides, right now it's either you or Andy."

I picked up a tea towel and started drying the dishes she was rattling into the rack at record speed. "Or Tony Rollins. Or Dr. Zampa."

"Let me see," she said, putting a forefinger coyly against her cheek. "Whom will they be more likely to pick to blow up a boat? A fine upstanding dentist, elder in his church and a member of Rotary, or the angry violent wife who works in a bar and shovels shit by the bucket full?"

"True, I'd rather kick ass than kiss it, but wouldn't you?"

"Depends on the ass."

"You are a truly wicked and perverted woman, Miss Hemming."

"That explains me. What explains you?"

"Stupidity."

"I'll buy that. You still aren't seeing how much trouble you're in." Both hands in the sink, she turned to me and said, "Get a lawyer and forget about everything else. Andy isn't your responsibility. You can't worry about him right now."

"He has a copy of the tape. The only thing which might actually save my ass."

"Okay, good point. But still you aren't responsible for him."

I kept quiet. I knew better than to argue with Juice. I went back to the table and picked up her cigarettes while she drained the sink and wiped it down. "Maybe we should try and figure out who was on the boat," she said.

"You try. I'm calling Andy again."

After about twenty rings I gave up and punched in Ruth Ann's number. Guilt. Fortunately she wasn't home either so I left her a message telling her that I was doing just fine but I couldn't make it today.

"When are you going to get a cell phone like the rest of the world?" Marley asked as I hung up.

"Never. I hate them more than I hate that damn blinking light on my answering machine. I get too many calls now. Just think how much more miserable I'd be if people could actually get me?"

"You're the most anti-social social person in the world."

"I have a busy inner life. I just want the world to leave me alone."

She humphed at me. "What are you going to do the rest of the day?"

"Work. But first I want to cruise around out at Windimere. I still think all this has something to do with Windimere. And Tony Rollins is at the head of my psycho list. He was definitely scaring the shit out of me"

"It takes a lot to scare you. If he gets your notice there is definitely something to pay attention to. I'll come with you."

"And miss another adventure in garage sales?"

She dumped her cigarettes into her purse. "See what a swell person I am?"

"And we can keep an eye out for Andy." I jogged down the stairs, waiting for her at the bottom as she locked the door and checked it twice. "I bet he's taken to the streets again, moving from place to place so the CIA can't find him."

"So far it seems to be working."

"There's one place I haven't looked for Andy," I told her as we came out the alley to the street. "A coalition of Southern Baptist churches runs a soup kitchen from a strip mall just off Tamiami Trail. It isn't far from Hess Street—within walking distance." We waited for a break in traffic and ran across the street. "Reverend Halliday might know where he is."

CHAPTER 25

David Halliday was closing the lid of a battered old upright when we came through the door of the Baptist food mission. The breakfast hour was long past and the utilitarian room was empty of people.

"Sherri," David sang when he saw me. This came with a big welcoming smile and an open-arm gesture. "Just the person I wanted to see." The widow peaks of his sand-colored hair were melting back to meet a small bald spot on the back of his head. Even his mother would admit he was short and a little pudgy, but his delight in the world made him one of the most attractive men I knew.

I smiled in response to his warmth. After the world beat you up, here was someone who made it better.

"I haven't seen you since Christmas. Let me buy you lovely ladies a cup of coffee." David put three white mugs on a tray and filled them from a gleaming urn. Then he carried the coffee to the nearest plywood table.

I introduced him to Marley and watched them checking each other out real close. Sparks were going off like a short in an electrical wire. Go figure.

"I'm looking for Andy," I told him. "Have you seen him?" I asked as I pulled out a molded turquoise chair from the table.

He tore his eyes away from Marley and canted his head to the right while he thought for a moment. "Earlier in the week. He was really agitated. Only stayed for about ten minutes. He's off his medication again."

"Where would he go if he didn't go home?"

"Are you more worried about him than usual?"

"Yeah." I picked up the cup of coffee and blew air over the top of the black boiling tar. I bet it had been percolating for hours.

He thought for a moment. "He might be out behind the big-box stores two blocks south. You know that big undeveloped area? Used to be a cattle ranch, the King Ranch. Now it's just wasteland."

"The one the development put on hold because of the nesting eagles?"

He nodded. "That's it. They're trying to get the zoning changed on it. They'd have it already if they hadn't cut down the eagle tree. Some of the county commissioners have dug their heels in and are holding up approval."

"Serves the fools right," I said. "Imagine thinking

you can just go cut down a tree with an eagle's nest to solve your problem with the environmentalists. What were they thinking?"

"I agree," David said. "I went out there to protest." He was talking to me but his eyes were on Marley. "Carried a sign and everything."

"I wish I'd been there too," Marley said. Her voice was all breathy and full of awe.

"And you think Andy might be there?"

He turned up his palms. "Some people live rough out there," he said. His eyes were focused on Marley as he explained. "They use big cardboard boxes from appliances and bits of wood from construction sites, anything they can find to make shelters. Not the best solution for homelessness, but some people prefer it to regular shelters." David Halliday looked deep into Marley's eyes and said, "Andy lived there once when he was evicted."

Hello, had I stopped existing?

"Or Andy might be in a shelter," he said. Marley was nodding in agreement.

I could have fallen off the earth and they wouldn't have noticed. I really wished they'd concentrate on my problem instead of their own itch. "Andy doesn't trust authority. He's more likely to live in the open than go to a shelter. I'll look out there."

"Be careful," David told Marley. "There are a lot of drugs and alcohol used out there."

"In that case, Sherri will feel right at home," said Marley with a big grin.

"Tell me everything," Marley said, as the door shut behind her.

"Everything about what?" Playing dumb is so pitiably easy for me.

"About David Halliday. Is he married?"

"Not that I know of. Probably gay."

She whacked me across the arm. "No he isn't. For sure." She started on a long list of questions and suppositions while I drove out to the abandoned ranch off Tamiami Trail.

"How'd you meet him?" she asked.

"Andy. I came out at Christmas to help serve dinner."

"You aren't," she waggled her fingers, "you know."

"David and I? Hell no."

She didn't look like she believed me.

We drove around behind the new superstores to the loading docks where the deliveries were made.

"I wonder where the eagles went," Marley said. "Not many places along the coast left for them."

Broken bottles and leftover packaging littered the pavement. The parking lot was separated from an empty field by a chain-link fence with grass growing though it and plastic bags and bits of paper blown into the metal webbing. Undeveloped acreage, where longhorn cattle had wandered two years before, stretched out behind the buildings. It was amazing that a prime parcel of land like the King Ranch had escaped development this long. The property fronted Tamiami and was across from strip malls with housing developments behind them.

A six-foot-square sign wired to the fence said "Gridiron Developments" with a St. Pete telephone number. I pointed it out to Marley.

"The name figures," she said. "A tree with eagles would be just one more opponent to be knocked down."

Marley and I drove along the chain-link looking for a way through until we came to a place where the links had been cut and the edges forced back to form a small breach in the fence. Someone had hung a used condom on the wire above the opening.

"Charming." We sat there staring into the jungle, hunting for courage or a face-saving reason not to get out of the truck.

"I don't like this," said Marley, looking anxiously about.

"There's only us."

"That we can see; you can't see beyond ten feet. The palmetto hides everything. We could be murdered and no one would know."

"Now who's paranoid?" I opened the door and jumped down with a great show of confidence.

Doves cooed in the thicket of thorn bushes. It sounded peaceful. Passing feet had beaten a sand path into the weeds leading towards a stand of pines. I dipped through the fence and stepped off the path, waiting for Marley in the knee-high dry grass. Even the air smelt dusty.

"C'mon, Juice, where's your sense of adventure?"

"Home with my mace."

She took one more glance around, gave a huge sigh and told me, "I would so rather be at a garage sale," then she ducked down to come through the fence. We stood side by side for a moment and looked at the strip of sand leading into the palmettos, and then I started down the trail with Marley right on my heels.

"How are we going to find him?" she whispered. It was that kind of place, a place where you didn't want to call attention to yourself.

"I haven't a clue," I told her as we rounded a clump of Brazilian pepper trees and came upon a campsite. I stopped so suddenly Marley bumped into me. A wild collection of garbage—bottles and cans, broken furniture and what looked like used car parts—was strewn around a ring of stones containing ashes. A heavy cardboard box, which once contained a refrigerator, lay on its side with a pair of worn sneakers sticking out the end. The inhabitant was a satin lump formed by a ragged wine-colored quilt.

The doves still cooed.

"Holy shit," Marley hissed in my ear. She took a big handful of my T-shirt. "Is he dead?"

"Why don't you go find out," I whispered.

She jabbed me hard in the ribs for the suggestion.

We tiptoed forward, two parts of the same silent animal.

The relief of passing our first test didn't last. We followed the path as it circled around some pepper trees to where two teenagers, male and female, blocked the narrow path in front of us. Dressed all in black, they looked as if they only came out at night. They were studded and pierced, eyebrows, lips and noses—their ears weren't just pierced in multiples but contained big metal plugs . . . I'm talking half-inch plugs at least, their lobes stretched thinly, just like those pictures in *National Geographic* at the dentist's office. Black hair, dyed and spiked, crowned gaunt white faces. Their clothes were shiny and stiff with grime. Everything about them was designed to smack fear into people like us.

CHAPTER 26

I could hear Marley hyperventilating in my ear; her chin was digging into my shoulder. I told myself they could be really very nice people.

"Good morning," I said and stepped aside into the tall weeds. Marley's skinny little body, pressed up tight to mine, shuffled sideways with me. Her damp breath filled my ear.

The Bat People didn't respond . . . didn't even blink. They just kept on walking.

"Have a nice day," I whispered as we watched them disappear around the clump of pepper trees without looking back.

"God," Marley sighed and plopped her head down on my shoulder.

"I wish I had an outfit like that," I told Marley. "And I wish I was wearing it right now."

"I hope they don't come back with their friends to rob us."

"They don't have any friends. They'd probably eat them. Besides, that's why we locked our bags in the truck."

"I've got to pee," Marley wailed and tugged at my T-shirt. "Let's go back."

"There's lots of room out here." I spread out my arm to illustrate the endless opportunities. "Feel free."

"You kidding? Not on your life."

She was still holding onto my shirt. I pulled her forward. "We should've asked those kids if they've seen Andy."

"We should have asked them to call a cop," replied Marley.

"I should have brought a picture."

"Good idea. Let's go get one." She tugged harder on my shirt, trying to turn me around.

"So you can run out on me? Not a chance."

"We don't belong here," she wailed in my ear.

"Makes the Shoreline Mobile Home Park look real upscale, doesn't it?"

"If that's your idea of a silver lining, can it."

"It's the first time I ever felt that I had an advantaged childhood."

"Oh yeah! With privileges like that, how could you have gone so wrong?"

"Hard work, my girl, hard work. Even with advantages it takes hard work."

Marley let go of my shirt. I didn't bother to turn around to see if she was making a break for safety. I had the keys.

"If we don't find him now," I said over my shoulder, "Let's come back tonight."

She yelped and slapped my back. "Forget it."

The path divided and I considered the options. On our right the track led to a large spreading oak while the left just went farther off into the scrub brush.

"Let's go home," Marley whispered. "We aren't doing any good here." Her chin was on my shoulder again as I tried to decide which way to go. "Please."

"That's where I'd take cover if I had to live out here." Live oaks don't drop all their leaves in the winter so enough remain to form a canopy. I headed for the oak. "We might find someone that knows Andy."

Marley grabbed my shoulders to hold me back. I turned my head to look at her.

"Aren't you scared?" she whispered.

"Petrified . . . paralyzed with fear."

"No, you're not. You're still moving."

True, I'd started moving towards the oak. Walking backwards, I asked Marley, "Do you want to wait here?"

She looked around judging if it would be safer to go with me or stay here alone. "No," she said reluctantly. "I'll come." She shuffled forward a few steps then stopped again. "What if we run into someone that's out of his mind on drugs?"

I had no suggestions. My feet slowed and my brain said, "Marley's right. This is crazy." I started back towards her. From behind us came the sound of running feet, coming down the path to where it divided. I saw Marley's eyes open wide with horror before fear galvanized me into movement.

We dove below a bower of vines at the edge of the oak and stood up in an open area under the canopy. Dappled light fell on five primitive shelters, made from a combination of plywood and cardboard. One of the shelters had Clay's Cypress Island Reality for sale signs tacked to its side. The sight made me smile for a heartbeat until I saw what else was in the clearing.

Two men sat on listing aluminum lawn chairs in front of a circle of stones. They were staring at us like we were lunch, a very good lunch.

"Whoops!" Marley said in my ear.

They may have been homeless but these two weren't beaten or downtrodden. Their eyes shone with sly malevolence; these were dangerous predators, not the victims we normally associate with homelessness—the sort of men you went out of your way never to be alone with.

"Hello!" I said, trying for the perkiness of a Christian zealot going door to door. "The Reverend Halliday is conducting a little survey on the needs of the people who use his mission. He's just over there . . ." I pointed behind me to lend credence to my lie, "and will be along in a minute, but perhaps you could answer some questions for us . . . if you wouldn't mind, that is."

They exchanged looks. The bigger one, the one who looked like he was wearing a fright wig left over from Halloween, along with his worldly possessions, turned his head aside and spat on the ground. "Halliday can go fuck himself."

"Well, I'm really sorry you feel that way," I said, edging backwards. "God bless you brother."

"I'm not your brother," he growled. This man definitely did not have a religious nature.

The smaller man smiled, which was unfortunate. He was missing his top teeth and it looked as if he would be better off without the bottom. "You can bless me if you want," he said, cupping his crotch, to make it clear the exact nature of the blessing he had in mind.

CHAPTER 27

He planted his hands on the arms of the chair and started to push up. My feet were already moon-walking out of the clearing.

The big man grabbed the little guy from behind as he reached his feet. "Forget it. You want to bring the law down on us?"

Mr. Teeth whined deep in his throat but sank back down.

"By the way," I said, suddenly brave again, "we were also requested to ask if Andy Crown is here." Their faces stayed blank. "He's about six foot tall with wild curly hair." I raised my hands in a circle around my head to help them visualize it. He's thirty-two years old with blue eyes." Even I wouldn't have recognized him from this description.

Nothing.

By now Marley was moving backwards faster than I was and tugging on my T-shirt to get me moving.

Not a good thing. They were getting a better view of my charms than was safe.

"Well, goodbye," I said, ever polite.

We turned and ran. I'd won more than one trophy for track, but still, when we rounded the pepper tree Marley was the one that ran smack into the man coming up the path.

Marley screamed and beat him with her fists while he ducked and dodged, putting his forearms up to defend himself and calling her name.

At the sound of her name she stopped her attack, stared at him for the flick of an eye and then threw her arms around the Reverend Halliday. She'd found her salvation at last.

"Marley," I said, yanking on her sweatshirt, "Marley." But she didn't let go, she was drowning and he was a giant rock above the raging sea. To be honest, he didn't seem to mind, seemed to be holding on just as firmly.

"After you left I started thinking that this was no place for the two of you to come alone," he explained over Marley's shoulder, rubbing her back and rocking her gently. "I came to make sure you were all right." He lost interest in me at this point and turned his face into Marley. "It's all right. You're safe," he soothed.

Marley was sobbing with her head tucked into the side of his neck and her arms locked around him. She was going to drown the poor guy if she kept this up.

Making shushing sounds, he slid an arm across her shoulders and with her locked to his side, he led her slowly away.

Oh for god's sake—a little fear plus a few hormones and control goes right out the window. I felt quite left out. I stepped around them and stomped up the path to the hole in the fence.

At the truck I dug out Marley's bag and helped myself to her cigarettes. I leaned against the pickup, waiting for Marley and trying to figure out what to do next. With the three of us together it would be much safer to go back into that jungle, but I wasn't sure that it would get us any further. The population beyond the fence was even less inclined to help than the people on this side. I dug around in my bag and found an old telephone bill, the second notice of an unpaid balance. I pulled the statement out of the envelope and stuffed it back into my bag for next month. I wrote Andy's name in big block letters at the top of the envelope and tried to find words that would reassure him. In the end, I wrote, "Call me, Sherri." I poked a hole in my note and tied it onto the fence with a bit of string from the pavement. Anyone going through the chain-link was bound to see it. Hopefully they wouldn't rip it down.

An idea hit me. I should have thought of it sooner. I could make up flyers and leave them everywhere Andy might be. It was a great idea. Maybe even add a picture of Andy and hand it out all over town with the promise of a reward. As quickly as this great idea came to me, sanity told me that you don't find a paranoid person by putting up flyers with his picture on it. It would feed right into his delusions.

I helped myself to another cigarette. It was taking them a long time to get to the fence.

I was about to lean on the horn when I saw them coming. Reverend Halliday still had his arm around Marley's shoulder. I kept my eyes on Marley, trying to figure out was happening. I didn't have to wait long.

When they dipped through the fence, Marley started talking. "That was terrifying. I'm really shattered," she told me. "David's going to take me home."

Oh really! David! I wanted to ask her why she didn't pick up guys in bars like the rest of us, but her eyes were warning me to shut up.

"Okay." I nodded my head in agreement. "Good idea." I reached into the truck and got her bag.

"I'll call all the shelters and see if they have anyone named Andy Crown," David promised.

I handed Marley her bag.

"And I'll ask everyone that comes in for food if they've seen him. I'll call if I hear anything."

"Now that's a great idea, David. Thanks."

I sank back against the truck and watched them walk to his car, watched him unlock the door for Marley, watched her smiling at him like he was

Superman. I felt a strange stab of jealousy, fresh and hot and unexpected. I wanted to feel like that again.

Ashamed, I scrambled into the truck. I was turning the key even as I slammed the door. I squealed out of the parking lot like a teenager downtown on Saturday night. So much for being a mature adult.

I stopped for groceries on my way home and was still putting stuff in the fridge when someone knocked on my door.

"Hi," Cordelia said. She tried a smile. "Sorry I'm not who you were hoping to see."

I laughed and held the door wide for her to enter. "Was I that obvious?"

"Yes." Cordelia settled gracefully into the bottomless couch. Man I wished I could do that.

"I was hoping you were Andy Crown." I told her the story as I went to the fridge for sodas. "I really want to find him."

"What can I do to help?" Her guileless blue eyes begged to be included, anything to keep from dwelling on the realities of her life.

"How about calling the hospitals?"

"Sure."

"I already went out to see his mother. I don't want to go back."

"We go to church together," she said. "I'll ask how Andy is dealing with Jimmy's death and ask if they've seen him."

"Thanks." I watched her turn the glass around in her hands. "So how are things with you?" I asked.

She just hunched her shoulders in response. "I'm getting through the day."

"You came by to check up on me, didn't you?"

She set the soda on the battered coffee table. "I didn't think I'd find you here."

"Why?"

"Because Noble is away until Sunday morning."

Well that explained where Evan had gone. "Sorry to disappoint you."

"I'm not disappointed. I'm glad you're not the one. I'd hate to lose you as a friend."

I winced. What kind of a friend keeps a secret as big as the one I was keeping?

"Anyway," she said with a delicate flick of her wrist, "I've hired a private detective. I know it sounds like a tacky thing to do but I have to know the truth. So far he has just followed Noble to normal places. Work-related things. And Evan's. That's why I thought you lied to me. I thought he was pretending to visit Evan and slipping in to see you somehow." Her delicately pale face looked apologetic.

"Is it so bad between you?" I asked. "Can't you just go on the way things are?" I knew it was a stupid question the moment the words were out of my mouth.

Her eyes fell. "We never . . . ," she paused, looking down at her gold wedding band. She reached out for it and took a deep breath. "It's been so long. Not since Robin was born." She looked up at me. "Do you think that's normal?"

"Not where I come from."

"No, I don't suppose it's a problem you've ever had. Men like you." If anyone else had said that it would have sounded catty, but with Cordelia it came out as high praise. "You don't know what it's like to lie in the dark, hoping he'll reach out to you."

"Cordelia . . . ," I started.

"You don't know what it's like to touch a man and have him pull away. Each time I try to make him want me, by wearing a new dress or flirting with him, I see him cringe. See him close in on himself and I feel like a whore, an ugly worthless . . . ," she searched for words, "hussy. It's like I'm cheapening myself and he can't stand to see it."

"Don't blame yourself, Cordelia. You're a beautiful, intelligent woman. If you weren't so fine and upstanding you'd see just how many men are attracted to you. Don't fault yourself for some failure in Noble."

She shook her head wildly. "No, no. It isn't Noble. It's me. If I were just more like you."

I laughed. "Wash your mouth out, girl. If your mama could hear you she'd fall down in a faint."

She smiled faintly. "My mama couldn't begin to know how I live and I can't tell her."

"Have you tried?"

"No! Never! I've only told you. I couldn't tell her or anyone else."

"But what do you plan to do if your detective does come up with some evidence that Noble is having an affair?"

"I don't know exactly."

"Well, there's lots of time to decide. In the meantime it's you I'm concerned about. Give yourself a break, stop slamming yourself."

I wanted to say more and put an end to her misery; or maybe it would start more misery, but it wasn't my secret to tell. Besides, Cordelia's detective would soon set her straight . . . if she made the connection. Cordelia was naïve, an innocent, and the truth of Evan and Noble's relationship might never occur to her. She'd just go on thinking they were good friends and that she'd made a mistake about Noble having an affair.

The wind had shifted to the north, bringing cold winds with it. The temperature dropped late in the afternoon and by the time I left for the Sunset the landscaping all over town was beginning to sport bed sheets, a sure sign we were in for a frost. I thought about Andy, hoping he wasn't sleeping rough.

CHAPTER 28

When I turned into the parking lot at the Sunset, only a few hardy tourists were still on the sand, huddling together under blankets waiting for the sun to go down. They must have been the ones down from Toronto. Those guys are always the last to leave the beach.

I was so glad to get to the bar that night you wouldn't believe. It says something when work is easier than living, but at the Sunset I knew how things worked and people only wanted things from me I could deliver. I ran all the way up the stairs.

Diana Krall's sultry voice filled the room, as the etched glass doors closed behind me and Bobby Lee, the manager, greeted me with, "I wasn't sure you'd make it in tonight. Can't stay away, can you Sherri?"

I grinned at him. "I'm just a fool for you, Bobby."

The three amigos were there though they don't usually show up on a Saturday. I took it as a sign of moral support. "Haven't any of you got a home?" I asked.

"Yup," said Peter, "and we're in it."

Between pulling beers, opening bottles of wine and mixing drinks I told them about the break-in. "Only four people knew I had the tape. You guys and Evan. So which of you broke into my joint and took the video?"

They each pointed a finger at the guy beside them and said, "Him."

"Very funny. I've got some orders to fill. By the time I get back I want you to tell me who did it."

When I got back they'd decided it was Evan who'd searched my apartment. "Well that was easy, wasn't it?" I said. "I'm glad we got that taken care of."

Brian pushed the wire rims back up his nose. "You should stay somewhere else until this is settled." His worry lines deepened. "Stay with a friend . . . stay at your mother's."

I made a face.

"No really, he's right," Peter put in. "Don't go back to the Tropicana. You can stay with me if you like." He waggled his eyebrows. "Safe as can be."

I laughed. "Honey, you ain't never going to get that lucky. I'd rather face Hannibal Lecter than a night fighting you off."

"Oh, I'd like it if you fought," Peter said, rubbing his hands in anticipation.

Clay ignored us and said, "Peter's right. I have a couple of rentals out on the beach. I'll go back to the office and see what's available. You can stay there for the next month."

"I can't afford the beach!"

"I'm not going to charge you." He seemed almost indignant.

I stopped in my tracks, a carafe of house wine in each hand. Clay, the cheapest guy in the world, was offering something for free. He was really worried about me.

"Thanks, Clay."

I put the drinks down on a tray and came back to him. "Thanks, but I'll stay put." I reached out to touch his hand and then quickly withdrew it. I made busy until I got my wonky emotions under control.

"You need protection," Clay said when I came back to them.

"Like a police car parked outside my door? My neighbors are already leery about inviting me to the annual cookout."

"Screw the neighbors," Clay snarled. This guy just takes things so literal it makes jiving him difficult. "At least stay somewhere else for a while."

"There is something you all can do for me," I told them. "Would you all keep your eyes open for that white SUV? The three letters to the right of the orange spell OFF. I'm sure it belongs to one of those guys on the video. If we know who they are, we may know why Jimmy was interested in them enough to video them."

"How be I check out Windimere?" offered Brian.

"I tried today but no luck."

"They'll be there Sunday morning if they're golfers. I'll check the Royal Palms as well."

"I can tell all my agents to watch for it," Clay put in. "They're up and down the island every day."

Peter turned to Brian and asked, "Can't you call someone in vehicle registration and see who that plate belongs to?"

"You watch too much TV. I am just a real estate lawyer. I don't know anything about getting a plate number. Hell, I can't even get my own tickets fixed." He stared glumly into his drink. Lately it didn't take much to sink him into a gray funk.

Marley strode in and settled her bony bottom onto a stool beside Brian, talking before she'd even sat down. "No luck on finding Andy. David checked all the shelters. I even called Mrs. Crown. He isn't in a private facility."

I would have liked to hear the conversation between Marley and Betsy Crown, liked to have heard Marley say, "So, have you got Andy stashed someplace?" Diplomacy wasn't one of her talents.

It was a wild night at the Sunset. It started out as people simply dropping in to express their condolences and then the memories started flowing along with the booze.

Skip Howard took the floor with people three

deep at the bar around him. "One time Jimmy and I were coming back from a basketball game up in Bradenton. We'd won so we'd kind of been celebrating. Jimmy was stretched out in the back seat, sound asleep, when this cruiser pulls me over." Skip started to laugh, a high wheezing laugh that leaves him helpless. His Santa Claus belly shook like a bowl of jelly while everyone waited, nudging each other and laughing along with him though they didn't know what the joke was yet.

"Jimmy is sound asleep," he repeated. "Sheriff's deputy has me spread-eagled on the hood of my car." The memory doubled him up with laughter. "Jimmy wakes up, gets out of the car and walks back to the cruiser. The deputy left it running, see?" Now everyone one was laughing, waiting for it.

"Jimmy gets into the cruiser." More wheezing hilarity from Skip. "Takes the deputy a few seconds to figure out what's happening here. Maybe it was just the surprise of seeing Jimmy when he thought I was alone. Or maybe he was slow at guessing what Jimmy intended to do. Anyway, the deputy finally figures it out when Jimmy is getting in the car. The cop is going crazy. Yelling at Jimmy to stop. Running back to stop Jimmy. Even pulling his gun. Honest to god, I thought he was going to shoot Travis." The whole bar was laughing now.

"Jimmy just pulls out around him and takes off."

Tears are running down Skip's face. Gasping for breath, he stammers, "The deputy . . . the deputy threw me in the back of my car . . . swearing . . . ranting. Takes off after Jimmy. Followed him all the way through town and out to South Beach. He's got no jurisdiction inside city limits but he wants his cruiser back."

Now the bar around him goes crazy but Skip isn't done. "When we get out to South Beach, the cruiser is parked in the Travises' driveway, door open, car still running but no Jimmy. The crazy son of a bitch just went into the house, climbed into bed and went back to sleep."

That was my boy all right . . . a crazy son of the bitch named Bernice.

From a wake it turned into a loud boisterous party that Jimmy would have loved, but things had started to quiet down by the time Tony Rollins came by. He wasn't smiling and he wasn't joining the "Remember Jimmy" party.

"I need to talk to you," he said.

"Come out to my office." I led the way down the corridor to the exit door. As my daddy would say, it was as cold as a witch's tit outside.

"Andy Crown called the club looking for Jimmy today."

"God!" It just about knocked me over. "Here I've been running around looking for him and he calls you.

You didn't tell him Jimmy was dead, did you? That would send him spiraling off the planet for sure."

"Nah."

I sagged back against the railing. "Did he say where he was? Leave a message of any kind?"

"He just asked for Jimmy and when I said Jimmy wasn't there, he said, 'Tell him Andy called.' I'm thinking he might be the one who took the blades off the pump."

I froze. It was a long fall off the narrow little platform to concrete below. "How did you know about that?"

"What?"

"How'd you know what caused the explosion?"

His face screwed up in distress. This boy really didn't come from a gene pool you'd want to dip your toes into, but you don't have to be real bright to kill someone. "You told me?" The fact that he put a question mark at the end of the sentence said he really wasn't expecting me to go for it.

I wrapped my hands tight around the railing ready to kick out if he moved towards me. "No I didn't."

"I guess I read it in the papers."

"Don't think so." The rough block bit into my shoulder as I wedged myself into the corner against the wall.

CHAPTER 29

"I guess the cops told me. What does it matter?"

It mattered. There was one for sure way he could know what happened on the *Suncoaster*.

"That nutcase, Crown, doctored Jimmy's boat. You should tell the cops."

"It's your story. You tell them."

His body jerked closer to me. "You're the one they're interested in. People saw you on the boat. I'm trying to help you here."

"People?" Things were getting better and better. "Who said?"

He leaned towards me. I could smell the mint of breath spray. "If you want this thing to go away, you have to give them something."

"It's nice of you to be concerned about me."

"I don't want cops snooping around."

"I can see that would make your clients nervous . . . interfere with business."

"Jimmy was fucking up everything."

"Well, he can't bother you now." I started to ease around him. He blocked my way with his shoulder.

"This Crown guy is perfect."

"Right now I have to get back to work." I pushed him away with my right hand but he grabbed my wrist and held me.

"I want us to be friends," he said.

"Sure," I lied. "I'll call you."

I stacked the last glass and wiped down the bar.

"C'mon," Bobby urged, his hand already on the light switch.

"You got a promise, Bobby?"

"Yeah, I promised myself a hot shower and bed."

In the parking lot Bobby's sedan sat beside Jimmy's red pickup. But there was another car still there. The last place I'd worked there was always someone sleeping a heavy night off in the back seat, but not at the Sunset. Another thing the Sunset is too upscale for. At this time of the night everyone should be gone.

Bobby hesitated. "Who is it?" He was thinking about the night deposit in his inside pocket.

The door of the Lexus opened and Clay stood up, looking at us over the roof.

"It's okay, Bobby," I said.

I went around the Lexus to where Clay was waiting, hands stuffed into the pockets of a leather bomber jacket and looking uncomfortable. He always gives the impression of being tall although he's not quite six feet. It's the stillness that makes you aware of him, no wasted movements, nothing over the top, steel in the presence of reeds.

"Did they pick you to babysit?" I asked. "I figure you three tossed a coin to see who saw me home from the party."

He hunched his shoulders forward. "I volunteered." He didn't look pleased to admit it.

I'd enjoyed them fussing over me, even encouraged it, but the joke had gone far enough. "Well, you're off the hook. There's no one waiting for me. They got what they came for."

"You don't know that. You don't have any idea of what's going on."

"True, but then I never do."

"It can't hurt to be cautious for a few days."

"Okay, but I want to go to Andy's before I go home."

"I'll drive," he said, turning on his heel and getting back in his car.

The leather seat was heated although my nether regions were hot enough and I really didn't need the help; but I wiggled my bum down into the warmth as it wrapped around me like an embrace. We cruised out to Tamiami with Chris Isaacs singing about getting lucky in Texas while I was thinking of getting lucky right here in Florida. I told myself Clay wasn't my type. Judging by Jimmy, my type was drunk, drugged out and totally beyond control while Clay was all about control and taking care of business. Where's the fun in that? Definitely not my kind.

Clay pulled up in front of number nine at the Palmetto Motel. Country music, overlaid with laughter and curses, boomed into the night. A party was in full blast at the end unit, with people spilling out into the parking lot. It was arctic cold but that didn't seem to be bothering them as they drank from long-neck bottles and cans that flashed silver in the light from the open door.

"Wait here and lock the doors," Clay ordered, his eyes fixed on the rowdy gang as his hand reached for the door.

"Staying with the car is more dangerous than going. It's the Lexus that will attract them." I jumped out and ran to Andy's door before he could stop me.

"Andy," I yelled and pounded on the door with my fist. Two big guys broke from the pack outside the party door and slowly drifted towards me. "Andy, open up. It's Sherri. We have to talk." My eyes never left my audience.

Now five guys were moving my way. I heard Clay's car door open behind me and I was gone back to the car. My door slammed shut just as the first guy leaned on the right fender. He stared through the windshield, growling obscenities.

The Lexus shot backwards. A can bounced off the windshield, spraying foam across the glass. The Lexus squealed forward and out onto the street.

"Clay, your car!" I wailed.

He turned on the wipers to clear the mess and grinned at me. "You know all the hot spots, don't you?"

"Yup. And I get invited to all the best parties. And that was a good one."

When we reached Tamiami he stopped for a red light. "Wanna go home?" he asked.

"I'm too wired to sleep."

"Are you hungry?"

"Let's cruise out to South Beach and Indian Mound. At this time of the night, everyone will be home. Maybe we'll find the SUV. An SUV says upscale neighborhood to me."

"Well, at least better than the one we just left."

"I'm thinking there's not great resale potential in that neighborhood," I said.

"See," Clay replied, "already you're thinking like a realtor."

He headed south for the bridge to Cypress Island. "Marley thinks Jimmy is still alive."

He turned to look at me. "Do you?"

"Yes."

"She also thinks he was the one who broke into your apartment."

"I don't know about that. It would be crazy to hang about here. I think he's far away."

"Maybe he needs the video before he goes."

I didn't want to think about Jimmy. I was enjoying the heat and trying to decide if it was time to take a risk, time to let someone inside my defenses.

"Sherri, if Jimmy shows up and asks you to go with him, will you go?"

"God, no! Never!" I sat up. "Are you out of your mind?"

He gave a harsh bark of laughter. "I'm beginning to think so."

CHAPTER 30

We drove slowly through the quiet dark streets of South Beach. "I'd forgotten that you can't see most houses from the street. And nobody lets their cars sit outside overnight."

"Still, it's a nice night for a drive," replied Clay.

I didn't remind him it was cold as a walk-in freezer.

As we drove along Beach Road listening to the music, I told Clay about Tony Rollins.

"Andy is an easy target. With Andy wrapped up nice and tight no one would look too close at what Tony is doing out at Windimere. I probably only scratched the surface of what Tony's up to."

"What if Tony Rollins doctored Jimmy's boat?" He turned to look at me. "And you were out on that stairs alone with him."

"It did occur to me."

"I think . . . ," he said and stopped. I waited. "I think you should go away for a while. Let this blow over."

"Great idea, but I'm the chief suspect. Styles would just haul my ass back here."

"Then you've got to be more careful. Go someplace secure."

"Yeah, like the Shoreline?"

"God no. Don't go to your mother's. Hell, you could get knocked off by one of the neighbors."

"The Shoreline isn't that bad. It's true the inhabitants are keen on taking the occasional shot at one another, but there's only been one actual murder. I'm not sure whether they're just bad shots or always too drunk to be accurate."

"Stay with Marley."

"What if you're right? I don't want to put anyone in danger. What if I stayed with Marley and someone came looking for me there? See what I mean? I think I should stay as far away as I can from everyone else to avoid . . . what's it called, collateral damage."

"Nice image."

"Well, my life's beginning to feel like a war zone."

"I've got an idea." It took him a while to get to it. "I live in a really secure building. Stay with me for a while."

"Hey, are you making a pass at me?"

"No. No. I just want you to be safe. I'm going up to Cedar Key to look at a piece of property tomorrow so you'll have it all to yourself."

I tried to decide if there was some hidden meaning. Any other guy I'd know what was happening, but not with Clay. I could never read this guy. "Safe is an interesting concept." Falling into bed with him probably would defeat the purpose of staying safe. "Now that Jimmy's video is gone, there's nothing else anyone could want from me."

"Don't bet on it," Clay said.

Clay took me back to the Sunset to pick up the truck and then followed me out to the Tropicana, parking and getting out of the Lexus before me, watching the deep shadows as I got out of Big Red. He was well and truly spooked.

"I'm going in with you," he told me. No arguments allowed.

Clay had never been to my apartment so at the top of the steps, I pointed to the right, and started to say, "Down here," but Clay had already turned. I froze. Sure, he knew that I lived at the Tropicana but that was all he knew. Now he just walked right up to the end unit. Fear crept up my spine. How did he know which apartment was mine? Something was happening here I didn't understand.

Clay waited outside my door. "Are you coming?"

"It's okay," I assured him. "I'm fine now. You don't need to come in."

"I want to check inside. You don't want any more nasty surprises."

Yeah, like the nasty surprise I'd just had. Something was wrong here. Something was going to jump out and bite me, I knew that.

Slowly, looking for the hidden pain, I went to join him.

He took the keys out of my hand and opened the door. How could I doubt Clay? He wasn't like other guys. He probably came by earlier to check out where I lived. And having him here suited me just fine.

He held the door wide and waited for me to go in. Then he followed me inside and locked the door behind us. "I'm going to have a look around."

I smiled. "That will take you about a second and a half."

He took his time, looking in the closets and even under the bed while I lounged against the door frame watching him. "If I'd known you were coming I'd have made the bed."

He grinned, "You and a rumpled bed are the things fantasies are made of."

The sparkle in his eyes lit a fire in the pit of me. "Tell me more about these fantasies."

He laughed and came towards me. His jaw had a slight darkening of late-night beard along it, making him look rough and dangerous. Rough and dangerous was just the way I wanted it. I flamed into one huge erogenous zone, itching for his touch. I reached out for him.

"Jesus," Clay said.

Who knew? Damn, but Mr. Cool turned out to be Mr. Hot as Hell and I couldn't get enough of him.

It had been a long time for me and maybe for Clay, too. There were no words, no promise of forever, not even of tomorrow, no tenderness; just a driving need for fulfillment. Only bruising kisses and frantic hands on two sweaty bodies: demanding access and climax and turning the unmade bed into a battleground of desire.

Later came soft murmurs of pleasure and gentleness, guarded endearments, later when our pulses had evened out. But just as quickly as peace was declared, war broke out again.

I lay on top of the rumpled sheets letting the air dry my hot body. Outside, a tropical storm was unleashed. Rain poured down. The drought was over.

I watched Clay stretched out beside me in lightening shadows of dawn. I thought he was sleeping until he reached out and gently circled the tattoo on my right hip. "I hate that thing," I told him.

"You could have it removed."

"Why bother."

"Oh, I don't know. Maybe you'll want a new name there."

I raised myself up on my forearms and looked down at him. "Trust me, if I ever have anything else tattooed there, it's going to say, 'Mine.'"

His hand grew still. I lay back down.

"Come to Cedar Key with me." His hand started caressing me again. "Have a little holiday and let the dust settle." He'd been born in Florida just like me but there's no sound of Dixie in his voice. Deep and rich, like melted chocolate, his voice sounds smart and important, like a newsman on CNN. I love the sound of his voice even when it's saying things I don't want to hear.

"Do you really have to go to Cedar Key?" I sound real down home no matter how hard I try.

"Yeah. There are other people involved. It's important."

I wanted to ask, "And what's happening in this bed isn't?" Instead I said, "I'll stay in Jacaranda. There are things I need to do."

"Why don't you go over to my apartment?" He held up a hand to stop me. "Just for a few days. I'll feel better knowing you're safe."

I turned it around and around, trying to see it from all angles. Lying naked beside him was one thing; this was another. "I'm safe here," I told him.

He rolled away, got to his feet and started dressing.

After he left I slept, but not for long. By nine I was up, restlessly pacing the apartment. Without Clay there, I started to doubt him, started to wonder. His slip of the night before took on a whole new meaning without his body to distract me. I was becoming desperate and obsessed with knowing what was going on. I needed to do something.

Evan showed up while I was under the truck, checking along the frame for a hidden video cassette. He kicked my foot sticking out from under the bumper. "Doing your own engine work now, Butch?"

I slithered out and smiled up at him. "Welcome home, Romeo. Where have you been?"

"We took the boat and sailed down towards the keys. Noble went home late last night and I slept over on the boat to do some repairs."

"Cordelia was here yesterday. She thought I might have gone away with Noble."

"The truth would be worse." He offered me a hand and pulled me to my feet. "So how've you been?"

"It hasn't been boring." I bent over to pick up the piece of cardboard I'd been lying on. "I've been thinking that Jimmy likely had a copy of that tape out on the boat. Andy has one and I had one. Maybe there are more copies. I need that tape."

He bit the inside of his cheek. Worry lines took away some of the freshness from his face, making him look less boyish. "Were there any pictures of Noble and me on that video?"

"Not that I saw."

He sighed. He looked tired and depressed. Either the cruise hadn't gone as he planned or he was really sorry it was over. Or he was very worried about something else. Whichever it was, I didn't want to know. Other people's love lives are just too stupid to bear and I had enough problems of my own.

Besides, there was something else on my mind. "Why did you really go out to Windimere?"

He looked embarrassed. He couldn't keep eye contact. "It was stupid," he said. He scuffed his toe in the crushed shells. "It was just a fit of anger."

If Evan, a very proper sort of person, could go out there and risk embarrassing himself, what else could he do?

His eyes looked everywhere but at me. "I got out of bed mad on Monday. Jimmy was lousing up your life."

Nice, but I wasn't buying it. "And you were worried that he'd ruin Noble's too. You'd do pretty much anything for Noble."

He said simply, "Yes."

"And Jimmy seemed to be a threat to Noble?"

"Noble met Jimmy coming out of the Jutebox. Jimmy said we were such a good story he was having trouble keeping it to himself. Jimmy thought it was a big joke." Evan studied the undergrowth. "You don't know how hard this is on Noble. Falling in love with me turned his life upside down. We met the first day of classes. It was a thunderbolt. Noble claims he didn't even know he was gay. That Thanksgiving he went home to tell Cordelia he couldn't marry her, their engagement was off. He never got the chance to tell her. Cordelia told him she was pregnant and they were married before he returned to school." He looked at me, the misery of every lost love etched on his face.

"Noble didn't think there was any other choice for him. Besides," his eyes went back to studying the toe of his shoe, "he always wanted children, the one thing I can't give him and if he leaves Cordelia, he's afraid he'll lose them."

He looked at me and smiled. "But for one little sperm traveling upstream Noble and I wouldn't be in this mess."

"And that's pretty much the story of all of us. Jimmy wasn't going to tell your secret."

His jaw hardened. "Jimmy thought we were a big joke. You've told me a hundred times he was capable of anything. He didn't care who he'd hurt."

"Did you rig the motor on the *Suncoaster*?"

CHAPTER 31

I wanted to take the words back as soon as they were out of my mouth. A week ago I would have trusted Evan to the ends of forever: now I was calling him a murderer. We stared at each other in shocked silence, not believing we'd come to this.

A yellow cab swung into the parking lot, spraying shells as it braked beside us. We swung away from each other in relief.

"Sherri," Eddy Ortiz called through the open window, his white teeth flashing in his dark face.

"Talk to you later," Evan said. He threw his duffle bag over his shoulder and jogged for the stairs.

"Evan," I called. But he didn't stop or look around.

Eddy got out of the cab. "I have good news and bad news."

"Gimme the good news first. I could sure as hell use some."

Eddy folded his arms and leaned back against the car. "I saw Andy."

"Great," I said.

He held up a hand. "But I couldn't convince him to get in with me."

"Bad. Where was this?"

"I was coming back from delivering a fare to the airport in Sarasota. He was out on Tamiami Trail near that big fruit stand. I called to him. He stopped. He knew me. I said you were looking for him, said I'd give him a ride but he took off."

"At least we know he's still around. The fruit stand is near the center where Marley and I looked for him. He may go back there."

"Sorry I couldn't help."

"There's someone else I'm looking for. He drives a white SUV with a license plate ending in OFF. The guy stiffed me for a bar bill." A lie was simpler than the truth but it was beginning to scare me how easy they were coming. "Will you keep an eye out for the SUV?"

"Sure. I'll tell the other guys to watch too." And they would. They'd all been done for a fare sometime and would stick together on this.

"Thanks, Eddy." A thought occurred to me. "Do you ever play golf?"

He laughed. "Not what you'd call golf. My brother, Angel, he's almost an accountant now, you know."

His voice was full of pride. "We rent clubs a couple times a year out at Hidden Lakes and tear up some turf."

"Good. I've got a little pressie for you. C'mon." I opened the lid to the bed of the pickup. "There," I said, waving a hand at Jimmy's clubs. Alive or dead, Jimmy wasn't going to need them and I didn't want them around.

Eddy looked at the clubs and then looked at me. "You're kidding!"

"Nope. I can't use them and I wouldn't feel right selling them."

He rubbed his upper lip with the edge of his hand while his eyes searched the ground.

Had I made a big mistake here? He was really uncomfortable about something.

"Look, if you don't want them, sell them. I don't care. I just don't want them around."

He nodded and stuffed his hands into his back pockets.

"Hey, Eduardo, what's happening? Have I screwed up?"

He laughed and looked up at me. "Nah, you didn't screw up. Not by a mile. It's just . . . well it's just a surprise."

"Good. For a minute there you had me worried." I reached in for the bag but he beat me to it. He pulled the black leather bag out of the truck and slung the wide shoulder strap over his left shoulder. The red embroidery of Jimmy's initials flashed at me.

"When I show up with these, my little brother's gonna shit himself."

"And if you want some lessons, I'm your girl."

"How do I look?" he asked, standing stiffly upright with the bag over his shoulder and grinning like a fool.

"Like a cab driver with a set of Pings."

"Not like a pro?"

"You've always been a pro, Eddy. You don't need a set of used clubs for that."

Clay called. Cool and reserved as if we hadn't been pawing at each other like ravenous beasts. "Just wanted to be sure you were still upright and taking nourishment," he said. "Had any more unwelcome visitors?"

"No one's interested in me."

"I wouldn't go that far," he said with a soft laugh. "I know at least one person you've turned upside down."

I smiled as I said, "Strange, I haven't thought of you once."

"There you go, women are tougher than men."

"Except, well except, I have this incredible itch."

"Which I'd be happy to scratch. Just don't have any strange visitors until I get back."

"They have the tape. It's over."

"Let's just hope Jimmy's tape was all they were looking for. I'll be back tomorrow. Are you working?"

"Mondays are always my night off."

"Oh, yeah." Like he'd forgotten. "Maybe we could do something," he suggested.

I roared with laughter.

"What?"

"Yeah, let's do something. You do it so well."

"It's a date."

Before I headed for the squatter's city behind the box stores, I picked out a nice clear picture of Andy. My plan was to ask anyone going in or out of the field if they'd seen Andy. How much trouble could that get me into right? Silly me.

The first person to come out of the wilderness was an elderly man who looked far too frail and ill to be living rough . . . or to be any danger to me. His left hand trembled and his gait was unsteady as he dipped through the fence and came towards me. "Excuse me," I said holding out Andy's picture. "Do you know this man?"

He rheumy eyes flickered over me. "Get lost, bitch." He staggered away.

"Charming. It was lovely to meet you too." This was a different crowd from the people David looked after.

Fifteen minutes later a pair of guys in their twenties came around the end of the building heading for the jungle. "Have you seen this guy?" I asked. I was a little more wary this time, staying way back and stretching out my arms to their limit. "Do you know him?"

They didn't even look at it. "Yooooo, mama. I'd like to know you." Baggy shorts moved towards me and his friend circled around to come up behind me. The fence on my left side held me trapped between them.

"I'm a cop," I warned. "Don't mess with me."

The guy facing me stopped. "You're shitting me." His eyes went sideways to his partner to see what he was making of me.

"Don't even think of it," I said.

Baggy pants backed off a step.

My heart was thudding against my rib cage; my voice was husky with fear. "Have you seen him?" I repeated.

He shook his head, sidling around me to the opening. The other guy was already through the fence and disappearing fast.

A slow learner I may be, but I'm not totally stupid. I went back to the pickup and dug out the nice heavy handle of the tire jack and laid it across the seat. Then I parked Big Red right next to the hole in the fence. If they wanted to go in or out they had to walk right along the driver's side of the truck. The window was up and the door locked. The keys were in the ignition, ready to go. If anyone got between me and escape I'd run them down.

I leaned over the seat to dig around in my bag for writing material. I block-printed "Have you seen this man? Five dollar reward for information." Cheap, but I didn't want anyone to decide they might like the reward without the information and bash out my window. I waited. Although it was only in the sixties outside, heat built up in the cab and made me sleepy— but I was too afraid of the animals coming out of the jungle to crack the window. What had happened to all the defeated tired people who asked for spare change on the street? Maybe only the strongest had the courage to live out here in the underbrush.

It was nearly an hour before a chubby man with wild hair came hurrying through the field, along the path to the hole in the fence. I started to hold my sign and the picture of Andy up to the window but there was something familiar about the way he walked, forward on the balls of his feet. I lowered the picture. He saw the truck, hesitated and then came on warily.

Still cautious, I rolled down the window and stuck my head out. He was bending to the opening when I called, "Andy?"

He jerked upright, still holding the wire mesh, frozen in indecision, off balance, one foot sticking through the opening, while he tried to decide if he was going to bolt back into the underbrush or go on.

"It's Sherri. Please don't run," I begged. I tucked the sign and the picture down behind the seat.

He drew his foot back through the opening, holding onto the fence with both hands, staring at me.

"It's Sherri," I said again.

"I know," he answered. Like how dumb do you think I am?

It was hard to see the old Andy in this person. He'd always been skinny, even emaciated; now his once strong and well-defined features were hidden and flattened under an extra layer of fat. His face and body were bloated and personal care and hygiene had gone out the window some time ago. Now Andy had his own kind of funky dreadlocks thing happening. A video could be hidden in that rat's nest, no problem. Betsy Crown would not approve.

"Hi, Andy." His jaw worked from side to side; his body tensed. I slid the tire iron under the seat and opened the door cautiously, afraid sudden movements might make him bolt.

"I'm glad to see you. I've missed you."

He pointed behind me. "You've got Jimmy's truck," he said. He walked along the fence to the truck, craning his neck to see inside. "Is Jimmy with you?"

"No."

"Are you two back together again?"

"No. Jimmy and I aren't together."

His head swung rapidly to the left as if a voice had called him and he was searching for that person. "I know, I know," he said, annoyed and impatient. His jaw worked from side to side and he bounced on the balls of his feet. Erratic movements and raw energy turned the once charming man into a terrifying individual.

"How 'bout going out to Hog Heaven for some barbecue?" I suggested. "I'm starving."

He shook his head wildly in denial. "Can't," he said, "can't. It's all poison." Letting go of the fence, he backed into the tall grass, his hands pumping up and down as if he held invisible bottles of salad dressing that he was trying to mix.

"I got your call about the tape."

He stopped. "Holy Grail," his head jerked spasmodically. "Jimmy said put it in a safe place."

"And did you?"

His face molded into a sly look of amusement like he'd put one over on me.

"Where is it? Where did you hide the tape?"

He charged the fence. Grasping the chain-link, he pressed his body towards me and whispered, "Casablanca."

"Where?"

"Casablanca."

"The movie?"

He pushed away. The fence vibrated and clanged with the force. "Gotta go, gotta go."

"Wait," I yelled. I couldn't let him go or I might never get another chance. "Do you want to go back to your apartment? I'll take you there."

Wild-eyed, he swung to face me. "Can't." He rushed back towards me, glaring, with his jaw clenched. "You know that!" he growled.

I felt real fear but as quick as it surfaced I tamped it down, telling myself this strange person was still Andy.

"Can't go back there." His jaw worked.

"C'mon, let's go for a drive," I begged, not ready to give up yet. "Have something to eat."

He canted his head to one side, listening. He nodded and came to the gap in the fence. He froze. I waited. At last he seemed to feel safe. He ducked through the wire and joined me on the pavement.

I jumped into the truck to unlock his door.

"Where do you want to go?" He didn't put on his safety belt and I sure as hell wasn't going to suggest it. I rolled the window down and leaned towards it, trying to keep the smell of him at bay.

As we headed inland to the Florida of cattle ranches and citrus farms, Andy turned on the radio, twirling the dial to stop at the Dixie Chicks. The music fit the landscape.

At first Andy ranted and raved and held long conversations with ghosts, but slowly his frantic motion eased and his conversation with the invisible men grew less strident.

"How come you're driving Jimmy's truck?" he asked.

"My piece of junk gave out again. Jimmy's taken the *Suncoaster* on a little trip. So he let me drive Big Red."

Near Caloosa we drove through a desolate burnt-off area from last summer's fires. All that was left of thousands of acres of pines was black poles poking skyward. This time next year it would be green again with saw palmettos. Even some of the pines would miraculously come back to life and once again wild pigs, small, dark and mean—rather like my daddy—would populate the thick and wild palmetto jungles. We passed two men on the side of the road, one of them carrying a three-foot gator by the tail. Andy pointed to them and said, "They've got dinner."

We bumped down a gravel road to a gritty barbecue place called the Firepit on the Myakka River, where we sat outside at a weathered picnic table under a live oak bearded with Spanish moss and ate burgers and fries. Andy was calm.

"There's a path along the water." I gathered up the debris of our meal and added, "Let's go for a little walk."

He followed me without replying.

At the beginning of the narrow meandering path,

a pair of otters chased and dived in the dark brown water around the gnarled roots of a Cypress tree, slipping away in the water at our approach. We walked down the twisting dirt path in single file as it followed the edge of the river. A heron lifted off and flew low over the water in front of us.

I walked in front of Andy, head down, weighing my options. I wasn't kidding myself that I was just thinking of Andy. I needed Andy, needed him lucid. He was all that stood between me and a murder charge. My chances of finding the tape without him were just about nil, and without the video I had no other evidence that the *Suncoaster* explosion was anything but me saving money on a divorce lawyer. Also, the fact was, if anyone could figure out where Jimmy was it was Andy. If Jimmy was going to get in touch with anyone, it was Andy. Let's face it, the only thing standing between me and the electric chair was Andy. I needed him out of Lalaland. I needed drugs, lots and lots of drugs.

I was vaguely aware of the quietness. Even the country rock spilling out of the Firepit had faded, but I was too deep in thought to realize I'd wandered into danger.

We rounded a curve in the path, hidden from the world. Andy reached out and grabbed me.

"Please," I begged. My hands went up to clutch at his forearm across my neck. I was going to die. "No, please, no."

CHAPTER 32

He held me tight to him. I let my body sag, turning my head and tucking my chin into my shoulder while pulling down on his forearm, hoping I could slip out from beneath his hold.

Andy's other hand grasped my left arm, his nails digging in. "Watch," he whispered. He let go of me and pointed past us. My eyes followed to where a large gator, sunning on the bank of the river, blocked our way. I sagged back against Andy.

"Shit." My heart was going like a jackhammer. "Thanks," I breathed and whimpered. "Let's turn back."

Shame washed over me. I was angry with myself that like everyone else I'd seen his difference as dangerous. I couldn't believe I'd doubted him and swore to myself I never would again. But the truth, hiding down deep in my gut, was far different from what I was telling myself. I was afraid of Andy, afraid of what he might do to me in his delusional state.

It was the old "Be careful what you wish for." I'd found Andy but what did I do now? I needed help to get Andy sane.

The men's room was on the outside of the restaurant, around the back near the kitchens. While Andy went there, I headed for the payphone out on the screened veranda overlooking the river. I called the Crowns and told Mr. Crown about Andy's condition.

"Our son is no longer our responsibility," Mr. Crown informed me in a cool professional voice, probably the one he used to tell people their life savings had just been wiped out by a correction in the market. "We've done everything we can for him. My advice to you is to drop him off at the nearest hospital."

Andy came out the screen door of the restaurant to stare at me. I gave him a little wave. He smiled and ambled over to a rough-plank table on the opposite side of the veranda. He plonked himself down and stared out the screen to the river. Around him a dozen bikers were sitting on top of picnic tables, their boots on the seats, laughing and drinking beer. Andy ignored them, but the bikers kept a wary eye on him.

"What about his doctor?"

"Dr. Steadman can't do anything if Andrew doesn't want help and it's been our experience that Andrew never wants to do things the easy way."

"Can you just give me Steadman's number?"

He did so reluctantly.

"I could really use some advice here," I told him.

"I've already given it. Drop him off at the hospital." The line went dead. Just like that. No goodbye . . . no nothing.

I slammed the receiver back into the cradle and snarled, "Asshole." A biker, overweight and nasty-looking, stopped in his tracks and gave me a startled look.

"Not you," I told him, flipping through the yellow pages of the telephone book. "I was talking to another asshole."

"Jacaranda Hospital no longer has any psychiatric beds," the person at the other end of the line informed me. "We converted them all over to orthopedics. Take your friend up to the hospital in Sarasota."

I called Peter.

"Do you have any motel rooms that go empty at night?"

He made growling sounds in his throat, the aging playboy still on the prowl.

"Not for me, you fool. I've got a friend who's in trouble."

"All of your friends are in trouble."

"This one is the best of show. A little psychotic: a little dangerous. I'm worried about taking him home. There's a newspaper on the bar with the story of Jimmy's death and white lilies with a sympathy card. Hearing about Jimmy is going to send him over the edge into Never-Never Land. Hell, I'm not sure he hasn't already passed the edge." I pressed my forehead against the rough paneling. A small throbbing headache was eating its way through my head. "I don't want to take him home." It was a confession of fear and inadequacy.

"God, don't take him to your place." The alarm in Peter's voice warmed me but his concern only lasted a second and then he went right back to being the same old on-the-make guy. "Tell you what—if there's an empty room tonight, it's yours. If there isn't, you dump him at your apartment and come and spend the night at my place."

I laughed out loud. "You never stop, do you?"

"When I stop trying with you, you'll know I'm dead. Please call the mortuary."

"Andy's in pretty rough shape. I hope he doesn't scare the rest of your clientele."

"They're all in rough shape. He'll fit right in."

"Thanks, Peter."

"For you, anything."

"Do you want to sleep on my couch tonight? I'll whip up a big pot of spaghetti and pick up a cherry cheesecake."

"No." Just the thought of it was enough to get him agitated. "They'll be watching there."

"It's my cooking, isn't it? You can be honest with me, most people refuse dinner invitations."

No answer.

"Tell you what. A friend of mine owns a motel. I know he'll let you stay in an empty room for a few days."

Andy tilted his head to the left, listening to a conversation only he could hear. "Good, good," he said, bouncing his knees up and down nearly to his chin with excitement. "They won't expect that. Let's go."

At least it was a temporary solution—time to figure out where the tape was.

CHAPTER 33

The three high-kicking dolls on the neon red sign of the Kit Kat Klub were left over from another era. As a little girl in the backseat of whatever clapped-out vehicle my mother was driving at the time, coming down from my grandmother's in Sarasota, the three Bettys were the signal that we were almost home. I pulled into the shared parking lot with the Pelican Motel next door, praying Peter had told his staff to expect us.

"Do you want to wait in the truck while I get the key?"

Andy nodded rapidly, staring out the side window and never once looking my way.

Would he be in the truck when I got back? I took the ignition key with me.

Everything about the desk clerk was thin—thin hair, thin body and thin cigarette-stained teeth with gaps in between them. I told him that Mr. Bryant had left a room key for me. He leered and licked thin lips. I didn't want to know what he was thinking but maybe I was just getting as paranoid as Andy. Or maybe Peter had a naughty habit that I didn't know about.

The room had last been decorated about the year I was born and, from the smell, that was also the last time anyone opened a window, but Andy was pleased.

"Good," said Andy looking around with satisfaction. "Good." He turned on the TV and settled down in front of a rerun of *Friends*.

"Andy." It took a moment for his eyes to focus on me. "Do something for me."

"What?"

"Take a shower. You're really developing a nasty pong."

He went back to the TV. But when the program ended he got up and went into the bathroom closing the door behind him.

Would wonders never cease? I opened the door and the window as the shower started to run. I swung the door back and forth to try and move in some fresh air. Then I called Marley. "Get in touch with Andy's doctor. I can't make that call from here."

"Sure," Marley said.

"See if he has any suggestions. I sure as hell don't

know what to do. If he was bleeding, at least I could put a bandage on it."

"Sherri, do you think it's safe? You hear all the time about paranoids turning violent."

I sighed. "I don't know." Hell I didn't know anything. "Husbands turn violent, wives and parents too. I don't know if Andy will. There's no use in denying it."

"At the first sign of trouble, promise me you'll get out of there."

I didn't tell Marley that Andy's condition was already bad news; I just swore an oath to run at the first sign of anything unusual, but how I'd be able to tell was beyond me.

I called Brian.

"Is there any way we can get him committed? There's no way he should be out walking around."

"Let me talk to a few people and get back to you."

"It's better if I call you. The phone ringing might set him off."

"Sherri, I don't like this."

"Me either. I'll call you."

"Wait," he yelled.

I waited.

"I tried to call you. I checked out all the golf clubs I could think of. Twice. No luck."

"Maybe he doesn't play on Sundays."

"I have to be in court tomorrow. When I finish,

I'll swing by and check them again. Call me. All right?"

"Yeah, Brian. Thanks."

"I really don't like this situation. Have you talked to Clay?"

"Nope."

"That SUV was spotted by one of his agents on the south end of the island. Unfortunately that's all there was to it. The agent had clients in the car and couldn't follow it."

"At least it's here, not down in Miami or over in Orlando. Sooner or later we're going to get him."

Andy came out of the shower with a towel wrapped around his midriff.

"Why don't I slip out and get you some clean clothes from your place."

"No," he shouted. He started hopping back and forth from one foot to the other in agitation. "Don't go there. They're watching that place."

"Calm down," I soothed. "Is Jimmy's tape there? Only I wouldn't want to risk losing it."

He smiled a small secret smile, looking suddenly sly.

I tried again. "The Holy Grail, is it in your apartment? Maybe I should move it."

"I told you it's in Casablanca."

"Casablanca?"

He smiled, confident now.

"Not at your place?"

He shook his head.

"It's in Casablanca?"

He nodded. "It's safe. No one will ever find it."

And I believed him. Not even I could find it and he'd told me where to look. I watched him pull back the covers and climb into one of the double beds, pulling the towel out from beneath the sheet and dropping it on the floor beside the bed. He picked up the remote from the night table and started rolling through the channels.

I dug out the cigarettes I'd bought with the barbecue at the Firepit. At least there was still one copy of the video and when I got Andy sane I still had a faint hope of finding a way out of this mess. Casablanca. What in hell did that mean? Had he dropped the video in the mail for foreign parts? A better idea was to get a map of Florida and see if there was a town called Casablanca. Or what about a store or a nightclub named Casablanca?

"Andy," I called softly. He looked at me. "Have you seen Jimmy?"

He shook his head.

"When did you last see him?"

He gave a soft shrug. "'Bout a week ago." His eyes went back to the action on the television, his teeth chewing at the edge of his thumb.

"Not since?"

He pursed his lips as he thought, as if the effort to remember something that only happened a week ago caused him pain. "Dunno."

"Try. It's important."

"When he dropped off the tape," he got out at last.

"Last Sunday?" I asked. "Only . . . that's when he dropped off my copy."

"Don't know what day," Andy replied.

"If Jimmy wanted to hide, where do you think he'd go?"

His head swung towards me. "Why would he hide?"

"Suppose he owed someone big money."

His body relaxed a bit. "He'd just take the *Suncoaster* on a trip until Dr. Travis paid up."

"What if they'd already taken the *Suncoaster* away?"

"Did someone take the *Suncoaster*? I thought you said Jimmy had taken it on a cruise."

Keeping my lies straight was heavy-going. "Yes, but I think he's in trouble. The boat isn't the best place for him. Where do you think he should go?"

He shrugged. "Jimmy knows lots of people. He'll do all right. Don't worry about him." The television called.

"What does Casablanca mean?" I asked.

He looked back at me. He smiled, a small teasing lift of the lips. "Don't you remember?" he asked.

"Should I?" His eyes were already on the TV.

"If you don't want me to go to your apartment, why don't I go to the Tiger Discount down the street and get you some clean clothes?" How much credit did I have left on my card? If they kept it, I would be embarrassed, but it wouldn't be the end of the world.

"Okay," he agreed.

"I'll take those clothes with me," I pointed into the bathroom, "And slip by my place and give them a wash."

I hurried into the bathroom to get his clothes while his forehead furrowed as he listened to his voices. The minute I picked up the bundle of clothes I knew I'd gotten a bonus, I could feel the outline of a key under my hand.

Quickly, before he could object, I rushed to the door. "Back soon with clean clothes and pizza." With no clothes, he was forced to stay. If he ran out naked, the police would pick him up for sure. Either way it worked for me.

I went to the Roach Motel, a creepy place even during broad daylight. Inside Andy's place it didn't get any better: dark and gloomy and smelling of Andy's unwashed body and stale food.

It was really just one large room with a futon, a

couple of wrecked chairs, a two-burner stovetop and a small refrigerator. A short stub wall with some cabinets below acted as an eating counter between the two spaces. Not a lot different from my place, but at least I had a proper bedroom.

To the left was a windowless bathroom. I flicked on the overhead, sending a roach scuttling across the floor for cover. The lid of the violet toilet tank was gone, the pink sink was cracked and the floor was missing half the tiles. There was no tub, only a tiny metal shower stall across one corner that dripped rust. I backed out the door.

By the window overlooking the parking lot, a television was fixed, high up on the wall. Underneath, on a battered folding TV tray, was a VCR with a wedding picture sitting on top of it, Jimmy and me with Marley and Andy on either side of us, smiling like we'd just won the lotto.

Six tapes were piled beside the photo. I knew I wouldn't find Jimmy's tape but I was hoping I might find a copy of *Casablanca*. I stuffed them in my bag to take with me. Perhaps Jimmy's tape was spliced onto the end of one of them. I'd just have to go through them and see. I stuck my fingers in the tape holder. Empty.

I went through the few cupboards and drawers quickly. I didn't find any more videos or the antipsychotic drugs I was also searching for. I had a desperate plan to crush them and put them into his food but either Andy's prescription had run out or he'd flushed them. It was a stupid idea anyway.

I eased back the curtains and carefully studied the few cars parked outside, all looking like they belonged there, which was to say they looked like my green wreck. There wasn't an SUV among them. The parking lot in the middle of the horseshoe-shaped motel was as desolate and ugly as always.

At the discount store, I rushed around and picked up a couple of pairs of underwear, a navy jogging suit, toothpaste and a toothbrush, comb and deodorant. I held my breath as the anemic clerk slid my card through the register. Wonder of wonders, it worked. Bring on the debt.

At my place, I quickly stuffed Andy's clothes in the washer. Then I ran up the stairs and popped in the first video, pressing the fast-forward and watching Mel Gibson and Danny Glover do their thing at triple speed. There was nothing on the tape that shouldn't have been there.

I listened to my messages. Two creditors, Ruth Ann, several friends and the bank manager . . . why did I even bother having a phone? There was also a message from Evan. Jimmy's parents were having a memorial service for him on Thursday morning at ten o'clock. Evan said he'd pick me up. Calling my friend a murderer hadn't broken the bond—a stronger relationship than I'd realized and something to be grateful for.

And Styles had also called. His message said he'd be in touch. A simple statement but scary: a relentless drip, drip of fear.

Back at the motel I rapped on the door with a knuckle and called "Andy" in the most cheerful voice I owned. "It's Sherri." Only then did I put the key in the lock. I turned the handle slowly and pushed open the door with the tips of my fingers. I didn't want to startle him and I wanted to have lots of time if he was going to do something crazy.

Andy was curled up in bed, pillows piled behind his head, watching Stagecoach with John Wayne. God bless AMC. His fingers were picking at the sheet and his foot jigged up and down, making the whole surface of the bed tremble.

"If I had a dollar for every movie we've watched together, I could pay off at least one of my credit cards," I told him. I went to the second bed and dropped my load of plastic bags.

"I slept," Andy said.

"Don't you usually?"

"Not much."

"I've got pizza and some goodies for you." I pulled the clothes I'd bought out of a bag and threw a pair of boxers at him. "It always comes down to the same thing with men doesn't? Doing their wash and bringing them food?"

"That and wild erotic sex." His comeback delighted me.

"Do you know the difference between erotic sex and perverted sex?" I asked.

"No."

"Well, erotic is when you use a feather and perverted is when you use the whole chicken."

He laughed.

Hee-haw, things were looking up.

He wiggled into the shorts under the blanket and said, "Jimmy says he noticed your hooters first, then your ass and then your sense of humor. I noticed your sense of humor right away."

"You've always been a gentleman, Mr. Crown."

I stretched out on the second bed and watched him eat his pizza and somewhere between the cheese and pepperoni I fell asleep. I woke in the dim light from the silent television. Andy was leaning over me, staring into my face.

CHAPTER 34

I nearly wet myself. "It's all right, it's all right," I whimpered. "It's Sherri . . . it's Sherri."

He turned away.

My heart was going like a pile driver. I swung off the bed, eyes fixed on Andy, ready for any sudden moves on his part as I edged towards the door, my bag clutched to my chest. "Can't sleep anymore." I dug the room key out of the pocket of my jeans and put it on the table by the door. "I'll be back," I promised, not knowing if it was true. "Stay here, Andy."

His eyes never left the silent television.

A maid, dressed in jeans and a tee advertising Spanky's bar, was using her key to open the door of a service cupboard to start her rounds. What would Andy do if she knocked on the door or, heaven forbid, if she used a passkey to enter?

"Just skip number twenty-one today, okay? My friend is ill."

"Sure, honey," she said.

At my apartment a white card was stuck in the edge of the door, a calling card from Detective Styles. He must have come for me at the crack of dawn. If he had intended to arrest me would he leave a card? I looked over my shoulder for the patrol car waiting to pick me up. Nothing. I turned over the card. He'd written, "My office—ten o'clock."

Yeah, right. Talking to Styles only made my situation worse. I flipped it onto my pile of mail. If Styles wanted me, he'd have to come and get me. I wasn't going near him voluntarily. I headed for the shower, Ruth Ann's daughter to the end. Ruth Ann thought being clean would make any situation better and as I stood toweling off my hair I decided that in this small thing, she was right. In nearly fifty years of living and trying, she was bound to get one thing right even by blind luck.

I called Marley.

"I haven't been able to talk to the doctor," she told me. "The first time I got the answering service and then I got his nurse. She won't even acknowledge that Andy is a patient of Dr. Steadman's and she says the doctor won't talk to me."

"At least they know there's a problem. I'm going to try calling him."

"Watch your tongue, Sherri."

"In case I annoy him?"

"I know your temper."

"If he's not going to help with you being polite then my being nasty won't make the situation worse."

"Just try the sugar before you pour acid on him."

"If I ever get near him."

"Call me when you can. Oh, I forgot, you're the one that doesn't have a cell phone. Why don't you stop by and pick up mine?"

"Now there's a good idea. For the first time in my life I actually want one."

"I have a patient waiting for me. Come by and pick this up, I'll leave it at the desk, and if you need support tonight I'm there, although to tell you the truth this situation scares the hell out of me."

"Me too." I was with him less than twenty-four hours but even that had been too much. I wasn't sure I could face him again but did I have any other choice? I remembered something else. "I picked up some tapes from Andy's. If I drop them off at the desk, will you go through them tonight and see if there's anything on them about Jimmy?"

"Sure," agreed Marley. "Anything else?"

"Since you asked, how's your love life?"

"Better than yours."

"Oh god, I'm not going to end up in something disgusting in pink satin, am I?"

"Never! I'm thinking blue," she said and hung up.

I dialed Peter's number. "I hate to ask you this but

can we have a couple more nights? I'll pay. Well, eventually I'll pay. I just can't pay you right now."

"Take what you need, Sherri." He didn't even offer to take it out in trade.

"Thanks, Peter."

I left a message with Dr. Steadman's nurse. "Andy is at the Pelican Motel, right next to the Kit Kat Klub on Tamiami Trail. Unit twenty-one. Would you ask the doctor to come by please? Andy's in real bad shape. I'm afraid he might become violent." Even saying it felt like a betrayal. If all else failed, was I willing to say Andy had attacked me to get him committed? It was an idea I was toying with. Betraying a friend to save my own ass didn't sit well with me, but what was a stay in a mental ward compared to death by electric chair?

"I'll pass on your message," the nurse told me. It sounded like it hurt her to say it, but then this was probably more than she should be saying—admitting that Andy was a patient—and breaking some kind of medical oath. Being mean-spirited, I wasn't real grateful for this small favor.

I went to pick up the damn cell phone.

Dr. Zampa was handing a file to the receptionist. He frowned.

"Hi, Sherri," Carla said and reached under the counter for the cell phone. "Marley's with a patient."

"We should talk," Dr. Zampa said and marched away. I guessed he expected me to follow.

"I don't want you to get the wrong idea," he said as he closed the door behind me.

His office was small and he was between me and the exit. I told myself not to annoy him. "What idea would that be?"

"I didn't have anything to do with Jimmy's death."

"Tell it to the police."

"There's a cop that plays golf out at Windimere. He told Rollins, who spread it around, that Jimmy's death was no accident."

He waited for me to confirm it. I waited for him to get to the point.

He sighed heavily. "Look, Jimmy and my wife were friends. That's all. I didn't like you coming around the house and suggesting anything more. I didn't like you upsetting my wife."

"How did you like Jimmy buying into Windimere?"

His jaw tightened.

"How much was it going to cost him to get a piece of it?"

His lips thinned.

"Maybe I should tell the cops just how upset you were about Jimmy and your wife."

"Don't threaten me."

"How much?"

"Jimmy was going to put up three-quarters of a million. We all had to give up some of our shares so he could buy in."

"Why? Why was everyone willing to let Jimmy buy in?"

"Because we're bleeding to death out there. We need money to stay afloat until we can start building houses."

"Where was Jimmy getting that kind of money?"

"He said he was in a land deal. The money would be available within three months."

Harry's Diner was just across the road from Dr. Zampa's office. A bonus. I went for coffee and stepped through the door as Harry was yelling through the passway at Val, "Fill those sugar containers." He started to turn away as she sauntered towards me, ignoring him. "And come and get this box of napkins."

She rolled her eyes to heaven. "Maybe I should just shove a broom up my ass and sweep the floor while I'm at it."

"I heard that," Harry yelled.

Not only was this the best java in town, it also had the best comedy act.

A handsome gray-haired man came up beside me as Val handed me the takeout.

"Hi, Sherri," he said.

Blank.

"I'm Hayward Lynch. Clay introduced us at the Sunset."

"Oh, yes. Sorry about that. I'm normally real good with names and faces but my brain is on holiday at the moment."

"A beautiful woman doesn't remember me." He placed his hand over his heart, "I'm shattered." He smiled to show he'd survive.

"Do all Clay's friends hang out here?"

"They do if they want to have lunch with Clay."

"Are you in real estate too?"

"Gridiron Developments. Have you heard of it?" There was something in his eyes, swift and fleeting, like the shadow of clouds skimming across water on a windy day. I was conscious of how closely he watched me. It must be important to his ego that I recognize the name.

"Yes, of course," I lied.

I was tempted to wait for Clay but it wasn't the time or place for a warm reunion. "Look, I've got to run. Andy is waiting. Say hi to Clay for me."

I was nearly back to the motel when the penny dropped. Gridiron Developments owned the property behind the box stores—the company that didn't like eagles getting in their way.

CHAPTER 35

I got my courage back, well most of it anyway, telling myself it was just the sudden waking up and finding Andy looming over me that freaked me out. Embarrassed now by my reaction, I was determined to banish my doubts, telling myself over and over, "Andy would never hurt you." With the "be nice" voice of civilization screaming down the voice of self-preservation, I headed back over the bridge to the mainland.

I called Ruth Ann while I waited in the takeout line at the Chicken Roast. "Where've you been, honey? I've tried and tried to get you."

"I know, Mom, I've just been busy with things."

"Oh my, this has hit you hard, hasn't it?"

"What do you mean?"

"You called me Mom. That means you're really upset. Do you want to come home for a bit?"

I started to laugh. "No, Mom. At the moment I'm

spending my time with Andy. He's going through a bad patch."

"Oh, Sherri, darling, I don't like that. That boy just isn't right in the head. He's liable to do any crazy thing."

"He wouldn't hurt me."

"Now you don't know that. It isn't safe." She'd once seen Andy in full flight and she'd never quite forgotten the sight. I think her Baptist background whispered of demon possession and she more than half believed those old superstitions. "There's no telling what he might do."

Frayed nerves hyped my uncertain temper. "Yeah, just like there's no telling what a drunk might do. But that never stopped you from bringing them home and holding on, did it?"

There was silence at the other end.

"Sorry," I said. "I haven't been sleeping too well. That was out of line."

"That's okay, dear." Her voice was a soft whisper that hurt more than a curse.

I wanted to tell her that it wasn't okay for people to dump on her, me included. But I already had enough problems I couldn't solve without trying to correct Ruth Ann's character flaws. She'd spent her life being a doormat, stepped on and beat on—she wasn't going to change now. Besides, the woman truly believed that there was goodness in everyone and it only took enough love from her to bring it out. It was only Andy that Ruth Ann was unwilling to cut some slack.

"Look, Mom, I'm in a checkout line. I have to go. I just wanted you to know that there's a memorial service for Jimmy on Thursday morning."

"I'll pick you up." Her tone of voice said there was no dissuading her without turning really nasty. I stilled the sharp words that sat on my tongue waiting to jump out and bite her.

I told her the details and added, "I don't know if I'm going."

"You have to go. You're still his wife."

"The clerk has almost finished running through my groceries. I'll call you and let you know what I'm going to do. Bye." I hit the End button. With foot-work like mine I should have tried out for football, not cheerleading.

Someone had taken my parking place in front of unit twenty-one so I parked across the lot and stared at the door, trying to decide what was waiting for me. There was no way of knowing, but a crab of anxiety was clawing at my insides. Andy's bizarre behavior was threatening at the best of times and today wasn't any-where near that. Normal had disappeared with the *Suncoaster*, leaving me swimming in peril, real or imagined, jumpy and ready to overreact.

And now, as I opened the crew door to get out the bags of food, my anxiety was triggered by a shadow approaching from my right. Something about the determined stride or some gut instinct told me that dark form was coming for me. I jumped behind the door, holding on to the handle and using it as a barrier between me and danger. A scream trembled in my throat.

"Sherri?"

"Clay!" I sagged back against the truck, weak with relief. What had I expected? "What are you doing here?"

Clay's hair looked like he'd combed it with his fingers, his clothes were wrinkled and there was dark stain of whiskers on his face. "Jesus, Sherri, Peter told me where you spent the night. I've been out of my mind with worry."

"Always the worrier." I tried a smile. "I'm all right." I closed the door so I could come around it. His hand went out to touch me before he thought better of it and withdrew it. I reached into the cab, got the food and closed the door with my hip.

"This isn't your problem," Clay said.

"Look, the only thing between me and the electric chair is that tape. That makes Andy my problem. He's the only one who can save my ass and right now there's no making sense of half what he says. I need to hold on to him until I can get him medicated and sane."

Over Clay's shoulder, I saw Andy. Naked to the waist, barefooted and with his hair standing out in a matted fan around his head, Andy charged towards us. He was making a keening noise high in his throat, his face a contorted mask of rage.

CHAPTER 36

Clay whirled and dropped into a crouch.

"Devil," Andy screamed. "Satan."

I dropped the plastic grocery bags and jumped between them yelling, "It's okay, Andy. It's okay."

"He's one of them, one of them," he screamed. "Evil, evil. He'll suck you in. Can't you see?"

"No, no," I said. "I know him. He just needs to know how long we're keeping the room. It's just about the room, Andy." I had my hands flat against his bare chest now, pushing him away.

"Go back inside." I pushed on him. "Go inside. Everything's fine."

He looked beyond me to Clay. "They always say something to deke you out. Can't trust him," Andy muttered but the violence was seeping away.

"Look, take our supper." I picked up the bags, one of them weeping soda. "See what you can retrieve out of this."

Reluctantly he took the bags out of my hands, but he didn't back away "Go on," I told him, pushing hard at his chest with my palms.

"Everything is fine and I'm hungry. Make yourself useful," I ordered like a bossy older sister.

Andy stepped back, watching Clay for any move, any twitch that might seem a threat. He walked backwards, watching us, all the way to the door of the unit where he stood staring at us with a dark malevolent look. Abruptly he went inside. The door closed behind Andy but the curtains opened.

"Jesus H. Christ," Clay whispered. "You can't go in there. You can't help this guy."

"It'll be all right. Besides I need him as much as he needs me."

"You're nuts. He's going to kill you!"

"Go," I ordered. "Before you upset him."

"Upset him!" he roared. "Upset him! That guy is crazy!"

"Go Clay." I backed away from him. "Just go. I'll be fine."

"Wait," Clay yelled. I swung around to the motel, expecting Andy to be charging out again.

"Wait," Clay said again, quietly this time. His hands were raised, placating. "I'll find a doctor." He came towards me and for one horrible moment I thought he was going to wrap his arms around me.

"Don't touch me," I whispered. "You might scare Andy."

I saw him take a deep breath. I was sure he was going to argue. Instead, Clay reached in his pocket. "Take this," he said. "Don't argue. You have my cell phone number. I'll have it with me all night. Call me if . . . well, I don't know what. Just call me if there's anything."

"Thanks, Clay." Tears stung my eyes. Shoving the folded bills he'd given me into my jeans, I ran for the motel.

Andy sat on the edge of a chair facing out the window to the parking lot. With his elbows on his knees and his feet bouncing up and down like pistons, he was hitting himself in the jaw with each upward movement. He didn't seem to notice. The white plastic bags were dumped on the floor at his feet, still oozing liquid.

"Zippy Stop and the Roast were crazy," I explained, all calm as though nothing unusual had happened. "But I've got all your favorites. Barbied gator bait." I pulled the chicken, in its greasy little cardboard tray out of the plastic bag and set it on the table like an offering. "There's coleslaw."

The top had come off the slaw. I just picked the shredded cabbage off the bag, shoving as much as I could back into the clear plastic container and put it out with the chicken. "And here's the potato salad."

The leaking plastic bottle of soda I left in the bag and took into the John.

"We keep eating like this and we won't have to worry about how we can manage to live on social security," I called out to Andy. I closed the bathroom door a little so Andy couldn't see me and pulled the wad of bills out of my pocket. I counted five hundred dollars before I shoved the bills back in my pocket. "We'll stroke out first."

I poured what remained of the soda into the two glasses in the bathroom, threw a bath towel over my shoulder and headed out. Setting the glasses on the table with the food, I tossed the towel on the floor, tapping at it with my toe to sop up the mess. Andy sat just as he had been when I left.

"C'mon, Andy, eat something," I urged like a mama with a reluctant toddler. His legs kept going and he stared out blankly at the parked cars.

"This junk will surely kill you but you'll die quicker if you don't eat anything."

I set a plastic fork and napkin on the table. "Destroy your arteries," I invited.

"You don't bug me about what I like to eat and I won't bug you about your cigarettes. Deal?" he said, still staring outside.

My hands stopped in midair, hovering over the chicken. "That's what Jimmy always tells me."

He swung 'round to the table now and held the

chicken with one hand while he broke off a drumstick, attacking the chicken, biting into it and pulling the meat away from the bone, licking the juice off the palm of his hand and sucking it off his fingers.

"What was your favorite part of *Casablanca*?"

In a flash he said, "The romance."

"Yeah, me too. I guess we all want a romance like that. Something grand. And I love those hokey lines, 'We'll always have Paris' or 'This is the start of a beautiful friendship.' They get to me."

"Shhh," a finger to his lips. He leaned over to me, his lips brushing my ear and whispered, "It might be bugged. Don't talk about it here."

So much for my sneaking up on his thought processes. Even totally psychotic, I couldn't fool him into telling me where my Holy Grail was and time was running out.

"I always thought Jimmy would make it in the pros," I told Andy.

"He could if he practiced every day, quit drinking and partying, if he gave up all the other distractions, he probably could make it." He nodded his head. "He has the natural talent and the temperament but not the discipline or the willingness to put off short-term pleasure for long-term gain."

My jaw must have dropped at this logical, reasoned group of words with no gobbledygook in the middle.

"And for one million dollars, Mr. Crown, was there anything I could have done to influence the outcome?"

"You mean like nag him more?" He looked at me, a sad sweet smile on his face. He raised his right hand and made the sign of the cross in the air. "I absolve you from all guilt and responsibility." He lowered his arm. "You nagged enough."

"Thank you, Father Andrew."

"You're welcome, my child." Again that sweet smile. "No one can control Jimmy or make him do something he doesn't want to do. Jimmy won't change until he wants to, which will probably be never."

"That's exactly the conclusion I came to."

He started humming softly to himself and bouncing his knees up and down in time to silent music.

"I have to go to work. Will you be all right here?"

He didn't answer. I let him go away from me.

I pulled out to pass a line of traffic and saw a white SUV with its blinker on one lane over on the right. Flipping my right signal on, I pulled back in, slipping by a black Saturn with inches to spare when the driver slammed on his brakes, and then I exited Tamiami Trail for the freeway, nearly taking out the steel barrier. My heart was pounding and the adrenaline was dumping into my blood like Niagara. I caught up to the SUV.

I'd nearly killed myself for the wrong SUV. I hit the gas and pulled out around it, heading for the first exit. I was days away from joining Andy in Bizarreville.

On any normal day not guilt nor kindness nor love could make me voluntarily seek out one of my family. This had been far from a standard day. Since I was already late for work and it was my day for the weird and unusual, I decided to stop and see Ruth Ann.

"She just went out back," one of the other waitresses in Dutch's bar told me.

"Thanks." I went outside, through the tables fronting the parking lot and around to the back of the restaurant. Ruth Ann was there and so was a man I didn't recognize.

CHAPTER 37

With all that has happened to her, my mother should look like a hag, but her skin is still smooth and pale, without lines or brown spots. And there's a kind of innocence to her face that reflects the inner woman. Too skinny, she's still full-chested and manages to look voluptuous. And she's still beautiful.

She was wearing a short denim skirt, studded with silver, and a pink frothy top that looked more suitable for the bedroom than a public place. Silver bracelets jangled up and down her arm and silver earrings caught the light shining down on her from above the door.

"Bitch," the guy looming over her snarled before he jogged down the three cement steps to the alley. At the bottom of the steps, he turned back to look up at her. "Stupid bitch."

Unruffled, Ruth Ann jutted a hip and looked down at him from her impossibly high stiletto heels.

Dressed in cowboy boots, a western shirt and a straw Stetson, the guy looked like an aging guitar player from a country and western band. Actually, knowing Ruth Ann's taste in men, he probably was. "Too bad your brain isn't as big as your tits," he yelled. "You'd be a frigging genius."

"Yeah?" Ruth Ann says. "Well, if your brain was the size of your prick, you'd be a gnat."

Woo . . . when nice girls turn mean, it's real nasty. This was a side of her I'd never seen before.

Mr. Country got very still, his eyes focused on her while I held my breath, sure she was going to be needing help here, but hers was the one comment guaranteed to set any man heading for the door double-time. She reached out for her cigarettes on the railing and lighted one as if he were already gone.

The war was over. He turned away and walked with great dignity up the alley, passing me without really seeing me.

Ruth Ann watched him go, one arm crossed over her waist and the other arm hanging straight down with the cigarette dangling from long slim fingers.

I stepped out from the shadows.

She straightened. "Baby? Is that you?" She threw away the cigarette. "What y'all doing out here in the dark?"

Everything was normal in Ruth Ann Land.

"That detective was here looking for you," Jeff said, as I tucked my pocketbook under the counter. "I told him I didn't think you were coming in, seeing how late it was."

"Sorry," I said, but I wasn't. Missing Styles made Jeff's frown bearable. Then I pissed Jeff off even more by hanging out with the amigos while he ran up and down the bar trying to keep the customers happy.

"I haven't got any good news for you, Sherri," Brian told me. "I faxed a strongly worded letter to Dr. Steadman. I took the liberty of telling him I'm your lawyer. You owe me a retainer of one dollar for that. And as your lawyer, I told him you would hold him personally responsible if anything happened to Andy Crown."

"Thanks, Brian. I take back all those bad jokes about lawyers."

"Don't do that." He adjusted his glasses and smiled. "What will we have left to talk about?"

When I told them about my night on Elm Street, Clay barked, "Enough."

We'd never heard him raise his voice before, so he had our full attention. "You're not going back there," he said.

The other two turned to look at me, waiting for me to put Clay straight.

But his words gave me an odd little feeling of joy: I was pleased he was worried about me rather than annoyed to be told what to do. "Relax. I've already decided I'm not spending another night with Andy." I could feel the laughter bubbling up inside me but with the other two as an audience I couldn't tell Clay how I planned to spend the night—visions of sugarplums were dancing in my head, erotic and sensual honeyed treats.

Clay wasn't done playing alpha male. "Don't spend another minute with the guy."

"Come on," I coaxed, "you're exaggerating. Andy won't hurt me." But was it true? He was no longer the person I'd known and I no longer knew what Andy was capable of.

"Besides," I told him, "He's the only one with evidence that there was more going on in Jimmy's life than our domestic battles."

I followed Clay into the body of the apartment—three enormous iron chandeliers were suspended from the eighteen-foot arched ceilings that were ribbed with heavy beams like the upside-down hull of a ship.

"Holy shit."

He was grinning at me and for once the normally guarded face was alive with pleasure.

"Who knew?" I said, spinning around and around. Opulent oriental rugs floated on cream marble floors. One wall, overlooking the gulf, was all glass. "I thought places like this only existed in the movies."

"Come on. I'll show you the rest." He was as pleased as a boy with a new toy and taking my hand, led me through an apartment bigger than most houses. Nothing had been spared, every detail, every luxury added. Trust Clay to do it up right.

"Wow," I said.

"Is that all I get? You're never at a loss for words."

"Until now. It's fantastic, Clay"

"I had a decorator down from Tampa. I told her what I wanted and opened my wallet and there you have it," he said with a wave of his arm. His joy was palpable. Mr. Cool was way over the top here as he showed me every nook and cranny of his opulent three-thousand-foot penthouse.

Clay didn't notice my silence, didn't notice I was edging for the door as he finished the tour. The beauty and elegance overwhelmed me, making me feel awkward and off balance. "What is it?" he said at last.

My soft shrug didn't satisfy him. "Tell me."

"I so don't belong in a place like this."

"Oh you belong all right."

With light kisses and velvet caresses he beguiled me and seduced me until I felt just fine. It seemed I'd been missing him. Later I could deal with being a donkey at a tea party.

We were already naked when he pulled away from me and asked, "What about Evan?"

"Why? What do you mean? What's Evan got to do with us?"

His eyebrows were drawn together in worry. He was thinking hard, trying to see where the quicksand was in this conversation. "I thought . . . you know."

"Evan and I were never together. This is for your ears only. Evan is gay. He and Noble are lovers."

At first he was silent, his body rigid with astonishment. And then he began to laugh. A rumble that started deep in his chest under my head and rose until it shook the whole bed.

When I opened my eyes he was gone.

"Of course," I told the ceiling, "today is the weekly meeting with all his salespeople. You didn't really think he'd miss that, did you?" I headed for the kitchen, and there was Clay, barefoot, in jeans and wearing a T-shirt even. A black shadow showed along his jaw; his raven hair was still tousled from sleep. Being unkempt made him look youthful and endearing . . . and sexy. Even more appealing, he was cooking.

I started to smile. "You're going to be way late for that weekly meeting you hold so dear."

He grinned broadly over his shoulder at me. "They'll have to get by without me."

"Is there anything here you can't leave?" I inquired as I undid his silk robe and let it fall off my shoulders and down to the floor.

With one hand Clay reached to turn off the stove while the other hand tipped the frying pan into the sink.

Clay couldn't skip out on all his meetings, that would just be asking too much of him, so here I was, dressed again in his silk robe and alone in fantasyland. I was going to enjoy it.

Everyone has to be good at something. Snooping is something I excel at. I walked through the apartment, opening closets and drawers. Clay must have had twenty suits hanging in a walk-in closet and double that number of shirts, neatly laundered and hanging exactly the same distance apart.

In the den the walls were covered in a material that looked like men's gray pinstripe suiting and although the other rooms were more glamorous, this room was most like him.

Photos hung on the walls. There were pictures of a teenaged Clay riding in rodeos and another of him accepting an award. On a table were family pictures, smiling and happy pictures. I studied them. His father was like Clay—dark with high, flat cheekbones that said somewhere in Clay's background was an ancestor who didn't come over on any *Mayflower*. Those hard angles were native grown.

Clay was raised on a cattle ranch east of Lemon Bay that had been started back during the Civil War by his family. They'd shipped boatloads of cattle north to the Confederacy, and the Union navy had sailed up the gulf to stop those ships from feeding the rebel army. Since then, Clay's family had fought to survive in the Piney woods off the mangrove swamps of Florida's west coast. They'd overcome hurricanes, disease and snakes, but in the end it was the cancer of development that spread inland and ate into their holdings, taxing and zoning them out of business. When Clay realized there was more money in houses than food, he'd joined the development side with a vengeance, turning the last hundred acres of the thousands his family had once owned into homes for the people pouring into the state, and becoming a rich man.

I sat down in his huge leather swivel chair behind the desk, twirling to take in the room. I reached out my hands to stop the spin. My flat palms landed on a spiral-bound folder. Gridiron Developments was printed in gold on the cover. I opened the cover and Hayward Lynch smiled up at me. I started reading.

The project was big, really big. Over a thousand acres. In the back of the prospectus were some loose sheets with calculations in Clay's handwriting. There was also a letter on Hayward Lynch's financial situation from an investigating firm. What it came to was Lynch was going to lose the whole development if he didn't get new funding, so Lynch was willing to sell half of his share to Clay for about a third of the real value. I closed the folder and pulled open the left-hand drawer. It was full of files. The first files, all blue, were household and personal financial files. I hurried on by. The next files in red were about the ranch Clay still owned east of Sarasota. Snooping through his private papers was even too much for me and I was going to close the drawer, honest, but at the back was a single buff folder.

I took it out. Jimmy's name was on the outside. A maggot of fear gnawed at me.

I opened the folder. It was a report from a private investigator.

CHAPTER 38

There were pictures of Jimmy—Jimmy on the *Suncoaster* and pictures of Jimmy with women. There was even a picture of Jimmy coming out of my apartment. Wrapped in a white towel, one bare foot resting on top of the other, I leaned in the open door to my apartment, watching Jimmy walk away. There wasn't much doubt what had being going on there.

And there were pictures of Evan and me—pictures of us out sailing, shopping and eating on the deck out at Big Daddy's Oyster Bar. It looked like a romance. And I looked like a busy girl. The truth was, other than Clay, Jimmy was the beginning and ending of my love life, but that's a secret I'll defend until death. I've worked hard for my reputation and I'm not willing to give it up. Like the ladies always say, "The only thing a girl has is her reputation."

Why had Clay hired a private investigator to take pictures of Jimmy? I read the written report carefully.

All of Jimmy's tricks were laid out there, chapter and verse, it could have been a book called *Cheating and Other Sins*. Some of it even I hadn't known about.

I shoved the pictures back in the folder and into the drawer, slamming it shut.

In the car I started to cry. Tears dripped off my chin and the cars coming towards me blurred and shimmered. I pulled off the road at Heron Point Beach and gave into bitterness and anger and hurt. I'd got it wrong again. I'd thought Clay was the last of the good guys. Fool that I am, I thought I was too wise to be taken in but my passion had turned into this disaster.

Why had Clay checked up on Jimmy? Jimmy had said he was in a land deal. Was it with Gridiron Developments? And what was Clay to Gridiron Developments?

The cold winds coming down from the north had been pushed away by a sweep of southern air giving us another sunny day. I watched a shrimp boat, with its nets held out on each side like graceful arms, dance up the Dresden-blue gulf and I dreamed of running away.

The librarian showed me how to go through back newspapers, searching for anything I could find on Gridiron Developments. There were lots of articles on Hayward Lynch—he hadn't exaggerated about his face being all over the papers. One picture showed him appearing before the municipal board for a zoning change.

"Bingo," I said aloud. I had it.

There, over Lynch's shoulder, was a face I recognized from Jimmy's tape. The face belonged to one of the county commissioners.

One thing was certain, I needed the video. I went back to the motel where Andy still watched TV. He was calm and quite rational but I didn't want to be alone with him. "How about going for a burger?"

It would be fine. Sure it would.

Three blocks away at the hamburger joint everything changed. He stopped just inside the door and looked around. A low keening noise began. I pushed him into an empty booth. "Wait here," I said and ran for the counter.

"Make it very fast food, will you?" I told the plump server in the too-tight navy uniform. "My friend isn't doing so well." I figured it was just having people so close to him that was freaking him out, but things would be better soon. Tables were emptying rapidly on all sides of him.

I got the order, grabbed a bunch of the packets of condiments and ran to Andy. "Do you want to eat in the truck?"

He reached for a burger without answering and began piling on the ketchup and mustard, ignoring the other diners. They, on the other hand, were all too aware of him.

He ate like a starving man but halfway through his burger, it all went wrong. Someone dropped a tray.

The soda flew out of Andy's hand and he was on his feet and running for the door before the cup hit the orange table.

I raced after him.

He hit the lock button and then buried his head in his hands. His whole body was shaking.

His head jerked up and he yelled, "I can't stand it anymore." He slapped his hands against the side of his head, beating on himself. "Can't stand it."

"Stop, stop," I begged, trying to hold down his arm.

He buried his hands deep in the thick mat of his hair, yanking on it. "I can't do this anymore."

"Then take the med . . ." I didn't get a chance to finish.

"No," he screamed, ". . . poisoning me with chemicals." He threw me away from him. My head slammed against the window.

He raised his right fist.

He meant to hit me. I could see it in his eyes. Clenched jaw, muscles quivering, it took every fiber of control he still possessed to keep his fist from slamming into my face. He swung away and drove his fist into the glove compartment instead. The door popped open and papers spilled out unnoticed.

"All right." With shaking hands I reached for the ignition. "All right."

"Why don't you help me?" he wailed.

"Refresh my memory here." I backed carefully out of the parking space and started forward. "What's happening?"

"I've been chosen. You have too but you won't listen."

At the street, I waited for the traffic to clear.

"You won't listen to the voices," he accused.

"I can't hear them." As the truck moved forward into traffic, Andy threw open the door. Horns blared around me as I slammed on the brakes and clung to the steering wheel with both hands, waiting for the feel of the human speed bump. I was sure he was under the wheels but through the rear window I saw Andy zigging and zagging between cars. I leaned over and closed the door.

CHAPTER 39

To make an all-round great day even better, Styles came down the steps from my apartment as I pulled into the Tropicana and parked the truck. Another minute and I would have missed him. I debated reversing out of there but he'd likely send cruisers after me and things were already exciting enough in my life without adding a police chase.

I leaned out the window and yelled, "I left you a message."

The shells crunched under his feet as he came to me and leaned down on the open window. "You missed our appointment."

"I just couldn't make it. Sorry."

"I'd like you to come down to the station and make another statement, Mrs. Travis."

"About what?"

"Just come with me."

"I'm working tonight and I'd like to catch a little sleep. I haven't had much the last couple of nights."

He opened the truck door. "It won't take long."

The police department was one street off Main and shared parking space with the post office. Everyone going into the post office sees who's walking into the police station. It would be all over town by nightfall that I'd been seen going in for a second time. Once, I could get away with. Not twice. That plus the news the *Suncoaster* had been tampered with and I wouldn't be considered a grieving widow for long, a new and interesting addition to my already colorful reputation.

Styles led me into the same tiny room as before and switched on the tape machine. The first questions he asked were easy. Finally he asked the big one. "Were you on the *Suncoaster* last Tuesday?"

"I've already answered that question and signed a statement."

"Just answer it one more time please."

"No."

"Did you tamper with the *Suncoaster* in any way?"

"Of course not." Now I was indignant. "I know what you think I did but I didn't do anything." Anger was a comfort and safer than fear.

"Did you cause your husband's boat to explode?"

"God no. I loved that boat."

"Did you have anyone else fix the *Suncoaster* so it would blow up?"

"Never. I didn't cause my husband's death nor did

I have anyone else do it." I leaned towards him. "Besides, I've already told you, over and over, Jimmy wasn't on that boat. Why don't you figure out who was and then you might be closer to finding out who rigged it." I had a sudden inspiration. "Maybe the guy who was fixing it up to explode made a mistake and blew himself up instead."

Styles said nothing.

"It's possible," I added lamely.

"Can you explain why two witnesses put you on board the Suncoaster the very day it exploded?"

"Two? They made a mistake, that's all."

"They're very reliable witnesses. Their testimony will stand up in court."

"Was there any insurance on the boat?" I asked, desperate to change the topic.

"No."

"Figures. Well there must be some reason Jimmy has disappeared. What was in the locked drawer of his desk?"

"How do you know about that?"

"Tony Rollins. What was in it?"

"Pictures."

"Pictures?" I repeated, getting that sinking feeling. "Was there a videotape?"

A small smile teased his mouth, about the first I'd seen on Detective Styles. "No video, just pictures. Pictures of you, Mrs. Travis."

"Shit."

It wasn't a small smile anymore.

"I want them back."

"They're evidence." His voice was prim and pious.

"Of what? How many pictures?"

"Six."

I was so sure I'd found them all. I longed to ask how bad they were but he was already enjoying this way too much.

I changed the subject, "I don't know why Jimmy has taken off but that son of a bitch is probably somewhere sunny right now, playing golf and romancing some rich tourist."

"We have reason to believe he was on that boat."

"Yeah, right. You told me, his truck was there. If you check you'll probably find out that that someone is coming to repossess it. Every time I park it I'm surprised when I come back and find it still sitting there."

There was something that had been bugging me. "We weren't legally divorced. I keep wondering if I'm responsible for Jimmy's debts. Do you know?"

"You'd have to speak to a lawyer about that, Mrs. Travis."

"I'm already drowning in debt without legal fees. Any new people wanting money out of me can just get in line. And it's a long one."

Styles sat there, turning a pencil around and around in his fingers and watching me. "Do you know a Mr. Huff?" he asked.

"He's been calling me but I don't know him."

"Mr. Huff is with Northern Fidelity Insurance." I didn't like the way he was watching me. Like a vulture checking out dinner. "Your husband was insured for a quarter of a million dollars."

I tried to laugh. "That's crazy. He didn't have insurance on his boat, why would he have insurance on his life?" I leaned towards him and spoke clearly in case he'd gone suddenly deaf. "He didn't have life insurance."

"Oh, but he did, Mrs. Travis. All paid up and with you as the beneficiary."

I went off like a rocket, jolting to my feet and sending the chair slamming against the wall in the tiny room. "That slimy son of a bitch, I knew he was up to something."

I yelled at Styles. "He probably thinks he can show up here a month from now and collect his money."

"Insurance fraud is against the law." Styles' disapproving air said being illegal should preclude anyone from trying it.

"Don't tell me. Tell him. I'm not involved in this."

"Why would he risk going to jail?"

I planted both hands on the desk and leaned down towards him. "Jimmy is nuts. Besides he probably didn't think he'd get caught. Jimmy never does. He likely thinks he has it all figured out." I turned away as rage made way for depression.

Styles rose to his feet and picked up the over-turned chair along with my bag, which had been hanging on the back of the chair. Setting the chair down firmly in front of the table, he said, "Sit down, Mrs. Travis." He dropped my black leather bag on the table.

"I can't believe that he let his parents go through this." I combed my hair back from my forehead with my fingers. "All those people coming to his memorial." Tears filled my eyes. "Well, I won't be there. When people find out, they'll think I was part of it." I collapsed onto the chair and sunk my head onto my hands.

Styles spoke softly. "Your husband is dead. This isn't some sort of plot. The insurance was taken out years ago, when you were first married."

I raised my head to look at him. "Jimmy is involved in something." I told him about the video and the SUV, about my apartment being broken into, about Andy, about the last two days with Andy. All of it. Then I told him about losing Andy.

When I ran down, we sat there, with me sniveling, while he thought about it.

"Am I under arrest?" I asked at last.

"Not yet, Mrs. Travis."

"Then I'm going home. And the next time you want to talk to me call my lawyer, Brian Spears." I got to my feet.

"Innocent people don't need lawyers, Mrs. Travis."

"My bet is they need them even more than guilty people."

CHAPTER 40

I ran through the shower and pulled on some clothes. Like it or not, I had to go to work, which meant I had to face Clay.

I wasn't looking or feeling my best when I got to the Sunset. When I brought Brian his drink he pointed out just how badly I looked. The others confirmed it.

"Forgive me," I said. "My beauty routine has failed me."

"You're still beautiful," Clay told me. "You just look tired."

"Well, a night without sleep can do that to you."

His eyes shifted sideways to the other guys. He was probably hoping I wouldn't tell them he'd taken the bimbo home. I wanted to tell him I got it. It wasn't a life-changing experience, no undying love but only a response to a basic need. Ruth Ann's parting shot was working on my imagination.

I lifted my hair off my neck. "Anyway, where do I stand in all this, Brian? Is Styles going to arrest me?"

Brian looked worried. I don't like it when a lawyer looks worried but then Brian always looks worried. It's his nature.

"Tomorrow you have to get a good lawyer and tell him everything," Brian advised.

"You're a good lawyer."

He shook his head and waved my words away with his hand. "You need a criminal lawyer." He adjusted his glasses, shifting his weight from side to side and looking uncomfortable. "If Jimmy really left his insurance to you, it makes you the prime suspect."

Actually I'd figured that out for myself.

I made it through the night by sheer determination. The last person had left the bar, the last dirty glass had been racked; now all I wanted to do was go home and crawl into bed with the covers over my head.

January is usually the driest month in Florida, but not this year. It was raining when the door swung closed behind me on the Sunset. Not just rain, that didn't describe it. Buckets, sheets and torrents were more what was happening and the drainage system didn't have a prayer of keeping up. Already every culvert was overflowing and water lay inches deep over the parking lot as I splashed out of the alley.

A man stepped out of the shadows at the mouth of the alley. I started away in terror.

"Sherri."

Clay.

"Hi," I said brightly, trying to step around him to avoid his embrace but his arms encircled me, pulling me to him. I turned my head and his lips fell on my cheek.

I pushed away. "We'll drown out here." I ran for Jimmy's truck but he ran me down and reaching out for me, pulled me into his body.

"Leave it. We'll take my car."

"Listen, Clay," I started.

He wasn't listening. With an arm tight around my waist, he pulled me towards his Lexus.

Inside the car he pulled me to him and kissed me again. My response wasn't what he expected. He held me away from him and asked, "What's the matter?"

If you don't have a good example, it's nice to have a really bad one. Ruth Ann, my shining example of how to handle a man, took over. "Listen, I think you're taking this too seriously. We had a little fun." I lifted the damp hair off the back of my neck, shaking it and letting it settle before I continued. "You know how it is with a girl like me."

"No. How is it?"

"Well," I ran my fingers through the sodden hair around my face, "out for a good time, not a long time." I slid over tight to the door, the handle in my hand.

"Has it been a long time?"

"Long enough. I'm just not into anything more than a little fun right now." I had the door open, sliding away from him. "See you," I yelled above the noise of the storm and ran like hell.

The rest of the population was safely home in bed and I should have been the only car on the road but a block from the Sunset I became aware of car lights following me. Clay! Damn him. What right did he have to follow me?

The driving was really wild. There was no way I could speed away from him but I decided to do a little maneuvering to see if I could lose him. I made a couple of right and left turns at random but the lights following me stuck close. At Orange Street, a broken palm frond blew across in front of the truck. I slammed on the breaks to avoid it, sending the ass end of the truck sliding to the left. The vehicle behind me stopped under a street light. I couldn't tell what kind of a car it was, but it wasn't a white Lexus. It wasn't Clay. Someone else was following me home.

I drove even wilder after that, plowing through dips in the road with three or four inches of standing water. I could feel the drag on the tires and knew water was spraying up on the underside. I prayed the truck didn't stall and leave me to the mercy of the guy behind me. The other set of lights stayed half a block behind me.

I made a decision. I took a right off Banyan, braking sharply and turning off my lights, I swung into the mouth of the alley past Marley's little red Neon and swung the truck in behind the stairs. I saw the other set of headlights go by the mouth of the alley. I was out of the truck and racing up the stairs, fumbling for Marley's key on my key ring as I went.

Marley's place was in darkness so it took some fumbling to get the key in the lock and I wasn't even trying to be quiet. I slammed the door shut and then pulled back the curtains to see if anyone had followed me up the steps.

The kitchen lights flicked on. I turned to see Marley standing over me with a raised baseball bat clutched in both hands.

"Jesus." I put my arms up to protect my head. "It's me, it's me."

"So I see." She lowered the bat. "You might want to call in advance next time . . . to keep me from killing you in place of a burglar."

"Someone was following me." I lowered my arms.

"Sit," Marley said, putting the bat on the table and going to fill the kettle.

I blame it on the coffee. Or maybe it was adrenaline. I was supposed to be sleeping on the couch but here I was going over the North Bridge heading for the mainland again, one eye on the rear view to make sure no one was following me, telling myself I'd lost him when I turned into the alley at Marley's.

The rain was still pounding down. Even at ten miles an hour, creeping along in the rain with the windshield wipers on high speed, I almost missed the entrance to the Roach Motel. I told myself I shouldn't be here, told myself to just drive on by.

I turned carefully into the flooded parking lot and stopped in front of Andy's unit. A light was on. He'd come back. I had another chance.

I ran for the motel and knocked once on Andy's door. No need to knock more because I felt the door move under my fist. Now a line of light showed around the door. I pushed it open a little further. "Andy?"

No one answered.

I pushed against the door with my fingertips and it slowly opened.

The light was coming from the bathroom. "Andy?"

I stepped inside. The first thing that hit me was the smell. Closed up for days, the unwashed body odor mixed with garbage stench hadn't improved in the heat.

I tiptoed into the kitchenette. This wasn't the way I'd last seen it. Garbage left in a plastic pail under the sink was now spread over the kitchen floor just like it had been in my apartment.

As I stood there looking at the mess, the storm backed off and the world grew suddenly silent. Some noise outside warned me. I didn't waste time trying to identify or categorize it, a well-honed survival instinct from a tumultuous childhood made me drop to my haunches behind the low counter. I stuffed my fist into my mouth to keep silent, just the way I had when I was a kid.

Footsteps entered the apartment. They stopped as my heart tried to burst out of my chest. There was no sound of the television being dismantled or anything being dragged out the door but maybe this guy was looking for something else besides what he could sell.

The footsteps went towards the bathroom. I heard the hollow thunk of the shower door being opened and closed. Then I heard movement back into the living area. I curled tighter, harder. I waited for him to find me. His steps came towards the half-wall I hid behind. There was a sharp metallic ring of something against the counter. Surely he could see me? I couldn't make myself look up to see if he was looking down at me. Could he hear my heart drumming?

The footsteps receded. The door creaked. Instinct, learned early and hard, took over and I stayed curled in the fetal position pushed up against the open cupboard, not moving, not making a sound so that I wouldn't give myself away. In the silence the refrigerator gave a little sigh and a shudder and grew still. I waited. The heavy silence grew oppressive.

I listened hard. I didn't hear a car start up. I waited some more. The rain started again. My body started to relax. Outside, something moved or was blown by the wind past the door. I froze. Rigid with concentration, hardly breathing, it was a long time before I could make myself move again.

Carefully, silently, I crawled to where the phone sat on the floor under the window. No dial tone. Andy probably hadn't paid a bill in months. I remembered the cell phone. I couldn't bring myself to turn my back on the door so I scuttled sideways, crablike, keeping low, to my bag on the floor behind the counter. I dialed 911 and reported a break-in.

"I think he's still here," I said breathlessly and hung up. I crouched behind the counter, the phone clutched in my hand and waited.

Two units responded but only one of the cops entered the room while the other stayed by the door with his hand at his holster.

"They're gone," I said to reassure him. I really didn't like his hand hovering so close to death.

The tall thin cop looked carefully around the room. I babbled on. "My friend is ill. I was just stopping by to pick up some things."

"You've got a key?" he asked suspiciously.

I nodded. "Yes." I held it up for him to see. "But the door was open and the light was on so I thought someone was still here."

He went to the bathroom and cautiously pushed the door open with his fingers before entering. "What's missing?" he asked when he came out and looked around at the jumble.

"I don't know."

"Have your friend come by and file a complaint." He headed for the door.

I was right on his heels. "Wait," I said. "I have to lock the door." I didn't want him leaving me here alone.

The thin cop waited but the other one kept going to his car and took off.

I followed the police car out of the parking lot, followed him all the way back to the Tamiami Trail, trying to make sense of what had happened. If they'd already searched Andy's place, why come back? Easy one. They'd played my messages, knew Andy had a copy of the video and they were looking for Andy. They wanted the tape as much as I did.

It never occurred to me while I was thinking my way through all this that someone tailed me as easily as I followed the cop out of the Roach Motel.

CHAPTER 41

Fear for Andy replaced my fear of Andy. I drove back to the Pelican Motel and pulled up in front of the last unit. The rain had slackened to a steady drizzle. The flickering light of the television shone through the curtains. Andy was safe. Time to go home.

I slept late. Ruth Ann woke me when she arrived next morning to pick me up for the memorial service. She tsk-tsked at the sight of the old Buccaneer's football shirt I was wearing. Ruth Ann always sleeps in black lace.

As always, her outfit was way way over the top. I figured she'd been shopping at Second Hand Rose again, her favorite place for what she calls her classy clothes. That's the only place I could think of where she'd get this outfit, a real classy setup. On her head was a perky little black straw hat with a veil that I'd never seen before. Actually, no one had likely seen anything like it since the fifties or sixties. She wore it set straight across her forehead with the tiny polka-dotted veil down over her bangs as if to say this is serious business.

Ruth Ann likes sexy clothes so I wasn't too surprised when she took off her short, fuzzy pink jacket. She was wearing a cocktail dress, more a dress you would wear in the evening than during the day and showing more cleavage than was polite at any time. Its one saving grace was the black color. Her heels, fuck-me six-inch spiked sandals, were also black, but they didn't look like they were designed to go to a funeral.

I put on a long black knit skirt that said hello to my curves on the way by but wasn't suggestive. A long-sleeved black turtleneck sweater was topped by a wide leather belt, studded with silver grommets and hung low on my hips. To finish the outfit I put on my black leather boots. Then I put in four-inch silver hoops. With our jet-black hair, hers dead ebony in memory of what used to be and mine for real and past my shoulders, we looked like two black crows called Hard Luck and Trouble.

We stood in the kitchen sipping coffee. There was a brisk rap on the door and Evan walked in. I hadn't thought to lock it after I let Ruth Ann in, but now I decided I'd reached a time and place where I didn't like people walking in at random anymore and I promised myself I would remember to keep it locked in future.

Ruth Ann squealed with delight. "Evan, sweetie." She set down her mug and minced around the bar with a big smile on her face. Evan took her in his arms. Over her shoulder he opened his eyes wide at me. I smiled in reply, but he still hadn't answered my question.

I didn't know about the rest of the country because I've never been out of the South, but down here, God definitely isn't dead. Florida is the buckle on the Bible belt, with salvation offered up on bumper stickers and billboards and religion pouring out of the radio, morning, noon and night.

Every other block has a church. In winter, when the cotton tops arrive, the churches have to double up on their services and hire off-duty police to handle the traffic so believers can get out of the church lot after the service. The way I look at it, this is a good thing. It keeps them off the golf course on Sunday morning so heathens like me can get on with our own praying.

A line of black limos stood at the curb and the parking lot was full of very expensive metal so Evan abandoned his car on the grass verge along the driveway at three minutes to ten.

The Jacaranda Unitarian Church on Pine Street

was where Jimmy and I had been married at his parents' insistence. Perhaps they thought an official white wedding would make me into the daughter-in-law they wanted or perhaps they hoped that the traditional ceremony could keep our marriage from turning into the train wreck they knew it would be. In any case, I hadn't been back since that Saturday in June and it felt like coming full circle walking up to the door, shaking with apprehension and dread, to say goodbye to Jimmy.

I wanted to slip into the very back pew but Ruth Ann wouldn't have it. Grasping my arm in a death grip, she clicked down the aisle with tiny little steps and unless I wanted to cause a scene, I had no choice but to go where she dragged me.

In the front pew the Travis family clung to each other and all the pews behind them were full, something Ruth Ann had failed to take into consideration.

Ruth Ann and I huddled together in the aisle staring at the out-of-town relatives and family friends. They stared back. I begged the floor to open up and swallow me. When it didn't happen, I tugged at Ruth Ann, trying to drag her back to the rear of the church.

"Sherri," Cordelia whispered and slid sideways, forcing the rest of the people in the pew to squeeze together and make room for us.

The rustle of bodies caused the witch to turn around. Eyes flashing with hate and malice, she would have cursed me but for Mr. Travis putting a comforting arm around her shoulders. "It's all right, Bernice." He turned her back to the front.

Still, the whole congregation heard her say, "I don't want her here."

Face flaming, I slipped in next to Cordelia with Ruth Ann right behind me. Cordelia took my hand and I clung to it like a life preserver.

After the service the minister asked everyone back to the Royal Palms for refreshment. Somehow I was sure the invitation didn't include Ruth Ann and me, but knowing Ruth Ann she was going to insist on making an appearance. What a perfect way to end this lovely social event.

The minister stood at the door shaking hands with the mourners as they left. As he shook my hand he leaned over to kiss my cheek, "I'm so sorry for your loss, Sherri."

"Thank you, Noble." I answered.

Cordelia slipped past me and went to stand beside her husband.

I kissed her cheek as well. "Thank you, Cordelia."

Evan showed up and took my arm. Smart man that he is, he must have been hiding out at the back of the church.

"Will you go to the Royal Palms?" I asked.

His face screwed up with distaste. "Why?"

"I don't know, except I really want to know what happens there. Talk to everyone and see if there's any hint Jimmy might be pulling a fast one. I keep asking myself who was on the *Suncoaster*? And where's Jimmy?"

"But Jimmy's dead, isn't he?"

"I'm not sure. Maybe not."

He stared at me in astonishment and then shot off to tell Noble. Marley took Evan's place. I asked her to go to the Royal Palms as well.

"I can't promise to keep my hands off Bernice's throat. She only has to make one little comment and there'll be blood on the floor."

Six feet away, Dr. Travis supported his grief-stricken wife to a black limo. "No matter what, Jimmy was her only son. She believes he's dead. I'll never forgive him for this."

Then over Marley's shoulder, I saw Cordelia standing alone, staring at Evan and Noble. The look on her face said she'd finally added two and two up to the right number.

CHAPTER 42

I touched her arm and Cordelia pivoted to face me but it took her a few seconds to realize who I was, and then her bewildered face formed into a hard mask of anger.

"It's Evan, isn't it?" she asked.

No more lies, no more cover-up. Even if I'd wanted to lie, it wouldn't have worked. She knew, and once you know, you can't unknow anything. "Yes," I replied.

"I've been so stupid."

"Cordelia . . . ," What could I say except, "This isn't the place. Come away with me."

"Why didn't you tell me?"

"Don't you think I wanted to?"

"I asked and you didn't say anything."

"Would you have believed me? Would it have been any easier?"

She gave a harsh bark of laughter or disgust and then raised her fingers to her lips as if to keep the sound in. Her eyes flew back to her husband. "I can hardly believe I didn't see it before." She turned back to me and her lips hardened into bitter lines of self-loathing. "It's so obvious. It wasn't you he wanted to be with, it was Evan."

She started to move away from me. I put out a hand to stop her. "Please," I begged. "Please forgive me." I took a deep breath, determine to keep my cool. "I don't want to lose you." I dug my nails into my palms. If I started to cry I wasn't sure I could ever stop.

She reached out to cover my hand with her own. "I'll call you."

"Come with me now. This is no place to go into this."

"Don't worry I'm not going to make a scene." She gave a little hiccup of a laugh. "I'm far too well bred for that." Her hand slid away and I watched her walk towards Noble. As he turned towards her, his smile slid away and his face crumbled into despair. She didn't say a word. There was no need, he knew it was over.

I was wrong about Ruth Ann. For once she didn't want to turn the other cheek and kiss ass. I think the reality of my relationship with the Travises had just come to her attention. "They didn't treat you very well, Sherri." Even this mild criticism was painful to her.

"Why didn't they ever like you?" She was so earnest I couldn't laugh.

"I think they had something else in mind for Jimmy."

She looked puzzled. Her scarlet lips bowed down in an unaccustomed frown. "But Jimmy loved you." For Ruth Ann, love was everything. She believed in romance: lived for it, even sacrificed her children for it. While watching her had molded me into a cynic at a very young age, lately I'd found myself admiring her unfailing tenacity and devotion to hope, hope that survived reality and experience. "You were the one Jimmy wanted. Surely that should have been enough for them."

She honestly believed that there's a soulmate out there for everyone. Each new love of her life had her trusting absolutely that this time it would work out . . . this time he wouldn't cheat on her, or beat on her, or leave her. This time her affair would be the culmination of what all those bodice rippers she devoured told her love should be.

Growing up, I'd never had any idea of what I wanted to be. I only knew what I didn't want: I didn't want to be like my mother. My life would be more ordered, more controlled and safe. I guess I pretty much blew that plan when I met Jimmy, no one's idea of any of those things, and now with Clay . . . well, let's just say I was batting a hundred.

"Never mind, Mom," I told her. "Let's go to the Sunset. I'll buy you a drink."

"But they never make you pay there, Sherri."

"I can't fool you, can I, Mom?" I tucked my arm through hers and took her along with me to find a ride home. I didn't think Evan was going to remember he'd brought us to the dance. Right now there were bigger events happening to him.

We didn't go to the Sunset. Instead, Brian dropped Ruth Ann and me off at my place before he went to the Royal Palms. Ruth Ann came upstairs and I made her a drink, telling her about Jimmy's tape but editing events so I didn't scare the hell out of her. I told Ruth Ann about Andy hiding the tape.

"I'd like to have it," I told her, "but all I can get out of Andy is the word *Casablanca*."

"Why don't you just rent the movie *Casablanca*? Perhaps you'll understand what he means when you see the movie."

"Aren't you the smartie?" I told her. "And I've always considered myself the family brain."

"That's all right, dear. You can be the brain. I like to think of myself as the family body." Her mouth tilted up in an impish beam and for once we spent time together and parted still happy with each other.

Even Tony Bennett's smooth sound in the background couldn't sooth my jangled nerves as I started my shift. My body was going through the motions while my brain was on other things. Around five o'clock, Brian and Peter came back to the Sunset. According to them there had been no happy stories of Jimmy at the Royal Palms, just hushed condolences and quickly sipped drinks.

"I asked Hayward Lynch if he thought Jimmy was really dead and he almost stroked out," Brian told me. "After that I was a little more discreet, but as far as I could see, everyone thinks Jimmy went up with the *Suncoaster*. But why would they tell me if they didn't?" He stared morosely into his drink. Even the smallest thing could make him feel rejected and dejected. His bitch of a wife had really done a number on his self-esteem.

"There's one thing," Peter looked warily over the rim of his glass at me. "I heard Bernice tell the minister that the DNA tests to identify the remains have come back. I couldn't hear what she said about the results or if she even knows them but if they had a service for Jimmy, surely they know he's dead."

"But if there's no body . . ." I still wasn't ready to give up my belief that Jimmy could defy or trick even death.

Peter's normal laughing charm gave way to concern. "Maybe you should ask Styles. That way you'll know for sure if it was Jimmy." He was telling me that like Ruth Ann I was gifted at denying reality.

Brian knuckled his glasses into place. "Bernice also said that Andy Crown called, looking for Jimmy. That's it, that's all I know."

About nine o'clock, I called the Crowns to tell them where Andy was.

"Would you call Steadman and ask him to come out? It'll have more impact if it comes from you."

A loud sigh blew down the telephone line and Mrs. Crown said, "We can't help you. My husband told you we are no longer responsible."

"I'm not talking about responsibility," I said, interrupting her. "No one is responsible. I just need all the help I can get."

"And we've given it. We've had over ten years of this. You've only been with him five minutes and you think you have all the answers—I'm really not impressed."

"Look, I'm not trying to be a hero. I don't know the right thing to do. It's Andy who's important here, not how you feel about me. I just want to help."

"What about us? Don't you think we deserve a little peace?"

"But if you could see him . . . I don't know what to do."

"Neither do we . . . that's the whole point. Please don't call again."

I left the bar early. At the Tropicana there was a parking place under the deep shadows of the trees. I hurried to get into it before the car following me into the parking lot took it.

The shells crunched under my feet and I was nearly to the steps when I heard the engine rev. Gut instinct and a misspent youth kicked in. I reacted.

CHAPTER 43

Leaping like a prima ballerina, I sailed into the air, landed momentarily, and then jumped again into the clump of Pampas grass at the bottom of the stairs. The sound of tires digging holes as the car braked and then slammed backwards propelled me forward. I rolled over the railing onto the concrete steps. Landing on my feet and moving, I raced up the stairs without looking to see who was trying to kill me or even if they were coming after me. I just ran.

The taillights of the car swerved out of the complex as I pounded on Evan's door, screaming, "Help, Evan, help," at the top of my lungs.

Evan didn't get a chance to invite me in. I charged through the cautious opening and then swung back to slam the door shut, pressing the deadbolt home before I slid down the door, melting into a puddle of tears, snot and babbling.

Evan stood there in stunned surprise as a confusion of words poured out of me. He listened while I regurgitated the whole nightmare, trying to make sense of it, and when I finally made him understand what had just happened, like any responsible citizen, he wanted to call the police. Not me. I just wanted to hide out and have my nervous breakdown without trying to convince anyone I had a good reason for it.

Always gallant, Evan gave me the bed while he slept on the couch. I came out of a nightmare to find him stretched out beside me, stroking my hair and murmuring soothing sounds. He gently untangled me from the death grip I had on him and rolled me away from him, shushing and comforting me along the way. His right hand went back to stroking my hair as he curled up behind me and held me close, whispering soft comfort.

I didn't care if he had killed Jimmy, I forgave him everything.

This sleepover was why I didn't know the cops had come calling early the next morning with more bad news.

Shortly before noon, Evan came back to my apartment with me. I made him barricade the door and promise to keep watch at the window while I showered.

I came out of the bathroom wrapped in a terry robe and with a towel around my head. The red light was flashing on the answering machine but I ignored it, wanting to get out of there as fast as I could.

"You can't stay here," Evan said. The look on his face said he was prepared for an argument.

"I know." I opened the fridge and got out the orange juice. "I'm about to pack a bag." I poured out two glasses. "I want to talk it over with you. Can I stay on your boat? No one will ever look for me there."

He grimaced. "Noble is there."

Well, there went that good idea.

"Pack a bag and call the cops. They need to know your life is at risk here."

"They aren't going to believe anything I tell them." I handed him juice. "They think I killed Jimmy."

"Don't exaggerate."

My handbag rang. We both stared at it, then at each other. "It's probably for Marley," I said as I dug through the junk for it.

"Hello," I said cautiously. I don't know what I expected from those things but it was never what I got.

"Sherri, it's Peter."

Alarm bells started clanging in my head. This was not going to be good news.

"Sherri, are you there?"

"Yes."

Now it was Peter's turn to go mute.

"What happened?" I yelled in the phone. "Why are you calling?"

"The police haven't been in touch?"

"For Christ's sake, Peter, what the fuck is it?"

"It's Andy," Peter said. "He's dead."

I moaned and slid down the wall to the floor, legs splayed out in front of me, the towel on my head listing and then tumbling to my lap.

"How?" I asked and then added, "I should have gone back. I shouldn't have left him alone."

Evan was beside me on the floor, cradling me in his arms and asking, "What is it, what is it?"

I turned to him, pushing wet strands of hair off my face. "Andy's dead. It's my fault."

He took the phone out of my hand and talked into it but I was sobbing too hard to hear what was being said.

When the first wave of emotion had flowed over me, I heard what Evan was repeating over and over like a mantra.

"It isn't your fault. You couldn't have helped him."

I leaned away from him so I could look into his eyes as if that would help me understand. "How did he die?" In my head I was counting the ways: hanging himself, pills or opening his veins. It had to be one of those. "Did he kill himself?"

"No. He was shot. Murdered at the Pelican Motel."

All Andy's delusions and nightmares had come true. I started sobbing all over again.

Evan hadn't told me quite everything yet. "Peter overheard the cops talking. Someone was in the motel with him, beating him, before he was killed."

I pushed away from him, onto my knees and then onto my feet. Staggering into the bathroom, I closed the door behind me and threw up.

When I came out of the bathroom the rich smell of coffee assaulted me. I hovered in the doorway to see how it would affect me, but the worst was over.

"Sorry." I leaned on the counter and buried my fingers in my damp hair.

"It's shock." Evan got out two mugs and poured milk into each of them. He put the milk back in the fridge. "I had nothing to do with Jimmy's death, Sherri." His eyes were fixed on the coffee carafe and I watched Evan move the handle from the right side to the left side.

"I know," I said. "I guess I always knew it. Things have been a little weird for me lately."

He looked over his shoulder at me and smiled. "No kidding."

Evan was finished waiting for the coffee. He poured the brew into the mugs, letting the last drops splatter on the hot burner, then he carried the mugs around the bar and handed me one. "What are you going to do?"

I set the mug on the counter and searched my bag for cigarettes. "I just want to crawl back into bed and pull the covers over my head 'til this all passes." I handed him the cigarettes and picked up my mug.

"But not here," Evan said. "And you'll have to call Styles now."

"Yes," I agreed. "But what if they think I killed Andy too?"

"Oh Jesus, you're as crazy as Crown. Besides, you were working, remember?"

I went to the police station as reluctantly as a nine-year-old boy going off to dance class. They didn't keep me waiting this time. I was shown right into an interview room and had hardly settled my behind when Styles shot through the door.

His eyes were red-rimmed from lack of sleep and his hair was uncombed. His bland suit was wrinkled. "I've been trying to reach you." The tone of his voice was somewhere between angry and accusing.

I was betting this wasn't a good time to tell him I'd spent the night with Evan. I slumped down in the chair.

"You know about Andrew Crown?" Styles asked.

"Yes. A friend called me this morning."

He leaned on the wooden table, towering over me and watching me intently. "Do you know who killed Andrew Crown?"

I shook my head. "If I knew anything I'd tell you.

Don't you think I want you to get the guy who killed Andy?"

"He was shot with a small-caliber gun. Do you own a gun?"

I sucked in air and tried to keep from screaming. "When my apartment was robbed, my gun was stolen."

"You didn't report it missing."

Why hadn't I? "I didn't know it was missing until later."

"You reported a break-in at Andy Crown's apartment too."

Once again the movies lied. The name I'd given was Sherri Jenkins. How had they gone from Jenkins to Travis and what had happened to all the stupid cops?

"Yes." I nodded in agreement. "I did call the police. It was a mess. Someone was searching for something."

"It's time you told me the truth, Mrs. Travis."

"Truth, what truth? I don't know anything I haven't told you. Jimmy is alive. Maybe he's trying to scam the insurance company and it went terribly wrong. I don't know. You'll have to find Jimmy and ask him, but you must believe he wouldn't have anything to do with Andy's death. He wouldn't hurt Andy."

Styles pushed violently away from the table and

left the room. Stunned, I sat there waiting. Was he coming back? Could I go now? I tried to decide. I picked up my bag, waffling. Was it against the law to leave the police station without permission?

As abruptly as Styles left, he was back. He had a zip-lock bag in his hand with a white label on it.

He handed it to me. I didn't waste time reading the black printing on the label because I recognized the object inside. It was a gold wedding band. I rolled it over in my fingers and through the bag I read the initials J and S with our wedding date in between.

Tears slipped down my cheek. "But maybe . . ."

He didn't let me finish. "The tide was going out when the *Suncoaster* blew up. It took most of the wreckage out with it but we found his hand with the ring on it caught in some mangrove roots." He took the baggie away from me. "We have DNA evidence. Even the insurance company is satisfied that James Elliot Travis is dead."

I couldn't deny it anymore. There would be no second chance for Jimmy.

CHAPTER 44

When I told Styles I was going home I didn't know that I was talking about the Shoreline.

I wheeled off the highway and went east on a secondary road for about a mile until a weathered plywood sign announced that I'd arrived at the Shoreline Trailer Park. There wasn't a shoreline within miles but none of the inhabitants were complaining. If you ended up in one of these aluminum-clad boxes, you had more than the view to worry about.

Along the road the property had been left to nature until the future development of some long-ago dreamer could kick in. The trailer park itself was another two hundred yards beyond this wilderness fronting the road. I turned onto the narrow rutted track where trees met overhead and made it into a long dark tunnel. The truck rocked through potholes deep enough to lose a small child in. At the end of the line, about fifty rusted-out single-wide mobile homes huddled together under a dark canopy of live oaks and Spanish moss.

The Shoreline had been a trash heap for people, old cars and drunks when I left at sixteen, and time had not improved it.

I parked beside Ruth Ann's twelve-year-old Toyota, switched off the engine and sat staring at the green vines and mold that grew over the sagging trailers. In the sharp clear air of a cold January day they huddled together, so close to each other that if you spat out your kitchen window you'd hit the lady doing dishes at her sink next door.

A poem we'd had to read in junior high floated into my head, "The Death of the Hired Man" by Robert Frost. I'd always remembered one line from it. It said home was the place that when you had to go there, they had to take you in. I looked out at the sad depressing refuse heap and said, "Welcome home." I'd come full circle.

Ruth Ann's door wasn't locked, but then her door was never locked. Some human disaster might need a place to land and she wouldn't want to seem inhospitable.

The aluminum door with the six-inch square window at eye level opened directly into the kitchen. I stood there a minute while my eyes adjusted to the darkness. The trailer was twelve feet wide and each room ran directly into the next; the kitchen led into the living room, which led to a narrow hall with a bath and tiny bedroom on one side and then down to a second bedroom across the end. Dark plywood paneling, low ceilings and small windows made it claustrophobic and oppressive, never mind that Ruth Ann had managed to cram a lot of junk into this small space. Each and every piece of crap us three kids had ever given her was proudly displayed and all the flat surfaces held dollar-store plaster figurines along with gap-toothed school pictures. We'd all grown up to be pretty decent-looking but you'd never have bet on it looking at these early shots.

I locked the outside door, not that it would keep out a determined seven year old. I also locked the door at the back of the trailer on my way down the passage, needing any tiny feeling of security. Then, in the back bedroom, all pink and fluffy like the inside of a Pepto-Bismol bottle, I kicked off my runners and climbed into my mother's pink satin bed where I gave in to defeat and despair.

After wishing the bastard dead a thousand times I'd finally got my wish only to discover it wasn't exactly what I wanted after all.

The thing was, I'd always been Jimmy's girl or Jimmy's wife. My identity had been tied up with Jimmy for so long, I no longer knew who I was. It was stupid but that's what it all seemed to come down to. His dreams had been my dreams. I had seen so clearly how life was supposed to be for Jimmy and in many ways I'd cared more about his success than he had, and even though I'd walked out I still hadn't forged a new life, hadn't found my own dreams. Maybe I didn't have any.

I was still in bed sorting through the pain two hours later when someone dropped Ruth Ann off. She didn't seem to think it was strange I'd crawled home to my mother's bed for comfort and I didn't protest when she got on the phone and told the Sunset I wouldn't be in for a few days. But when I heard her talking to the doctor's office I dragged myself out of the pink haven. This was serious. She hadn't even called a doctor when I fell off the roof and broke my arm. It hadn't been until the next day, when my teacher had the school secretary take me to the hospital and they did the x-rays, that we found out it was broken.

"Well, who's to know? You're always so dramatic," Ruth Ann said when she came to the hospital to pick me up.

The truth, at least my truth, was that she was so busy with the latest "love of her life" that she wouldn't have noticed if I'd expired at her feet. Ruth Ann believed in love, believed that love could conquer all, even though her life was a bad soap opera of wasted chances, broken promises and failed relationships.

Now what I once thought of as stupidity was beginning to seem like bravery in the face of a brutal reality.

I padded out to the kitchen. "Forget the doctor. I'm fine."

"You're not. I just want to get something to settle your nerves." It must be the hormone changes that were making Ruth Ann act so impulsively and motherly now.

I pressed down the telephone rest of her old pink princess phone. "Just leave it. My breakdown is over." I wasn't at all sure it was true but as long as I didn't think too closely about what had happened over the last week I might just squeak by.

"Can I do anything for you, darling?"

I thought about it for a heartbeat. "Yeah, you can. How about going out and getting *Casablanca* for me?"

She stared incomprehensibly at me.

"You know the movie . . . Bogart and Ingrid Bergman."

"You want to watch a movie? Now?"

"That's just what I want. Take the truck." I dug the keys out of my jeans and skidded them along the table to her.

She wrung her hands, afraid to argue with me in case she set me off again, the same fear I'd had with Andy. At last she picked up the keys. "All right, sweetie."

Being nutty definitely has some advantages.

While she was out I called Marley and told her both Andy and Jimmy were dead for sure.

When we stopped crying at each other she asked where I was. I told her.

"I'm coming," she said. Maybe it was just so unbelievable that I'd run home to Momma that she had to see for herself. "I'll just cancel the rest of my appointments."

"Isn't necessary," I protested.

"Maybe not for you but it is for me," she said and hung up the phone before I could argue.

The three of us had a group hug, a communal bawl and a discussion that went nowhere. Then we sat lined up on the sofa watching *Casablanca* and crying our heads off for lost love and wasted romance, while eating popcorn and drinking cold beer.

It wasn't until the last frame of the movie that I figured out where Andy had hidden the tape.

In the movie the exit visas from *Casablanca* were hidden in Sam's piano. That's where Andy had hidden the tape, in a piano, and as sleep crept over me I remembered where I'd recently seen a piano that Andy had access to.

A hand covered my mouth and a hushed voice breathed, "Shhh," and then, "Get up."

"What's happening?"

"There's someone outside," Ruth Ann whispered. "And I smell gasoline."

CHAPTER 45

She whipped back my covers and tugged on my arm, repeating, "Get up." Going to the window and sliding open the glass, she pulled out the screen and tried to hoist herself up on the ledge. I was mesmerized by black lace slipping up over a black satin thong.

The window was too high. She darted to the desk and grabbed the small chair. Setting it beneath the window, she looked back to me and whispered, "Hurry."

I was awake now. I rolled forward onto my feet and catapulted off the end of the bed. My bag was hung over a spindle at the bottom of the bed. I grabbed for it and finished up next to Ruth Ann at the window.

She was already on the chair. Turning sideways she planted her behind on the ledge, swung one bare leg over the sill and then the other one and dropped out of sight.

I slung the bag strap over my head and threaded

my left arm through it as I climbed onto the chair. I braced myself on the sill, the metal channels biting into my hands. Below me in the dark, Ruth Ann crouched. I swung over the sill and dropped down beside her.

She pointed to the next trailer and dashed across the ten feet separating the units, dropped down to her belly and started shimmying into the fourteen inches of space beneath the trailer. I followed.

I was halfway under when there was a giant whoosh and the night lit up. I moved like lightning, scuttling up beside Ruth Ann. Debris rained down on the tin roof above us, making a hell of a racket, as she reached out a hand to stop me from going any further.

"If this trailer catches on fire we're going to fry here," I protested.

"Just wait," she replied, never letting go of my arm.

It wasn't easy to stay still. When it stopped raining junk, Ruth Ann said, "Okay," and shimmied forward on her elbows like she'd been practicing for this her whole life. And maybe she had.

I was off like a shot until my hand touched something, something soft and living.

It yowled and shot away from me into the blackness beneath the trailer. I cursed.

"Shhh," Ruth Ann warned.

Ruth Ann held me back again at the edge of the trailer, sticking out her head to look around. Outside, an excited and frantic voice began calling and giving orders. "Okay." She squirmed out from beneath the trailer.

I followed but slower, hesitating with only my head protruding, prudence overcoming panic. Out there was still someone who had tried to burn us alive.

Ruth Ann didn't hesitate. She was already at the next trailer. I shimmied the rest of the way out and cautiously followed.

Ruth Ann tried the door before retrieving a key from over the light, opening the door and going in. I couldn't figure out what was happening so I hunkered down in the shadows, waiting for Ruth Ann to reappear.

Around us doors opened and people in various states of undress piled out. Then the overhead lights went out. Now the only illumination was from the fire but it was still enough for someone to find me by. I slid down the stairs and pressed deeper into the shadows of a shrub, wrapping my arms around myself to stop the shivering. It was cold, probably only in the forties, but that wasn't the reason I was shaking.

People came towards the fire like bugs drawn to a porch light and I watched for anyone familiar, sure that someone was out there waiting for me but not knowing who it was. But then again, maybe they'd gone, thinking they'd taken care of me just like they had Jimmy and Andy. They hadn't counted on Ruth Ann . . . Rambo in a thong.

She appeared now, carrying an armload of clothing and a flashlight, although the fire spread a dim light around us.

"Here," she said, handing me half of her bundle. "Ken and Joanne are both deaf. I had to wake them."

I wondered, in our little adventure, when she'd had time to think of that.

"They gave me some clothes for us. You must be freezing."

An hour later most of the Shoreline people had drifted away, back to the warmth of their own dwellings but here and there little groups talked in hushed tones. Even though it was frigid, Ruth Ann and I refused all offers of shelter. Wrapped in blankets we sat on the concrete steps of the trailer next to Ruth Ann's, watching the three remaining firemen patrol the embers of Ruth Ann's home. The oversized man's tracksuit and the heavy pair of sport socks I'd pulled on did little to keep out the chill and not even the acrid smell of burnt wiring, plastics and other carcinogenic things I didn't want to think of could drive us away. We were compelled to hang in until the bitter end.

Ruth Ann's hair hung in ragged hanks around her face. In the harsh morning light with no makeup she looked every day of her age and more. "Sorry, Mom."

She put her arm around my shoulder. "What for?" she asked.

"This is my fault. I brought this on you."

She gave a small shrug. "Perhaps it was George." She saw my questioning look and responded with, "The guy you saw me with the other night. The pig. I think he did this."

Seems we had our choice of nut-case arsonists.

"It could be worse," Ruth Ann said.

"How? How in flipping hell could it be any worse?"

"I could have owned that piece of junk."

"Still you've lost everything."

"I was due for a new wardrobe." She wrapped the blanket tighter around her shoulders. "But I'll miss the pictures of you kids."

"I won't. How come I had so many teeth? That's all you could see, great big teeth."

"I read that the nose is the only part of the body that keeps growing throughout your life." Her voice was full of amazement, like she'd just found the solution to world hunger.

Silence.

"And?" I asked.

"And what?"

"What's the point of the nose story?"

"Maybe as your nose grew it balanced your teeth. Your teeth weren't too big; your nose was too small."

"Gee thanks. I feel loads better."

"You're welcome, dear."

Crazy giggles bubbled out of us. The trailer folk standing in small clusters broke off their soft conversations and looked at us. The firemen turned to look at the mad women. Their blank expressions sent us off into uncontrolled laughter, tears rolling down our cheeks, our bodies convulsing.

I wiped the tears from my cheeks with the flat of my hands. "I don't know if it's safe to stay at my place. Jimmy was mixed up in something bad. I think the trailer was set on fire because of Jimmy."

She took it like Ruth Ann takes everything, like it was just what she expected out of life and one more thing to be endured. "If there's bad stuff going on, you should go stay at your daddy's."

The crazy Vietnam vet with the hair-trigger temper was the meanest son of a bitch in the valley, with nothing to fear from anyone. Besides, he lived among an arsenal of assault weapons. "You'll be safe there."

"Yeah, but will Daddy?" This set us off once more. When I could breathe again, I told her, "I swear, in twenty-four hours I'd cut his heart out."

"Then come to Bodilla's with me. She'll put us up 'til we find something."

I thought about it. "I have a place." No more collateral damage.

We watched the fire marshal bag some stuff. We'd already been interviewed upside down and backwards. Ruth Ann said, "I'll have to get new cards for everything."

"You can do it from my place."

Ruth Ann shook her head. "I'm going to work. It's payday. I plan to take the whole thing and buy clothes from the skin out. I'm looking forward to it." She'd definitely spent her whole life getting ready for this one bizarre tragic moment.

Ruth Ann's Toyota was toast. The paint was bubbled and the right side tires had melted into the stones of the drive, leaving it sitting on a weird angle. Jimmy's truck was unscathed but I wouldn't let Ruth Ann inside until I'd started it, just to make sure it didn't blow up, caution slipping into paranoia.

We swung by the Tropicana, took showers and dressed. My clothes hung on her but she took it well. Her only comment was, "You should wear brighter colors."

Then we went out with a pair of scissors to get her transportation. We cut the drooping ceiling cloth away from the roof of the Green Puke and dropped the gray dusty material onto the floor in the back seat. I handed over the keys and Ruth Ann headed for the Crab Shack for her lunchtime shift. She worked three shifts a week at the Crab Shack and five nights a week at Dutch's.

Alone and out in the open, I felt vulnerable and small. Fear goosed me up the stairs two at a time. I slammed the door shut behind me and locked it, wishing I'd asked Ruth Ann to stay with me until I'd packed. How humiliating is that? Needing my momma to protect me and willing to put her at risk. Not the tough girl I thought I was.

Tiredness, fear and loss were catching up to me and I knew I was about to fly apart into a million pieces. It was time to hunker down somewhere safe and take a timeout, but first there were a few details to take care of.

I dug out Mr. Huff's business card from the pile of unpaid bills. He answered on the first ring and filled in the particulars. Seems Jimmy had a small trust fund from an aunt. Turned out Jimmy had set up automatic payments from the trust fund account to pay for the insurance and never canceled the payments, another sign of Jimmy's laziness. Or maybe this was his one act of unselfish caring.

I needed the policy. From the closet, I took down the cardboard box filled with tax receipts and canceled checks and removed the fake brown leather folder with the gold embossing. When I left Jimmy, I left behind the hand-me-down furniture and crystal wedding presents, taking only my clothes and this folder. It contained my birth certificate and our wedding certificate, something I figured I'd need for a divorce when I got around to it, which I never had . . . another sign of my laziness or maybe of a tiny iota of love that had been fatally wounded but wasn't yet dead. I untied the ribbon holding the folder together and opened the envelope containing the policy. There it was. I was a rich young widow. At least until I was arrested for Jimmy's murder . . . one more of life's nasty little jokes.

I threw the folder in the bottom of a suitcase and raced around the room, piling clothes and shit in on top of it. Sooner or later someone was going to figure out that I was still alive and come back for me. I intended to be long gone.

I searched cupboards and closets for the can of mace I carried when a customer at the Sunset had been giving me unwanted attention. I found it at the bottom of a discarded handbag. I felt safer already.

I crept silently up to the door, listening for any sound to say someone was waiting outside the door for me. All I heard was the squawk of the scrub jays waiting on my balcony for their chance at the feeder. I tiptoed to the window and peeked out. No one was near the truck, and unless they were pressed tight against the wall, there didn't seem to be anyone on the concourse either. I was ready.

My hand was reaching for the knob when I heard a small sound, perhaps a pebble rolling on concrete under the bottom of a shoe. I cowered by the door, sweat popping out in my hair and trickling down the nape of my neck. "Don't be stupid. It's broad daylight," I told myself. But I couldn't drive myself forward with harsh words. I'd already faced up to being a coward.

I considered the options. Could I do what Jimmy did and drop down from the balcony? Yeah, right, and anyone outside would die laughing and I'd be home free.

If I called the cops, would they get here in time? Take care of yourself was my family motto and my instinct. With shaking hands, I reached into my bag for the mace.

I pressed my ear up against the door, trying to hear. Down the hall, a door opened and shut. The nurse who lived on the other side of Evan called out to someone. There was a muted reply.

My scary piece of death outside the door was just someone waiting for a neighbor. I tucked the mace in a side pocket of the suitcase, picked up the handle of the suitcase and opened the door.

Wrong again, Sherri.

CHAPTER 46

I tried to jump back in and close the door but he was too fast, shoving his way in and locking the door behind him while I turned and fled. Behind me, I heard him stumble over the suitcase, but still he was on me when I got to the bedroom.

He grabbed me from behind and yelled, "Stop."

I kicked him. He turned sideways and my foot connected with his leg. And then he picked me up around the waist and threw me on the bed. Straddling me, Clay held my hands above my head and stared down at me.

"What the hell has got into you?"

I was breathing too hard to answer.

He searched my face. "I heard about the Shoreline on the radio. Heard about Andy. What's going on?"

If I screamed, would anyone hear me? The nurse was long gone and everyone else was at work. "What do you want? I haven't got the video."

His hold loosened and he leaned back from me but still sat on my pelvis, impaling me to the bed with his weight. "Why would I want it?"

"I saw the file on Jimmy." He looked confused, so I added, "The one in your desk."

"Oh, yeah?" His obsidian eyes snapped and danced. "You accidentally looked in my file drawer?" If the romance hadn't been over already it would be after this confession.

"Somethin' like that."

We grew still, staring into each other's eyes and adjusting to a new reality. Then he gave a soft roll of his shoulder and a rueful smile. "Time to fess up, isn't it?" He ran his hand over his face.

"It's my own fault." He rubbed his forehead with the fingers of both hands and said from the cover of his hands, "I'm out of control." He lowered his hands and said, "You have to believe this has never happened to me before." Ashamed and embarrassed at this admission, it seemed important to him that I believe he wasn't always this crazy. "I just don't understand what happened, but I was lost from the get go."

He smiled wistfully down at me and said in soft amazement, "From the first moment I saw you, I wanted you." His face said he still couldn't believe this unfortunate turn of events. "You lit a fire in my belly and it was consuming me. I couldn't eat, couldn't sleep, couldn't stand to be around you and could-

332

n't stand to be away from you. I would have done anything to have you but I had no idea what to do."

Well, this was a new and interesting twist. For a moment I forgot to be afraid of him.

"You and Jimmy . . . well, you kept us entertained with your godawful husband stories but it was torture watching you go back to him. And you always went back. No matter what he did."

He swung his leg off me and rolled onto the bed, staring up at the ceiling. "As long as Jimmy was around, I didn't stand a chance, nobody did."

His words sent a chill through my body. Was I listening to a murderer's confession? "What did you do?"

"I hired a private investigator" He looked at me. "In my business, knowledge is power and money. It's all about what you know and who you know. I thought I might find something out to make it easier for you to leave Jimmy." He looked away and stared up at the ceiling as if he were looking for answers in the fine veining of cracks. "Dumb. It didn't take me long to realize you knew every bad thing about Jimmy. There was nothing to add."

"There were lots of pictures of Jimmy and women. Why didn't you show them to me?"

He snorted with disgust. "I hadn't fallen quite that low. Besides I soon realized those pictures wouldn't tell you anything about Jimmy you didn't already know, but they'd tell you a whole lot about me I'd rather keep to myself." He looked into my eyes and said simply, "I'm sorry." His black eyes tempted me to forget but I'd been charmed by the best. I was immune.

I rolled off the edge of the bed and stood looking down at him, "And Lynch?"

He looked confused.

"I read the file on Gridiron. Then I went to the library and read everything I could on Hayward Lynch and the King Ranch Development. I found a picture of one of the guys on Jimmy's tape, a county commissioner. There's a tie-in," I counted them off on my fingers, ". . . Jimmy, King Ranch, Lynch," I pointed a finger at him ". . . and you. You're the key, the one that ties it all together."

He was on his feet protesting, "I didn't have anything to do with Jimmy's death. Nor with Andy's."

"Did you break into my apartment?"

"No."

I blew a raspberry. "You almost had me convinced. Only four people knew about the tape. You mean to tell me one of the others, for some unknown reason, broke in here?"

He thought about it, rolling it around in his mind and then he said, "Oh, shit." He dragged his hands through his hair. "I told Lynch. In the bar the night you told us about the tape, I told Lynch who you were, told him about the tape."

And I remembered turning on the blender to block out his words.

"Hayward is in deep shit. He came into the Sunset to get me to buy into Gridiron. He owns a thousand acres of the King Ranch and he's been trying to get a zoning change to develop it. He'd have had it already but for cutting down that tree to get rid of the eagles. The city didn't like his end run. He'll get the change, but the question is will it come in time to save his ass."

"So Lynch stands to make a lot of money if the zoning changes?"

"Yes. Lynch has about seventeen million of his own money into that property already, everything he and his family owns," Clay told me. "If that zoning change doesn't go through quickly he will lose it all. He's desperate. Each day the decision is held up just brings him closer to bankruptcy. His creditors are already in court to seize his assets. He's as thick as thieves with most of the commissioners—Dunton and that lot—that's why he thought the zoning change would be a shoo-in, but a couple of county commissioners are being sticky. This will set a precedent. All hell will break loose and they won't be able to close the floodgates on development out there. Until they solve the sewage and water problems even I don't think it's a good idea."

"What if there was a scandal involving a member of the county commissioners?" A worm of an idea was digging its way out of my brain.

Clay shrugged, "I'd say he was shit out of luck if it involved this piece of property. The county would put off making any commitment for months and that would screw him."

"Would he be willing to pay someone to make it happen?" I asked. "To get the approval?"

"What are you saying?"

"Would he pay off one of those guys who were being difficult?"

"Definitely. They were only shy one vote the last time it came up. If someone hinted that they'd be willing to stop dragging their feet and vote yes Hayward would grab at the chance."

"Well, say Jimmy saw Lynch paying off one of those guys, perhaps when he was trying to fix the camera, and say Jimmy knew what it meant when he saw those guys together." I was going slow, thinking out loud. "He taped it. And say Jimmy demanded . . ." I shrugged my shoulders and picked a number out of the air, ". . . a hundred thousand dollars. Would Lynch pay up to keep anyone from knowing?"

"He would if he had the money."

"Surely he could raise that amount?"

Clay looked doubtful. "I bet he's maxed out every piece of plastic, every overdraft and every friendship. Do you know how much it costs to finance his debt?"

"Fortunately not, my own is enough to disturb my sleep."

"But he might give him something and offer him a small piece of the action when the zoning went through." Now it was Clay's turn to ask a question. "Would Jimmy try blackmail?"

I didn't hesitate. "Yes. But why kill Jimmy? Why not just pay Jimmy off?"

"He might once. But Hayward is all about being in control. He wouldn't be at anyone's mercy. He plays to win . . . all or nothing. Plus it's my guess he wouldn't trust Jimmy. Wouldn't trust him not to come back again and again."

"Blackmail would tend to make you untrustworthy in most people's eyes."

"Well, unless you have the tape, there's no proof."

"I want the guy that killed Andy and Jimmy to rot in jail. Even better, I want him to fry." I turned away. "I'll find the proof."

Clay came to me and wrapped his arms around me. I let him.

"Look," he said, "you've got a lot of reasons to be angry with me." He turned me around to face him. "Please forgive me."

And then I was in his arms and he was kissing me. My pride in being different from Ruth Ann, stronger and more controlled, was broken, completely shattered in the fires of desire. Oh my, I'm my momma's girl all right. Give me a little pat on the head, well actually that wasn't what he was patting, and I'm willing to forgive anything. The old brain just disconnects and the hormones take over.

Someday soon I was sure to be saying, "Gee, how could I get it so wrong?" but right now my blood was hot and my body was saying, "Bring it on."

CHAPTER 47

Sex couldn't distract me from death for long.

Betsy Crown grimaced when she saw me at the door but stepped aside to let me in. She shut the door quietly, paused and then lifted her face to me, bracing herself for what was to come.

The first words out of my mouth were not the ones I'd rehearsed on our drive down the beach. "I'm sorry," I said.

With a small moan she wrapped her arms around me, grasping me tightly to her hard little body. A patch of dampness bled into my shoulder. Then she regained her iron composure and led the way into her magnificent white living room with the white baby grand.

She waved at a couch and went directly to a chrome bar cart. "I was just going to make myself a drink. What can I get for you?"

I know drinkers. I can tell within a sip how close they are to having a skin full and I knew she'd already had more than one. If she were in my bar, I wouldn't serve her.

"Whatever you're having is fine," I answered.

She dropped ice cubes into two glasses and then poured two inches of Stolichnaya vodka in her glass and an inch in mine. As she handed me the glass, Mr. Crown walked into the room.

He frowned at me and said, "I didn't expect to see you here."

In a voice that yelled, "Don't mess with me," Betsy Crown said lightly, "I want to talk to her."

I perched on the edge of a benchlike white sofa to let him know I intended to stay.

Mrs. Crown settled on the sofa across from me. "Tell me about Andrew," she begged.

"I don't know who killed him but he didn't kill himself. I don't want you to think that." I set the glass down on a glass-and-chrome table.

Mrs. Crown held her hands up before her face as if she were praying while Mr. Crown sat with his elbows planted on splayed knees staring at the deep white rug as I told them every detail of finding Andy and of our time in the Pelican Motel. When I finished, they sat in their separate islands of silence digesting it and making it part of their own history and memory bank while I got up and walked to the baby grand piano.

The lid was open. I had a good look around. I

walked slowly around the piano looking at the black interior from all angles and running my fingers along the curve in case my eyes missed something. A black video case taped on with black electrical tape could easily be missed.

"Do you play?" Mr. Crown asked. He looked mildly curious at my strange behavior but that was all. His son was dead and nothing beyond this fact could penetrate his mind.

"No," I replied, still checking. Nothing. Wrong piano.

I went back to the couch. "When did you last see Andy?"

"Thanksgiving," said Mr. Crown. "He was already delusional. He wouldn't listen to us, wouldn't go in for treatment. We decided to try tough love." Misery washed over his face. "To set him free, to find his own way."

"Tough love, soft love, true love: none of that would work. Love just wouldn't cut it. The only thing that would bring Andy back to us was the drugs. If you need to be angry with someone, save it for Dr. Steadman. I called him and begged him for help."

"I called him too," said Mrs. Crown. She swiped tears off her cheeks with the flat of her hands. The look she gave her husband kept him quiet. "Dr. Steadman reminded me that Andrew was his patient, not me. Dr. Steadman said he couldn't discuss

Andrew's illness with me without Andrew's written permission. He did, however, suggest I bring Andrew to his office."

She gave a whimper. "Quite impossible."

Each of us in our own way had tried and failed. Forever after, we would ask ourselves what we had left undone.

"I'll leave you now," I said.

"But you'll be at the service, won't you?" Mrs. Crown pleaded. "You were always so good to Andrew, you and Jimmy. You're the only ones who never forgot him." She gripped my hand in both of hers. "You're the only friends he had left."

They'd soon know that Jimmy had caused Andy's death, maybe not directly but Jimmy's greed had set all of this in motion. Sooner or later they were going to figure that out and hate us.

"I'll be there," I promised.

The door closed behind me. The exit visa, AKA Jimmy's tape, was not in the grand piano at the Crowns'. So where was it? Was it in any piano? Did I have any better idea?

I looked at the pink stucco castle next door. Ignoring Clay waiting in the car, I walked down the drive, along the road and up the flagstone path to the front door.

CHAPTER 48

"What are you doing here?" Bernice had lost weight. The skin on her face looked parchment dry and hung in great folds, but her eyes still blazed with hatred.

I pushed past her. "We need to talk."

"Talk? Talk? If I never talk to you again it will be a blessing."

"Someone murdered Jimmy. It wasn't me. Someone murdered Andy. It wasn't me. Don't you want to know who it was?"

She jolted upright like a steel rod had been shoved up her spine. "Come," she said and marched off to the small sitting room off the kitchen, always the most used space in the four-thousand-square-foot house.

It had been redone in apple green and white since I'd last been in it.

"Sit," Bernice ordered while I was still taking in the pretty new color.

I sat. Then I told her everything I knew or thought I knew.

"Hayward? You're saying Hayward Lynch killed Jimmy?" Her face warped into hard cruel lines.

"Or had him killed."

She hadn't even denied the possibility that Jimmy could be a blackmailer. Maybe she knew him better than I'd realized. "Did Jimmy leave a video with you?"

She shook her head. "He hasn't been around lately."

"Why?" And why was I asking?

"You," she spit out. "You were always the problem. He wouldn't listen."

Yada, yada, yada.

She took a deep breath and started down a well-trod path. "You destroyed him. And you couldn't even do what your sort does best . . . breed. At least I'd have something of my beautiful boy left."

As if I'd ever let the bitch get close to any child of mine.

"Do you think Jimmy might have come in when you weren't here and left a package?"

She thought it over. "I don't know, but I'll look."

"Without evidence we'll never prove Lynch did it."

She gave a sharp little nod of her head. "I'll look."

I started to leave and then turned back. "I have some things of Jimmy's, pictures and trophies, I'll drop them off."

With Clay still playing chauffeur, we fought the traffic over the bridge to Tamiami, but there weren't any music stores in the mall across from the box stores.

"Where to now?" he asked.

"There's a mall two blocks from Andy's apartment," I answered, "near enough for him to walk to. If there's a piano store there he might have stashed the tape inside of a floor model." The truth was I was desperate and willing to go on any wild goose chase just to be doing something. "Let's try there."

It was an older mall where the pavement competed with the façade for the speed they could crumble at and it didn't look like the ideal place to find what we wanted. But there, between Hollywood Nails and the American Terminator Pest Control Company, was a lovely little store selling all kinds of instruments. It seemed like an omen. The sign on the door said the Highnote offered music lessons as well.

A plump man in his forties, with thinning hair combed over a bald spot, came out of the back room just as I lifted the lid on a small Japanese piano by the front door. The clerk hurried over, rubbing his hands in anticipation. Lifting the lid on a piano must be comparable to kicking tires on a car.

We looked inside, gave it a good look, but there was no tape to be seen. At the second piano the clerk exposed the insides for me and explained what we were looking at. There was no videotape contained in the innards of this piano either. The two other pianos also came without videos.

"Do you sell many of these?" I asked.

"Oh, yes," the clerk assured me.

"How many in the last two weeks?" I asked. "I was just wondering if there was a piano here in the last two weeks that isn't here now."

"Well, no." The clerk's answer was hesitant. Perhaps he didn't want to admit that he hadn't moved one of these babies in two weeks or maybe it was the weirdness of the question that shook him.

I reached into my purse for the picture of Andy. "It's really my friend who knows about pianos." I showed him the picture. "Has he been in?"

His face told me that this was very odd behavior but he was willing to play along if there was a chance of a sale down the line. He studied the picture of a neat and clean Andy, with no dreadlocks, and shook his head.

"No," he said regretfully. "I don't think he is one of our customers but I'd be happy to meet him."

"Call Styles." Clay ordered.

"I really hate being told what to do."

We were on the balcony of his apartment, a warm tropical oasis of lushly flowering plants and bamboo furniture. Below us, six-foot breaking waves gave the azure blue horizon a jagged look and set bright-colored beach umbrellas trembling and dancing on the sand. I sat enfolded in Clay's silk robe with my feet resting on the bottom support of the table.

We'd been at it for hours. Clay wouldn't let it go while I wanted to sit here, enjoying the good feelings and banishing the rest from my mind. That wasn't Clay's way. His hard dark face had a take-no-prisoners look. "You have to tell Styles about Lynch."

"Why would he believe me?" I lifted the carafe and poured more coffee. "I haven't come across as any too credible."

His lips thinned into a straight hard line. I knew this stubborn and unyielding look. "I'll go with you."

"No. This is my problem not yours." He started to protest. I reached out and took his hand with its long slender fingers and raised it to my lips before I laid it along my cheek. "Never mind, Styles or Lynch or anything else. Let's just enjoy this."

Clay wasn't having any of that shit. "Lynch has got to be stopped."

"Give it a rest, Clay," I begged. "I need a little time."

He sighed.

"Doing nothing just isn't your style, is it?" I asked.

He gave a jagged little laugh that tugged at my heart. "I've never done enough of it to know."

"Well," I nodded at the apartment behind us, "working like a fiend gave you all this."

"I've missed a few things."

"I never thought you wanted anything but money."

"Neither did I until you came along." He frowned, unhappy to be at the mercy of emotions. "I still can't believe it." He got up abruptly from his chair and left the room.

I debated going after him but decided to hell with him. Whatever his problem was I didn't need it. I didn't need him. But not needing Clay was a lie I couldn't sustain.

He returned with my handbag and dropped it onto my lap. "Go ahead," he said.

"What?"

"Have a cigarette," he said. "I know you're dying to." Clay hated smoking with a passion.

"Thank you."

"You're welcome."

Clay dropped into the rattan chair and went back to studying the horizon. "I don't want to make a fool of myself."

"In what way a fool?"

He shrugged. "By going into the Sunset and hanging all over you or crowing or . . . I don't know what. I'm out of control." Again the shrug. "You'd think it would be easier at my age. But it's worse than when I was a teenager. I want to stand on the bar and announce it or send out e-mails or something. I warn you, Sherri, I might really do something embarrassing."

I laughed in delight. "That's about as likely as the Pope doing the can-can on Easter Sunday, but I live in hope."

CHAPTER 49

Clay got his way.

"You're fond of conspiracy theories, aren't you, Mrs. Travis?" Styles said. He was wearing another brown suit, darker than previous days but still anonymous. Today he'd gone wild and opted for a pale green shirt with a black tie with three small white diamonds across the middle.

"Lynch killed Jimmy and Andy."

"Let me see, first it was Mr. Rollins who was responsible for the explosion on your husband's boat, something about double billing, then there was this SUV on a mysterious tape that disappeared and now a blackmailing scheme. Are there any of your theories I've missed?"

I beat back the anger, trying for calm. "Are Jimmy's and Andy's deaths just theories?"

"You were on the boat the day it blew up. You're the only person who gains by your husband's death."

I tried to keep my face as bland as his but I hadn't had the practice. I'm sure he knew he'd scored heavy. "Except for Lynch. He stopped Jimmy from black-mailing him."

"And Mr. Clay Adams," Styles added, "with whom you spent the night. He got you. And now he's using this cock-eyed story to put pressure on Mr. Lynch so he can take over his land development project." Styles pressed his palms together and tapped his fingertips against his lips as he watched me. "Mr. Adams is a man who plays rough. Everything you said about Mr. Lynch's financial situation says Mr. Adams stands to benefit from the bankruptcy of Gridiron Developments."

"And Andy? You think he killed Andy?" I croaked. "Or do you think I killed Andy? Why?"

"You're the one who took Mr. Crown to that motel, the one who kept him there. You obviously had a reason to do so."

"I was working when Andy died." I was trying to break free of the web he wove around me. "Lots of witnesses."

"You have another friend, Mr. Peter Bryant. He's at the bar you work in every night and Mr. Bryant has lately acquired some new partners from Miami. Our little backwater is changing and Mr. Bryant's new partners are introducing a different element to the Kit Kat Klub. Personally, I think Mr. Bryant is a small-time hustler who is in way over his head. He's sailed close to the wind before but now he has lost control to his partners. But it gives Mr. Bryant access to a whole new set of muscles. Mr. Crown was tucked up nice and secure at Mr. Bryant's motel. His killer knew where to find him. Perhaps there was something you wanted out of Mr. Crown or maybe you wanted to make this story of yours believable; either way, his death muddies the water. I think you excel at spreading confusion."

"And my mother's trailer?"

"Your mother doesn't think torching her trailer had anything to do with you." I threw my hands in the air and got to my feet. "Well, I'm so glad you have it all worked out. There's only one thing. If you're wrong, someone is still out there trying to kill me."

CHAPTER 50

By seven o'clock that night I was in Clay's bed, sound asleep. But when exhaustion wore off I woke to stare into the dark for hours, all of my thoughts waking nightmares. Alone, on the dark side of midnight, there are no good thoughts.

I slipped from Clay's bed and walked barefoot through the intimidatingly beautiful apartment to the balcony, the only place I felt comfortable in Clay's home, and sat in the dark looking out to the gulf.

When would Styles come for me? In a few hours or a few days? Soon. Freedom was flying away from me. And how many of my friends would I take down with me?

I watched the twinkling lights off to the north on Shark Point as I searched the starless ebony night for answers, for a way out of the net winding tighter and tighter around me. Everything I knew to be true had been twisted and warped, and evil crouched in the shadows, waiting to consume me.

Was Clay involved? It was the question that stole my sleep. Trust didn't come easy to me, and Styles had made huge holes in what had been built slowly between me and Clay. I told myself none of Styles' theories could be real, but doubts, once in your head, are hard to erase. And would Clay find it any easier to trust me unconditionally when Styles messed with his brain?

And now I knew about the source of the deep worry lines that had been etched on Peter's face over the last months. He was living in his own hell. Night after night, I'd put his drink beside the twenty he laid on the bar. I wouldn't remove the bill until he drank it up or stood to go home. Most nights he laid another twenty down beside it.

Jimmy's idea about disappearing south into the islands teased and tempted me. Without money could I make it happen? Running, leaving my family and friends behind to deal with the fallout seemed cowardly but if they were all called into court to testify, to have every piece of their lives cut open, dissected and laid bare for anyone to pick through, was that any better? The big question was who would come looking for me and how hard would they search?

I needed to move. I left the condo.

The sun, creeping over the edge of the world, turned the shallow water near the shore a bright pink. The dawn beach was empty except for the tiny birds, legs scissoring frantically, that ran forwards and backwards at the edge of the water searching for food—a life and death struggle, hour after hour, of retreat and charge.

I had been on my own for almost a year, but I hadn't really gotten on with my life. I'd just drifted in some sort of limbo, and twice, out of loneliness or lust, I'd fallen back into Jimmy's arms. No wonder Jimmy had a hard time believing I was really gone. But now, dead or fled, Jimmy was out of my life and all the wasted emotion was swept away like smoke from my cigarette.

Watching the shorebirds, I realized that all life was pretty much the same. We're caught in the currents that take us where they will—if you try to stand still, a wave of change will sweep over you and drive you forwards or backwards. Either way, it will move you. The only way to keep your balance and gain a little bit of control is to keep moving, pick a target and pull towards it with all your might. But even when you gain your goal, it quickly moves away from you and you need a new sighting, a new star to make for. It was time for me to find my own star and pull towards it.

Could I trust Clay? While I was in his arms I could believe, but I'd lost all confidence in my own judgment—except for the strong conviction that no matter what the truth turned out to be, Clay was not a murderer. I turned around to walk back up the beach to the condo. Fifty yards ahead of me Clay stood watching me. I walked towards him.

CHAPTER 51

The chances of collecting on Jimmy's insurance were looking slim at best so I had to go to work. When you're as insolvent as I am there isn't much choice. Besides, if I was honest, it was the place I most wanted to be.

Clay came with me.

About five o'clock, Cordelia came into the Sunset, this time with boldness and a new air of defiance. It was as if everything had just loosened up inside her like the elastic on pantyhose left in a drawer too long.

"Fancy meeting you in a joint like this," I said. "What are you drinking?"

"How about a margarita? You always say they help you see the world from a new angle." She stood on tiptoe to slide up on the stool.

"Yes, I know I've preached that in the past, but do you really want to see the world from toilet-bowl level?"

"Let's risk it."

"And so?" I asked, as I positioned the coaster in front of her and set the salted glass on it.

"Noble is at home with the kids. I had to get out. I can hardly stand to be around him."

"Understandable."

"I've started doing the strangest things." Her tongue flicked at the salted rim. "Today I was going to dust his stupid basketball trophies. Instead I put them in a trash bag and I took them outside and smashed them. Very liberating."

"Well, it's better then smashing Noble."

"Oh, I've thought about that too."

"But are you making plans to do it?"

"Not yet. But I'm keeping that option open."

I'd make sure she stayed away from Brian and his stories. "Have you got any other plans?"

"No. I'm just going through one day at a time." She sipped her drink. "Delicious! Why haven't I tried these before? I think I could get addicted to these."

"I wouldn't recommend it."

Peter sidled down the bar and set to work. He always moved in on any female within sniffing range and Cordelia was well within range. I saw the pink spread up her cheeks and blessed him. It probably had been a long time since she'd thought of herself as an attractive female. Before long Peter motioned for another round.

"Not only hanging out in a bar but chatting up men—your reputation will suffer," I warned her, setting down their drinks.

She smiled and tucked her hair behind her ear. "It will make lovely gossip, won't it?" She canted her head to the side. "Which will get more attention, a minister's wife in a bar or a gay minister?"

"I don't know. This story just has so much going for it."

"My life has turned into tabloid material."

"We must compare notes but I may not have too much time. I could get arrested at any second for two murders. You might not want to be seen with me," I warned.

She smiled and her delicate features suddenly lifted and she looked more alive and animated than I'd ever seen her. She lifted her glass to me. "Let's swear to stick together. No one else will ever believe it."

"Sherri," Jeff called and held up the telephone receiver. "Oh Sherri, I forgot to tell you there was another call for you. Well, several actually, a man wanting to talk to you. He asked if I knew where to find you but he didn't leave a name."

I had a pretty good idea who it was . . . the guy with the gas can, wanting a second date. Who says men never call the next day?

I held the phone away from me, cautious and leery, "Hello?"

It was Andy's mom. "I just wanted to tell you Andy's funeral is tomorrow."

Marley came in, digging for details. "I expected you," she said, really curious about where I'd spent the previous night but she'd have to wait for that information.

"I went to see Bernice," I told her instead.

"What?" My story totally distracted from the trail she was sniffing along.

"It was a crazy thing to do. I bet she's torn every inch of that house apart." I pointed a finger at Marley. "Think before you leap, girl. This just shows what acting without thinking can do. We'll probably hear tomorrow that there's nothing left of the Travis home but rubble."

"Good," Marley said. She looked real sweet but it was a lie.

Tony Rollins slid onto the stool next to her. He gave us his "Can you believe how hot I am?" smirk and asked, "Who's your friend, Sherri?"

Well, he deserved everything he got. I introduced them and added, "Tony is the pro out at Windimere I told you about, Marley."

"Oh really?" Marley said.

Come to Jesus, boy, you're about to be done over, but not until he bought her at least two more Corona and limes.

Someone must have called a reunion 'cause Lara

360

Zampa took a stool near the door. There were tables open but they were served by wait staff. I was figuring that the only way she could talk to me was by sitting at the bar. I put her out of her misery and went down and took her order for a Perrier.

She didn't look good. Her eyes had black circles like bruises under them. Her hair was unwashed and barely combed. She wore no makeup. "Have you heard from Jimmy?" she asked.

Oh shit. "We're not going to be hearing from him."

Her eyes did a shift that told me she knew what was coming.

"Jimmy is dead," I told her.

She squeezed her eyes shut. Her lips pursed against the pain.

"Hey, I'm sorry."

She nodded and opened her eyes. "John said Jimmy was dead. He seemed sure of it."

"Maybe Dr. Zampa just wanted it to be true 'cause he wants you back. That's all."

"Yeah?" She stared at the bubbles in her glass. "But what if he was the one who killed Jimmy? I can't stand not knowing."

"He didn't do it. I'm sure of it."

Her eyes said she wasn't believing me.

I tried again. "Truly, Dr. Zampa had nothing to do with Jimmy's death."

She gave me a weak little smile. I'd tried. I went back to work. The next time I checked on her, Dr. Zampa was sitting down beside her.

"Oh, mother, this is going to be a long night." I headed down the bar to deal with the coming disaster.

I arrived as she snarled "What are you doing here?" at him.

Softly, as if she'd shatter if he spoke too loudly, he said, "I saw your car."

"You followed me, you mean. Go away." She turned away from him and he flinched in pain.

I put a coaster down in front of him.

"Bring me a Jack Daniels," he ordered. His eyes never left his wife.

The Sunset is generally a mellow sort of place with only soft music, the clink of glasses and the sound of light laughter to disturb the calm surface. Not that night. The bar was packed. Crowds take on moods and this one's state of mind wasn't good. Voices were raised at a table. Bodies moved restlessly around it until the atmosphere settled and then loud laughter erupted across the room where a chair was over-turned as someone left abruptly. The air was charged with energy as if an electrical storm was about to crack open the room. Every conversation bristled with emotion and everyone was hanging in as if they were expecting something big to happen. Waiting and drinking hard.

Tony Rollins, his face beet red, as if he'd been holding his breath way too long, got up from his seat and moved further down the mahogany. Marley gave me a sunny smile and went to join Peter and Cordelia.

As I passed a fresh drink to Tony Rollins I asked, "So when did Jimmy fire you?"

His eyes opened in surprise but he answered my question. "He told me the day he died that I was gone. He said he was buying into the club and he didn't want trash like me around his golf club." He was astounded. He really didn't get what Jimmy was objecting to.

Styles came in. A path cleared around him as he walked to the bar. Even drunks have a sense of self-preservation.

"Are you working or is this a social call?" I asked.

"Bring me a club soda," he said.

"Ah, the wicked aren't resting."

"What time do you get off?" he asked when I set down his glass.

"Are you asking me for a date?"

"Not likely."

"Too bad 'cause I bet I could put some color in your cheeks." Maybe I was as crazy as everyone else in the room tonight.

"What time?"

I watched him drain his glass and leave. I went down the bar to Marley and told her, "All I need to make this fine evening complete is Bernice." I turned a nervous eye to the door. "If that bitch comes in I'm going to faint dead away. A girl can only take so much."

"Nah, don't worry. She's probably still home destroying property. It'll be days before she figures out what you did to her."

I beamed at her in delight.

But it was Eddy who came in right after this, who really put a smile on my face, his own look of delight saying good news before he opened his mouth. "We've got your license plate." He slid a piece of paper across the mahogany bar towards me. "That's his name and his address. His name is Gregg Ganoff. One of the guys followed him home. Another driver knew him. Ganoff's wife teaches his kid over on the mainland. Hope you get your money back."

CHAPTER 52

"Ganoff, Gregg Ganoff," I told the amigos.

"Yeah, but who is he?" Brian asked.

They all got on their cell phones and started making calls to find out what they could about Ganoff.

Brian was the first with information. "He works for Hayward Lynch."

"So it's all true?" Why was I surprised? My hard surface cracked.

"Hey come on," Brian pleaded softly.

"Can I get a little service down here?" a guy called down the bar.

"Hold your fucking horses," Brian roared. The bar went silent.

I'd have been less shocked to hear Noble swear from the pulpit. I gulped down a laugh. "No more language like that Mr. Spears or I may have to ban you."

The big guy was frowning along the bar at Brian, trying to decide if he wanted to make something of it.

I sauntered down. "I wouldn't if I were you," I told him. "Not only is he a lawyer but he's a personal friend of the chief of police." I gave him my sunniest smile. "Now how about a drink on the house?"

When I came back, my amigos were in a heated discussion of what to do "Call that cop . . . what's his name?" Brian asked.

"Styles," Peter told him, "His name is Styles."

"Yeah, Styles. Call him," Brian ordered.

Clay was turning his mug of beer around and around.

"Well?" I asked him.

"Sure, call him." His eyes flicked up and then back to his glass. There was only an inch left in the bottom so I couldn't see what he was finding so interesting.

"But?" I urged him on.

He shrugged. "Without proof we go nowhere. Maybe the police will get lucky."

I watched his face closely and asked, "What are you thinking?"

"Lynch doesn't know he got your only copy. Maybe we should run Jimmy's scam and see what happens."

They got even louder now, shouting and arguing with each. I went off and pulled a couple of pints and mixed a Tom Collins while the idea percolated.

"It's too dangerous," Brian told me when we

picked up the conversation again. "Don't listen to these guys."

"Maybe Brian is right," Peter said. "Leave it to the cops."

"And let Lynch get away with it?" I lifted his glass and wiped the bar under it. "Besides, I'm still the one the police will arrest if there are no other choices."

"Lynch already has your copy of the video," Brian reminded me. "Why would he try and pay you off?"

"He doesn't know it was the only one. Besides, he's already tried to kill me twice. I won't be safe until he's in jail."

It was the wrong thing to say.

There were about twenty seconds of horrified silence and then they were on their feet firing questions at me.

"Sit down and shut up," I ordered. When they finally settled down, I said, "I guess I forgot to tell you about the first time."

"That's a pretty big thing to forget," said Peter.

"Can I get a carafe of house white?" Jessica Blair, our cute little waitress, asked from the end of the bar where she waited for the order.

I went to the wine fridge to get it. Intent on convincing me, Peter followed me along the bar to where Jess waited. For once Peter didn't even try out one of his lines. Jess was fresh out of high school and gorgeous, so it was clear Peter was upset.

"Go to the police," he advised me. "You can't deal

with this on your own. You need their help if you're going to get Lynch."

"Maybe," I said.

But Clay had a better idea. "We could get you miked and then you make a pitch to Hayward. I know a good investigator who'll take care of the details." He grinned at me. "Tell Hayward you want the same deal Jimmy had or you'll blow the whistle on him."

My mind had been going in the same direction. Hadn't we all seen this in the movies dozens of times?

"Are you trying to get her killed?" Brian yelled. He slammed his glass down hard on the bar, liquid splashing over his hand. His face was crimson and a thick vein stood out on his left temple. He looked like his head was about to explode.

"Okay, Brian," I soothed, "I'll do it your way." I reached out and patted his hand to try to calm him down. "I'll call Styles. Don't worry, it'll all be fine."

"You'll stay well away from Lynch?" He pushed at the bridge of his glasses. "Promise?"

"Hey, I'm no fool."

"Maybe not, but you are foolhardy. Promise me you won't call Lynch or have anything to do with him."

"Why don't you come with me to meet Styles? Then you can tell him what's worrying you."

He was on his feet now. "You aren't saying it,

Sherri." He turned to the others. "Do you see what she's doing? She's trying to change the subject." He put the flat of his hands against the bar and leaned forward. "Promise me you won't call Lynch or go anywhere near him." Each word was enunciated clearly.

"Don't be silly," I said, dismissing his fears.

"Promise," he insisted.

I laughed at him. "It sounds like we're back in school."

"You aren't going to put me off that easy."

"He's right, Sherri," Peter said.

"Let me talk to Styles before I go making any promises."

Jeff was giving me the evil eye. I hadn't been pulling my weight all night and his patience was running out. I went back to work.

As I pulled pints and mixed drinks, my mind explored the options. Lynch had nothing to lose. He'd already killed two people and if he thought I was a threat, I was dead. And if I did nothing, the police would arrest me for Jimmy's death. There was only one other choice . . . find Andy's copy of the tape.

The night from hell finally ended at the Sunset.

Clay opened the door and we scanned the parking lot. Clay had pulled the Lexus right up to the bottom of the stairs. Another car was parked beside it, a beige sedan. The door opened and Styles got out, letting us see him in the overhead light.

"What's he doing here?" I asked Clay.

"Who cares? At least we know he isn't trying to kill you."

"I can believe anything at this point."

Styles got back in his car.

Clay unlocked the doors of the Lexus with the remote. Then with his left arm across my shoulders and holding me tight to his side, he said, "Let's go." We ran down the stairs and he pulled open the door, hustling me inside.

"I feel like a movie star," I told him when he slid behind the wheel, "With a bodyguard. Well, two bodyguards. Do you think that's why he's here?"

"That or making sure you don't blow town or kill someone else."

"All comforting thoughts."

He was too busy searching for danger to pay any attention to me. I reached out to the right pocket of his jacket and felt the hard outline of a gun. He gave me a brief glance and then focused on his driving.

When we pulled into the underground parking at the condo, Styles kept going.

CHAPTER 53

I still had to get through Andy's funeral, had to hold myself together. Clay and I timed our arrival at the Unitarian Church for just before the service was about to start.

Styles stood outside the church, hands clasped in front of him, watching stragglers entering—judging and calculating. My legs wobbled as I passed him, pretending I didn't see him and didn't know him.

Inside, the church was cool and dark after the glaring sunlight and the sunglasses I wore left me blind. I slipped off the glasses but kept them in my hands. This time I slipped into the first pew inside the door, keeping my head down and making my body as small as possible, trying not to be seen, with my eyes firmly on the hymnbooks in the rack in front of me.

But we were barely seated when one of the ushers came down from the front of the church. People in front of us turned around to see what was happening. He leaned over and whispered, "Mrs. Crown would like you to join the family."

Oh god no! I couldn't do it.

Clay stood up, stepping out of the pew to wait for me.

"No," I whispered. "I'm fine here."

Clay leaned over and said, "C'mon." He held out his hand.

I took his hand, rose on weak legs, stepped out in the aisle and froze, trembling, unable to make myself move forward. Clay gave me a gentle push, starting me down the scarlet runner towards the front pew.

I went along, seeing questioning faces turn to me. Evan was there at the end of the aisle a few pews in front of us. A few pews further still I saw Cordelia. And then I saw Dr. and Mrs. Travis. I stopped. Bernice had a look on her face like someone had given her a permanent wedgie.

Clay placed a hand on the small of my back, a gentle pressure propeling me forward. I wobbled on until I saw Hayward Lynch, sitting two rows back from the Crowns. Hate, like I'd never felt in my life, raged through me. How dare he sit here at the funeral of a man he'd killed?

I felt Clay's hand squeeze my waist. "Let it go," he whispered.

"Sherri," Betsy Crown called softly. Her smile

welcomed me and her fingers beckoned. I walked forward and collapsed into the space waiting for us at the end of the front pew. Clay reached out for my hand and I clung to him, staring at the dark wood floor.

I sat there feeling loss and anger and pain. The hurt went on and on, never ending, beating on me, swamping me. The service was awful . . . worse than Jimmy's, odious and cruel and I thought Noble would never shut up and let us go.

At last Noble walked down the steps carrying the urn with Andy's ashes and handed them to Mr. Crown.

Clay nearly had to lift me to my feet. Then he dragged me out of the pew and off to the side so the Crowns and their daughter could get by us. I slipped on the dark glasses.

"Are you all right?" Clay asked when we cleared the shadow of the church.

"I might never be all right again," I croaked. "Let's go. I want to get as far away as possible."

"I'll take you home," he said.

Home. Ruth Ann always says, "Home is where the love is."

"Sherri," a man's voice called behind us.

I swung to face Hayward Lynch.

"Get away from me," I hissed. "I know all about you. Know what you did."

His mouth tightened into a thin white scar and his piercing eyes grew colder.

"You killed Jimmy and Andy."

I would have struck out at him but Clay held my arms as he spun me away from Lynch. And then Marley was hugging me and kissing me before passing me over to David who did the same.

David held me at arm's length and said, "We had a little moment for Andy yesterday morning." None of the sad funeral behavior for David, his face was happy, inviting me to share in his joy of life.

"Andy and I were talking about funerals once and he told me about a scene from the movie *The Big Chill* where the dead man's friend plays this Rolling Stone song on the organ at the guy's funeral."

He waited to see if I was following him. I've only seen that movie about a hundred times so I nodded to show I was keeping up.

"Andy thought that was a neat idea so at the service yesterday I rocked out 'You Can't Always Get What You Want,' on the piano and then we had a moment's silence for Andy." David grinned at me. "I'm sure my parishioners thought I'd lost my mind but I know Andy would approve."

I remembered David getting up from a piano when Marley and I went to the shelter. I knew where the tape was. I threw my arms around David and kissed his cheek and pounded his back. I swung around to search the crowd for Styles. Lynch was right behind me, a worried expression on his face. I grinned and said, "Got ya."

I didn't wait to see how Lynch took this. Dodging in and out of people I searched for Styles. When I found him, I grabbed a handful of his suit jacket and tugged. "You have to come." When I was sure he was moving in the right direction, I ran back to David. Lynch was talking to him but left before I got there.

"Can we get into your building?" I asked David. "Is it locked?"

"Yes," he said. "Mr. Lynch was just asking about the center too." He looked bemused by this sudden attention for a place normally so overlooked.

I snatched his hand. "Then you have to open it." I headed for the parking lot hanging on to David, Styles right beside me, and Marley bringing up the rear. Everyone was talking at me. Marley caught up and jogged along beside me, firing questions. David was going on and on saying that he didn't understand, when Clay pulled up in front of us and swung open the passenger door.

We went over the bridge so fast we were actually airborne. At Tamiami and Hope, Clay cut through a parking lot and came out the other side rather than waiting for a light. Styles didn't object to Clay's driving, although it was scaring the hell out of me.

At the shelter, we all tumbled out while the car was still rocking to a stop. I think it was in relief more than anything else, and while David went to the front door, Styles headed around to the back.

"Hurry," I urged David as he fitted the key in the lock. I looked around, searching for Lynch. It just didn't seem likely that he'd give up so easily, but maybe he was already leaving for parts unknown.

When we poured through the front door, we could see the back door hanging open even before we saw the raised lid of the old battered upright.

"Oh no!" I wailed, but the words were barely out of my mouth when Styles goose-marched Lynch through the open back door.

In his hand, Lynch held the videotape.

CHAPTER 54

Two days later I unloaded a tray of drinks at a table and went back to Peter at the bar. "The long and the short of it is this, the police are watching your partners, just waiting for them to do something wrong. Why did you get hooked up with them in the first place?"

"When these guys ask, you don't say no." He stared into his empty Scotch glass.

"Look," I said, "I have a little idea." I picked up his glass and poured him another drink. "Do you know Big Daddy's Oyster Bar?"

"Yeah, Morgan Davies owns it."

"Right. He's seventy-two and still working seven days a week. Can you imagine that? I hope that doesn't happen to me." I pondered the future for a moment. It seemed real likely.

"Anyway, we were talking last fall. He says this is his last season. He wants to sell. He asked me if I was interested in taking it over. He even offered to hold a mortgage."

"Why don't you?" Peter asked. "You've got Jimmy's insurance money."

I shrugged. "I'm not sure it's for me."

Peter laughed. "Face it, you just like the Sunset. They'll have to dynamite you out of here."

I took a bag of limes out of the fridge and spilled them into the bar sink. "We're talking about you." I turned on the tap. "The location of the Oyster Bar has always been great, but with the new houses being built out there that restaurant is a little gold mine. Sell out to your partners or just walk away, but get out. Get your name off everything and then go see Morgan Davies and tell him I sent you."

I saw movement at the entrance and looked up to see Styles standing in the door of the bar. He looked around, hands easy at his sides, making sure of what he had.

He was smiling. Hot damn, the man could actually smile. I picked up a cloth and wiped my hands as I walked down the bar to join him.

"Of all the gin joints . . . ," I began and his smile broadened. "Can I buy you a drink?" I asked.

"Nope."

"Well, this isn't working out the way I'd hoped."

He hitched himself onto a stool. "But I'll buy you one."

"Well," I said taking a wineglass down from the rack behind me, "Unaccustomed as I am to public drinking, I'll take you up on it." I poured myself a glass of the

378

most expensive white wine on the bar. "And what about yourself?"

He hesitated and then ordered a beer.

"This must be a special occasion indeed," I said as I pulled his dark ale.

We toasted each other over the rim of the glasses. "I arrested Hayward Lynch today," Styles told me, setting his glass down on the center of the coaster.

"Did he admit to the murders?"

"He's never going to admit to anything, but Ganoff confirms his boss borrowed his vehicle. Ganoff wasn't involved."

"Have you got enough to convict Lynch?"

He nodded. "Lynch shouldn't have kept your Beretta after he killed Crown."

"He probably was waiting for a chance to use it on me," I shivered.

"The county commissioner has admitted to the bribe, so we have Lynch sewed up pretty tight."

"So it's over."

He nodded and reached inside his jacket. He pulled out a brown manila envelope and slid it across the mahogany to me.

I knew what it was but I opened it anyway, counting the six photographs inside.

"Your husband was a mighty fine photographer," Styles said. "Mighty fine."

The End

Coming in spring 2009 from McArthur & Compmay

SEX IN A SIDECAR

by Phyllis Smallman

CHAPTER 1

Florida has two seasons. In the rainy season we get hurricanes: in the dry season we get tourists…both can be nasty.

October was early for tourists, and with Hallowe'en coming up, it was late for hurricanes. This should have been our quiet time but down in the Bahamas a tropical depression was forming. We weren't unduly worried. Hurricanes need warm water to sustain them. At that time of the year, we reasoned, the Atlantic Ocean would be cooling, so the further north the swirling mass traveled, the more likely it would starve for waters hot enough to feed it. Blinded by optimism, we ignored the fact that South Florida was in the grip of a record-breaking heat wave, with temperatures in the nineties, making it more like sultry July than October.

Hurricanes could feed further north. But really, at the tail end of the season, how bad could it be?

Circling in the steamy waters of the Caribbean, slowly gathering strength, the storm laid its plans. When it was ready, it started to move. West of Jamaica its wind speed passed thirty-nine miles per hour, making it officially a tropical storm. It was given a name now. The thirteenth named storm of the year: her name was Myrna.

When they give a storm a name you start to pay attention. The word hurricane begins to shimmer at the back of your mind. There's nothing like a hurricane hovering off shore to remind you that life is pretty much a crapshoot. You assess your options, check in with family to see if they need any help, and start making a list on the back of some unpaid bill of things to take with you and things to do before you run.

For me, Sherri Travis, family wasn't a problem. My mother, Ruth Ann, was in North Carolina visiting my half sisters and as for my father, well, let's just say we weren't real close and leave it there. And after living my whole life in Florida, thirty years of hurricane seasons, I really didn't need a list but a list is always comforting…like I was actually doing something besides sitting there waiting to have the shit kicked out of me.

On Tuesday morning we woke to find Myrna lurking malevolently south of the Florida Keys, barely moving but growing in intensity minute by minute. Even while we watched, anxious to see whose fate she held in her eye, Myrna surged to a category two hurricane.

Lines at the lumberyard grew longer as the wiser and the more nervous among us began boarding up windows. At grocery checkouts every shopping cart held half a dozen jugs of water along with some batteries and everyone filled up their gas tanks while comparing strategies and offering advice to the person at the next pump.

By noon the circling mass arced northwest, leisurely heading for the entrance to the Gulf of Mexico: good news for Miami and the Gold Coast, bad news for those of us living along the West Coast of Florida. Moving a little faster, dancing into the Gulf, Myrna sang, "Look at me, look at me!" We looked.

Myrna's winds increased. In a few hours she could blow up our coast for a real good visit. Everyone had a plan now and what was important in life shrank to those items we could fit into the family vehicle. All those other possessions we'd coveted and worked so hard for were about to be abandoned to the mercy of the storm. Around town, businesses closed and a cavalcade of cars crept slowly up to the entrance of the schools. Parents weren't waiting for any official closing to pick up their kids.

Now that she had everybody's attention Myrna stalled at the mouth of the Gulf, coyly hiding her intent. Ready for flight, we hovered between panic and false bravado. Late Tuesday, spinning north by northwest at eight miles an hour, she veered sharply to the West into the Gulf, heading towards Texas and Louisiana. A collective sigh of relief blew out behind her, not that we wished anyone any harm, you understand, we just didn't want Myrna to hit us. Living on a barrier island off the west coast of Florida, storms slam us hard. Only fifteen miles long tip to tip, Cypress Island had barely cleaned up the debris from the last storm. We figured it was someone else's turn.

All over town cars were emptied of treasured photo albums and heirlooms before the outdoor furniture was dragged from the family room back out to the patio and someone was sent out to replace the milk dumped down the sink two hours earlier.

But we celebrated too soon.